Thos ...

*Three broth...
whe... ...pect it.*

Three brothers, three young men from a privileged, aristocratic background. All are expected to uphold the Rosemont family name—which means giving up their roguish ways and marrying well. But are they ready to make convenient marriages where love is second to duty? That is when they each meet a woman who challenges them and convinces them that love is the only way to find true happiness.

Read Ethan's story in
A Dance to Save the Debutante

Jake's story in
Tempting the Sensible Lady Violet

Available now!

And look for Luther's story
Coming soon

Author Note

Tempting the Sensible Lady Violet is the second book in the Those Roguish Rosemonts series and features the middle son, Jake, who, like his two brothers, is happily single and wishing to remain that way for as long as possible.

However, Jake's plans are all undone when he meets the sensible Lady Violet, and Lady Violet's sensibilities are upset when she finds herself in a compromising position with Lord Jake during a parlor game.

Parlor games were a popular pastime for adults in Victorian times and provided them with a rare opportunity to flirt. Young women could escape their chaperones during games such as sardines or indulge in some forbidden touching during blind man's buff. And sometimes, young women would reward gentlemen who got the correct answer during blind man's buff with a kiss, as Violet's sister, Bianca, does in this story.

Tempting the Sensible Lady Violet follows on from the first book in this series, *A Dance to Save the Debutante*, where one dance ruins the plans of the youngest Rosemont, Ethan, to survive another Season without becoming romantically involved. The third book will feature Luther, Duke of Southbridge, who is in search of a future duchess and will settle for nothing less than the elusive goal of perfection.

EVA SHEPHERD

—

Tempting the Sensible Lady Violet

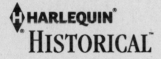

HARLEQUIN®
HISTORICAL™

Recycling programs
for this product may
not exist in your area.

ISBN-13: 978-1-335-72338-3

Tempting the Sensible Lady Violet

Harlequin Enterprises ULC
22 Adelaide St. West, 41st Floor
Toronto, Ontario M5H 4E3, Canada
www.Harlequin.com

Printed in U.S.A.

After graduating with degrees in history and political science, **Eva Shepherd** worked in journalism and as an advertising copywriter. She began writing historical romances because it combined her love of a happy ending with her passion for history. She lives in Christchurch, New Zealand, but spends her days immersed in the world of late Victorian England. Eva loves hearing from readers and can be reached via her website, evashepherd.com, and her Facebook page, Facebook.com/evashepherdromancewriter.

Books by Eva Shepherd

Harlequin Historical

Those Roguish Rosemonts

A Dance to Save the Debutante
Tempting the Sensible Lady Violet

Young Victorian Ladies

Wagering on the Wallflower
Stranded with the Reclusive Earl
The Duke's Rebellious Lady

Breaking the Marriage Rules

Beguiling the Duke
Awakening the Duchess
Aspirations of a Lady's Maid
How to Avoid the Marriage Mart

Visit the Author Profile page
at Harlequin.com.

To Romance Writers of New Zealand
and Romance Writers of Australia.

Chapter One

London 1891

Lord Jake Rosemont tapped the green baize table, signalling for another card. His fellow gamblers exchanged disbelieving glances. Jake knew what they were thinking. The cards laid out in front of him totalled eighteen. Surely it was better to sit on that number than to risk going over twenty-one and losing everything.

Even the unflappable dealer rose one eyebrow as if questioning the wisdom of the move.

As usual, Jake wondered how they could not see what was so obvious to him. The game was well-advanced. Many cards had been dealt, but few twos and threes had been played from the deck. His chances of winning were high. The risk was low.

The dealer turned over a card. A three. As one, the men seated at the table groaned, while the young ladies watching twittered and fluttered their approval, letting him know how much they appreciated a winner and how happy they would be to show their appreciation to him.

'You really do have the devil's own luck,' a sailor bearing an anchor tattoo on his brawny forearm said before clapping him on the back, as if hoping to capture some of Jake's good fortune.

Jake nodded his acknowledgement of the praise and dragged in the coins and notes on the table, adding them to his growing pile.

He could inform the sailor and the other men seated around the table that if they took the time to watch what cards were dealt to each player and performed a few quick calculations, they, too, would know when it was wisest to take a risk and when best to err on the side of caution.

'My friend is indeed lucky,' Herbert Fortescue exclaimed. 'Lucky at cards and lucky in love. Unlike me. I have no success in either area.'

Once again, the men at the table groaned and, once again, Jake knew exactly what they were thinking. *Not this again.* All night, as they moved around the gambling houses of London, Herbert had told anyone foolish enough to listen about his unrequited love for the beautiful Lady Bianca Maidstone.

Two heavily made-up young ladies sidled up to Herbert and linked their arms through his, cooing in his ears that they knew the perfect way to divert his mind from his troubles. But his lovesick friend would not be consoled and shook them off.

Jake turned back to the cards, knowing that his friend's assessment of him was wrong on two counts. Luck had nothing to do with it, in either cards or love.

With cards, he just played the odds. And when it came to love, that was an area which thankfully remained a mystery to him. Yes, he'd had many women in his life, but love, never. And that was the way he liked it. And as for marriage, the state that Herbert was so desperately seeking, Jake could see no reason why any sane man would want to tie himself down to one woman for the rest of his life. Pure madness.

Some people, including his mother, would say that at twenty-six he should be actively in search of a suitable bride. Jake would beg to differ. He'd seen enough disastrous society marriages, including his parents' own, to know that such a fate was best avoided.

Fortunately, his mother's marriage-making focus was currently on his older brother, Luther. Eleven years ago, their father, the Duke of Southbridge, died and Luther inherited the title along with the responsibility of running the estates. All he needed now was the perfect Duchess who could continue the lineage.

Unlike Jake, Luther was eminently suited to the role of Duke. As their father had never failed to point out, Luther possessed all the superior qualities of a nobleman, while Jake had never been anything other than a total disappointment.

He tossed his cards on to the table, causing them to scatter in all directions. Only the quick actions of the dealer prevented them from falling to the ground.

More cards were dealt. Jake continued to win more than he lost and the pile of money continued to grow in front of him. It was coming close to the time when he should leave this low dive. His winnings had attracted the attention of the gaming house owner. Several hands ago, the gruff man had emerged from his lair on the balcony above the gaming floor, where he usually surveyed his domain. He was now intently watching Jake from the bar.

Complimentary drinks had already been sent over to the table, presumably in the expectation that inebriation would ruin Jake's good fortune. Now a young lady had placed herself on his lap and was running her fingers through his hair while whispering in his ear all the ways she could help him spend his money. All he had to do was leave the table now and disappear upstairs with her.

'You're very pretty and extremely tempting, my dear,' he said, giving her rouged cheek a quick peck and gently lifting her off his lap. 'But not tonight.'

While these diversions were amusing and were not impeding his ability to win, the owner was far from amused. Like in all gaming houses, winners were appreciated only if it encouraged others to gamble more and only if they went on to lose all they had previously gained. But gamblers who took more from the house than they gave back were never welcome.

In most gaming houses, being the son of a duke would be all the protection Jake needed from the owner's ire. But in a dive such as this, even if the owner knew his lineage, it would mean nothing. Money was money. It mattered not whether the winner was the son of a duke or a dustman, if he was taking money off the house he was not wanted there. Such anonymity was rather refreshing and another reason why Jake preferred to frequent such low establishments.

Another pile of money was pushed Jake's way. Out

of the corner of his eye, he saw the owner give an all but imperceptible flick of his head to the beefy fellow standing at the entrance.

The man swaggered across the packed room. The carousing patrons fell silent and hastened out of his way, giving him a clear path towards Jake.

He stared at Jake, down the crooked nose that marked him out as a fighter. 'This table is now closed,' he said, crossing his arms over his enormous chest, the tattooed muscles of his arms bulging.

The other gamblers threw down their cards, scuttled off and disappeared into the throng. It was now definitely time to leave.

Jake flicked a coin towards the dealer as a tip, scooped up his winnings and, with a sleight of hand, placed them in the bouncer's pocket.

'Thanks, Lord Jake,' the broken-nosed pugilist whispered out the corner of his mouth, while keeping his face suitably aggressive. 'Just doing my job, you know.'

'I know,' Jake whispered back. 'And, yes, I'm leaving. I wouldn't want to get you into trouble.'

The bouncer gave a quick nod and took Jake's arm, as if forcibly ejecting him from the room.

Jake had known Bill since his days as a bare-knuckle boxer. He'd won a tidy sum on the man, who had been both fleet of foot and strong of arm. But after a life taking more punches than he could stand, Bill had retired from the ring and had found the only job open to him, throwing drunks and dandies out of gambling clubs.

The man had been a great success in the ring, winning many a bulging purse, but a charlatan manager and poor investment advice had left him with no financial compensation for the battering he had taken for others' entertainment.

He needed this job, but did not need to get into any more fights. Bill had a family to support and was trying to establish a boxing gym so he could provide greater financial security for them than the tenuous existence of a bouncer ever would.

'How are the children?' Jake asked, as Bill performed a convincing act of dragging him out of the club.

The man almost broke character and smiled. 'Wonderful. Little Maisy won a writing competition at the Sunday school last week. Teacher says she shows real promise and is a right clever little girl.'

'Good to hear it,' Jake said, still assuming the posture of a man cowering in the face of a beating. 'Use those winnings to buy her a present as a reward.'

'Will do and thanks again, Lord Jake, you're a proper gent,' Bill whispered. 'And you're not welcome back here,' he added, loud enough for the owner to hear, as he opened the door and thrust Jake out into the night-time air.

A contrite Herbert joined him and stared anxiously at the door, as if he expected a band of ruffians to jump them at any moment. 'That was a lucky escape. You wouldn't want to be on the receiving end of that man's fists. Did you see the size of them? And as for his arms, like legs of ham, they were.'

Herbert looked up the alleyway, then at Jake. 'So, what shall we do now? We're running out of places like this that will let you play.'

Herbert, unfortunately, was correct. Jake possessed

only one skill, the ability to win at cards. But there was no point having a skill if no one would let you exercise it. Now that he had been ejected from this particular back alley den, he was fast running out of options.

He looked up at the sign hanging above the door and laughed. The Queen Victoria. Last time he had visited it had been called the Hangman's Retreat. It seemed it had been changed in a misguided attempt to give it some class. If the ageing Queen knew that such a low establishment frequented by gamblers, thieves, vagabonds and ladies of the night bore her name, she would be putting her nose in the air and declaring 'we are not amused'.

'I know one thing we could do,' Herbert said, his face lighting up like a puppy who had been given a toy to play with. 'We could go to Norfolk this weekend for the Maidstones' house party.'

Jake groaned in much the same way as the men at the gambling table had and commenced walking up the dimly lit alleyway.

'Don't be like that, old chap. It will be fun,' Herbert said, racing to keep up with his friend.

Jake doubted that. The Season was about to begin. The house party would merely provide an opportunity for young women to get in ahead of their peers and try to secure a future husband as quickly as possible. Jake avoided as much of the Season as he could and was not about to subject himself to the unwanted attentions of the many husband-hunters on the prowl. Luther might be the main prize, but as the second son of a duke he, too, was in more demand than he would wish.

They turned into a side street and Herbert grabbed

his arm, his eyes pleading. 'You'd be doing me such a favour. I'd be in your debt for ever.' He blinked repeatedly and, to Jake's horror, he was sure his friend was holding back tears, but in the dim light he could not tell. 'All I need is some time alone with my beautiful Bianca to tell her how I feel, and I can't do it without your help.'

Jake shook his head in pity at what so-called love did to a man. One pretty little debutante had reduced this somewhat sensible man to a blubbering wreck.

'Please, Jake. You must come. Her sister is the most overbearing chaperon I've ever met and she's made it clear she doesn't like me. I'm sure Bianca has some attraction to me. All I need is for you to distract the chaperon so Bianca and I can have some precious moments alone together.'

They emerged from the labyrinth of side streets into a bustling main road and Jake hailed a hansom cab to take them to their private club. As they rode through the busy London night, Herbert's expression changed from sorrowful to chagrined. 'If it wasn't for that sister, I might even be betrothed to my darling Bianca already. When we met during their visit to my parents' estate, it was love at first sight for me and I'm sure it was for her as well. But I never got a chance to find out for sure. That sister was always there, getting in the way.'

It was a tale of woe Jake had heard many times already and would no doubt hear again before the night was out.

Herbert slumped down on the bench. 'She's such a miserable old maid and she just wants everyone else to be as miserable as she is.'

'And that's the woman you want me to spend the weekend entertaining? A miserable old maid?'

'Only you could do it,' Herbert said, sitting up straighter. 'I've never seen a woman who was able to resist you once you turned on the charm. All you have to do is keep the spinster occupied so I can get some time alone with Bianca.'

'And what of the spinster? How do you think she's going to feel about a man she's never met trying to charm and distract her?'

'Oh, I'm sure she'll be delighted. It will give her some nice memories to cherish on her long, lonely nights. She'll think back to those few precious days when one of London's most eligible young men flirted with her and she will sigh with contentment.'

The cab pulled up in front of their club and Jake paid the driver.

'Please, please say yes,' Herbert cried out as they entered the club. 'I'm desperate, Jake. I really do need your help. Please.'

'Oh, all right,' he said, to save his friend the embarrassment of begging in front of the other club members, and, heaven forbid, from starting to cry again.

'Thank you, thank you. You're the best friend a chap could ever have. Perhaps Bianca and I will name our first child after you.'

Herbert followed him into the billiards room, still smiling like a gormless lovesick fool, and commenced listing off other potential names for their future children.

Jake racked up the balls and took a shot, amazed at how love could ruin a man, and pleased he had never experienced such a debilitating condition.

* * *

'You've done what?' Violet stared at her younger sister, who continued to smile as if she had not a problem in the world.

'I've organised a house party for this weekend,' Bianca repeated. She had stopped Violet as they passed each other in the hall and imparted this piece of information as if it was something rather unimportant that only needed a casual mention.

'And what exactly has your organisation entailed?'

'Well, I sent out invitations to all my friends and several eligible gentlemen. They've all agreed to come. There will be about twenty of us. It will all be such jolly fun. Oh, and I've thought about what sort of parlour games we should play.'

'And?'

Bianca shook her head, her brow furrowing. 'And what? That's enough, isn't it? Or do you think we should have some dancing as well? Yes, you're probably right, dancing will be so much fun.'

'How do you intend to feed them?'

Bianca looked as bewildered as if she'd asked her how she intended to fly to the moon. 'Well, the servants will do that, won't they?'

'If you remember correctly, Bianca, we gave Cook the week off to visit her sick sister in Scotland.'

Bianca smiled. 'Yes, she was so pleased about that. Cook said her sister has been poorly for some time and what she needs is feeding up with plenty of healthy broth, and nobody makes more delicious soup than Cook. I'm sure her sister will be better in no time at all.'

'Bianca, with the cook away she won't be able to

prepare food for your friends.' Violet forced herself to rein in her impatience. 'Plus, there will be the servants your friends bring with them. Each young lady will most likely be accompanied by her own maid and each gentleman his valet. That will be at least an additional twenty people who will need feeding. And some are likely to bring their own carriages. They'll have drivers and possibly footmen with them, plus, there might be additional chaperons as well. And we have no cook.'

'Well, someone else can do the cooking, can't they?'

'Who?'

Bianca shrugged one slim shoulder. 'I don't know. One of the other servants. We do seem to have an awful lot of them. Some of them must know how to cook.'

As if to prove her point, two maids hurried past, carrying brooms and dusters, and Bianca smiled at her sister as if the problem was solved.

'Cooking is a real skill and preparing breakfast, lunch, dinner, morning and afternoon tea for forty or more people takes a lot of experience and expertise. That's why we have a cook. She has the specialised ability to do this.'

Bianca's face went blank. 'Oh.'

'Yes, oh.'

Bianca shrugged again and smiled. 'You'll be able to sort it out, though, won't you, Violet? You're so good at that sort of thing.'

'No, I won't. You're going to have to uninvite them.'

'No,' Bianca cried out, tears springing to her eyes. 'No, no, I can't. I just can't. Anyway, they're probably already on their way and will be here this evening. You have to make this better. Please, please.' She gripped Violet's arm, her eyes beseeching.

As much as Violet loved Bianca, sometimes she really was exasperating. It was often hard to believe they were actually sisters. They were both tall, but that was where the similarity ended. Bianca was willowy and elegant, with the fair complexion, blue eyes and blonde hair of their mother, while Violet was buxom, with brown hair and eyes, and an unfashionable olive complexion, but their personalities also couldn't be more different.

But perhaps Bianca's temperament was Violet's fault. She had been the closest thing Bianca had to a mother since their own mother died ten years ago, when Violet was sixteen and Bianca only eight. She had pampered and indulged her younger sister in a desperate attempt to make up for being left motherless at such a young age. Was that why she was now so impractical and overly emotional?

Violet had no time to find an answer to that question. 'Oh, all right, but don't invite anyone else, will you? And next time you think about doing something like this, consult me first.'

Her sister clapped her hands together and resumed smiling. 'Thank you, thank you. Oh, this weekend is going to be fabulous. I'm so looking forward to it and so are all my friends.' She wandered off down the corridor, singing a cheerful tune as if she had not a care in the world, while Violet strode off in the other direction towards her father's study.

She knocked on the door and entered before he had a chance to reply.

'Bianca has invited twenty people to the house this weekend and Cook won't be back for another week.'

Her father looked up from the piles of astronomical charts spread out on his table. 'Oh, that's nice, dear. I hope you all enjoy yourselves immensely.'

Violet sighed. Why did she even bother informing her father of anything? He seemed to think that the estate ran by itself, or at least, that's what he wanted to think. As long as she took care of everything, he was happy to be left alone in his chaotic study, buried in his piles of books and charts. That had been another reason Violet had felt the need to assume the mantle of caring for Bianca when their mother had passed away. Her father might be a loving man, but he had never been up to the task of raising two young girls. He was much more comfortable in the company of academic men, discussing the latest scientific advancements, than he ever would be consoling a little girl because she had lost her favourite dolly.

'We need to get someone from the village to help over the weekend, or even several someones. Women who can cook for large numbers of people.'

'Yes, you organise it, there's a good girl. Oh, and we also need to do something about finding a new estate manager, the sooner the better, and to fix up the problems at the tavern.'

Like Bianca, her father mentioned this as if he was merely indulging in a bit of idle chatter, but Violet's shoulders tensed, knowing more demands were about to be placed on her.

'What problems with the tavern? What's wrong with the estate manager?'

Her father moved from the charts on his desk to the bookshelf, ran his long finger along the titles, searching for some elusive tome. 'Ah, there it is.' He pulled out the book and rifled through the pages.

'Father, what happened at the tavern and what's wrong with the estate manager?'

'What?' He looked up as if surprised to see Violet still in his study. 'Oh, that. Yes, it seems Charles has left us. Bianca knows all about it. One of the young women in the village told her that Charles was...' He screwed up his face as he struggled to find the words. 'Shall we say, romantically involved with the barmaid at the Golden Fleece.'

That, at least, was one thing Bianca was good at. She loved nothing better than a good gossip, which meant the family always got to hear about any grievances the tenants might have. Not that Bianca ever did anything to solve those grievances, other than occasionally remembering to tell Violet.

'Isn't the barmaid married to the tavern keeper?'

'Exactly. Rumour has it that Charles and the barmaid have run off to parts unknown and the tavern keeper is not too happy.'

'I'm not surprised.'

Her father replaced the book and pulled another off the shelf, then looked up at Violet. 'He's in a bit of a funk, apparently, and is refusing to open the tavern. The men in the village are furious. Or so Bianca said. The local women told her there might be a riot if it doesn't open soon. And not just from the men who can't wet their whistle. Apparently, the women are sick of having them under foot while they're trying to prepare the evening meal. It's quite unsettling for the entire village.'

'Well, the tavern keeper will just have to open up and tend to his broken heart at some other time.'

'Yes, yes, quite. Perhaps you should sort that out, Violet.' He waved his hand in the air, as if such things were achieved by magic. 'And the sooner the better. We don't want the tenants rioting in the streets, do we?'

'So you want me to find a cook by this evening. Hire a new estate manager. Mend the tavern keeper's broken heart, make sure the tavern opens again and as soon as possible to prevent the villagers from rioting in the streets.'

'Yes. I know you'll find the time. It's not as if you have anything else to do.' Her father turned his full attention to her for the first time since she'd entered his study. 'I don't say it often enough, Violet, but I don't know what we'd do without you. Thank goodness that man...' He paused and looked upwards, as if searching his memory for a name, then lowered his eyes and smiled. 'Thank goodness that Randolph Simeon fellow left you at the altar. Bianca and I would be so lost if he'd actually gone through with it, married you and taken you away from us.'

Vice-like pain gripped Violet's chest, but she clenched her teeth tightly together in a well-practised manner and waited for it to pass. Her father hadn't meant to hurt her and she would never let him, or anyone else, know just how humiliating that memory was.

'I suppose I had better get busy then,' she said through gritted teeth.

'Very good, dear.'

She left the study, leant against the wall, closed her eyes and breathed slowly and deeply to release the tight knot lodged in the middle of her chest. Then she squared her shoulders and marched down the corridor, trying to think of which problem to fix first.

Chapter Two

Violet would start with opening the tavern, it being the easiest problem to solve on the list of things that needed her immediate attention. But she certainly would not be attempting to mend the tavern keeper's broken heart. Despite her reputation for resourcefulness, that was surely asking too much of her. When it came to her own hurt feelings, she had learnt through bitter experience that it was best to ignore them or bury them so deep that most of the time she was barely aware of their existence. But she would not be imparting this hard-won wisdom to Mr Armstrong. He would have to discover it for himself.

She pushed open the tavern's heavy oak door. The wattle and daub building, with its distinctive black timber frame, had stood on the same spot since the Tudor period and for many years had been a coaching inn. While most visitors to the village now arrived by train, the first stop for many a weary traveller was the local tavern, either for a drink or a meal. It provided accommodation above the bar and was a social hub for the local men. While the tavern keeper had the lease, like much of the village, the premises were owned by Violet's father, the Earl of Brookside. Just as they had belonged to his father before him, going back countless generations.

Her father had little to do with his tenants. His estate manager collected the rents and ensured all repairs were done, while the villagers got on with running their businesses. And that was what they usually did. But not tonight. It was late afternoon. The tavern should be bustling, full of locals and visitors. Instead, only one man was present. The unkempt tavern keeper was sitting hunched over on a bench in the bay window. Violet was tempted to grab Mr Armstrong by his lapels, give him a good shake and tell him to pull himself together, but suspected that would do little good.

'We're closed,' he mumbled, not looking up. This was hopeless. Mr Armstrong was going to be of no help whatsoever and, once again, it was all going to be up to Violet.

'That's what so-called love does to you,' she muttered to herself as she went behind the bar and lifted the cloths off the beer handles. Thank goodness she was now immune to that fickle, destructive emotion. It made you weak and vulnerable. Two conditions by which Violet vowed to never again find herself afflicted.

Several men appeared at the door, curious to see what was happening.

'The Golden Fleece is once again open for business,' she called out to them.

They didn't move, but were joined by more men, all peering in, but seemingly unable to pass through the open door. Violet knew what was wrong. They were frightened of her. She was sure if Bianca was behind the bar, the local men would have no hesitation in entering and would take delight in being served by the Earl's friendly younger daughter. But Violet had a formidable reputation and they were scared of her. Usually that was to her advantage, but not today.

'Due to the tavern being closed for several days, the first drink will be on the house,' she announced and prepared for a stampede of enthusiasm.

The crowd continued to grow, but they all remained hovering outside.

'All right. The first two drinks will be on the house.'

A few of the bravest, their cloth caps tightly clasped in their hands, tentatively crossed the threshold, but were stopped by Tom Watson, the local blacksmith. He stepped in front of them and held up his hands to halt their progress.

'The first three drinks on the house, I believe, would satisfy the thirst the men have been building up since the Golden Fleece shut down.'

Violet glared at him, sorely tempted to tell him what she thought of his attempts at extortion. But she still had to find a cook before Bianca's guests arrived and had no idea how she was to go about finding a new estate manager. The sooner this first problem was solved the better.

'All right, the first three drinks, but only if you, Tom Watson, show me how to work these things...'

she pointed to the beer handles '…and find a replacement barmaid as soon as possible.'

'Right you are, my lady,' he said, waving the men forward. 'Come on, lads. We've got drinking time to make up for.'

A cheer went up and they eagerly rushed forward. Tom retrieved the pewter tankards hanging on hooks, lined them up on the bar then used his own mug to demonstrate to Violet the correct way to draw a pint so it had not too much or too little foamy head on top.

He took a long, satisfied drink. 'This one doesn't count,' he said, lowering his tankard and wiping the foam away from his upper lip. 'It was just to show you what to do. I'm still entitled to three free drinks.'

Violet stifled her annoyance and started filling up the mugs. After a few false starts, she got the hang of things. The men all knew which tankard belonged to them and eagerly grabbed theirs as soon as it was placed back on the bar. They then downed the contents in one long swallow, as if they had been lost in the desert for months, rather than having gone without beer for a few days.

Once their mugs were refilled with their second free drink, they took their seats. Several patted the desolate tavern keeper on the back as they passed and one placed a drink in front of him. But they said nothing to the man, who wouldn't have heard any words of sympathy anyway.

The tankards kept coming back and Violet had to keep a good eye out to see who was on his second, who on his third and who was trying to sneak in a free fourth drink.

* * *

When Tom returned for his fifth drink, she put out her hand for his coins. He smiled and pulled a few pence out of his pocket. 'You're really getting the hang of this, aren't you, my lady?' he said as he handed her his coins.

'Yes, but I'm needed at home, and you promised you'd find a barmaid. That was part of our deal.'

Tom thought for a moment. 'I suppose my daughter, Rosie, wouldn't mind filling in.'

'Excellent—can she start tonight?'

He nodded.

'And also we need a cook up at the house. Are any of the women in the village able to cook for about forty people for two days, breakfast, lunch and dinner, plus morning and afternoon tea?'

Violet could almost see Tom's mind calculating. 'That's a big job. Whoever takes it on will be wanting generous compensation for such a lot of work.'

'But do you know anyone?'

'My missus could probably manage it, but she'd need a lot of help, mind. Maybe her sister would be willing. But it's such short notice and it will take them away from their own families. Let's say twice what you'd pay the cook for a week's work for each of them. That should be enough to get them to agree to doing it.'

Violet had no choice in the matter. 'Yes, all right, but can they please start straight away? The guests have probably already started to arrive and a meal needs to be prepared for tonight.'

'Oh, in that case, I suppose it will have to be three times what you pay the cook for a week.'

Once again, Violet had no choice but to agree. This was all Bianca's fault and, if there was any justice in the world, the money would come out of her sister's dress allowance. But the outcome of that would be tears, tantrums and more trouble than it was worth. Not for the first time, Violet wondered whether she really was up to the task of providing her sister with the necessary guidance and instruction that a young woman like Bianca required.

Tom departed and Violet went back to filling up tankards. After three drinks apiece, the men had lost their reservations at being in the company of the Earl's elder daughter and were now talking and laughing loudly, playing cards and dominoes, and the tavern had taken on a lively ambience.

'A mug of your finest beer as soon as you're ready, darling. I'm in desperate need of refreshment,' a man's voice cut through the hubbub of thirty or so men all talking loudly.

Violet handed some change to one of the farmhands and turned to the man, whose well-bred accent made it clear he was not a local.

He smiled at her and the air seemed to leave her lungs. Handsome did not begin to describe the man looking down at her. At five foot ten, Violet was taller than most of the men in the bar, but this man towered over her. Looking up, she estimated he must be several inches over six feet. And when had she ever seen eyes that colour? They must be brown, but in the dim light of the tavern, they appeared as black as a raven's wings. And those dark eyes were staring straight at her.

'What? I mean, sorry, what did you want?' Violet asked, uncharacteristically stumbling over her words.

'A mug of beer.' He smiled again, a slow, cheeky smile that drew her gaze to his full soft lips. 'I'm getting rather desperate. And while I know that making a man wait only increases his eventual satisfaction, I am in something of a hurry.'

Her gaze shot back to his eyes. He was flirting with her. The audacity of the man. Well, that might work on other women, but it wasn't going to work on her. Lord knew she didn't have much to thank Randolph Simeon for, but at least he had made her immune to handsome men. She now knew that an attractive appearance and a smooth manner could hide a cold, calculating mind and a cruel heart.

'Well, you're just going to have to get used to waiting. Other men were here before you.'

She turned to the other customers and for the first time that evening there was no one lined up at the bar.

He gave a low laugh. 'I can see you really do want to tease me first before you give me what I want.'

She grabbed a pewter mug from the shelf and pulled a beer, not caring how big a head it had on it, and slammed it down on the bar, the foam spilling over the top and slowly sliding down the side of the mug.

'Thank you.' He placed a pile of coins on the bar. 'And have one yourself. You look like you need cooling down.'

Violet scooped up the coins and threw them all in the drawer, furious that he was right. His teasing had indeed caused heat to rush to her cheeks.

Instead of taking a seat, he remained standing at

the bar, watching her while he drank his beer. Violet wanted to look away, but instead she watched, transfixed, as his lips touched the rim of the mug, then her gaze followed the liquid as it moved down his throat. Smiling, his eyes still fixed on her, he lowered the mug and wiped the foam off his upper lip, drawing her gaze back to his lips. 'Best I've ever had and well worth the wait.'

Violet fought to think of something cutting to say back, but for once her sharp tongue let her down and no insult would come.

'I've been forced to come to this part of the country under duress,' he continued. 'But if I'd known the young ladies up here were as pretty as you, I wouldn't have put up so much objection.'

Her burning cheeks grew even hotter, along with her temper. Did he think just because she was behind the bar that he could talk to her in any manner he wanted? Well, he was about to discover just how wrong he was in that assumption.

Violet drew in a long breath as insults whirled inside her head. Like all smooth-talking men, he deserved to be put firmly in his place, but the words continued their spinning and refused to settle into coherent sentences that would cut him to the core. She had to say something, anything. He needed to know she was one woman who did not appreciate his teasing manner, was unaffected by a man's good looks and refused to be trifled with.

'Hopefully, I'll see a bit more of you before I leave.' He looked her up and down, still with that lazy smile on his lips. Heat moved from Violet's cheeks to consume her entire body. He really was the limit.

She closed her eyes briefly to focus her attention, not on her embarrassment, or on the thought of this man seeing more of her, but on the anger seething inside her.

She leant towards him, so no one else could hear. He mirrored her actions, leaning uncomfortably close, their heads almost touching. Heat engulfed her, as if she had moved too close to the fire, but she forced herself to stand her ground. 'Listen here, you,' she seethed, pleased her voice contained a suitable level of disapproval. 'Just because I'm working behind a bar, don't think that gives you the right to talk to me however you like. I'm here to do a job, not to put up with your nonsense.'

Still smiling, he raised his hands, palms upwards, along with his eyebrows, as if he had no idea what he could have done wrong. 'I agree entirely and I most certainly did not intend to give offence. But I have to say, you look lovely when you're angry. It makes those big brown eyes shine and your cheeks glow.'

Violet looked around for the nearest object with which to crown him over the head, but a loud cough from a crofter waiting at the end of the bar drew her attention.

'Looks like someone else wants the pleasure of one of your tongue lashings.' He gave her a quick wink, picked up his drink and walked over to the only empty seat in the room, the one at the tavern keeper's table.

'What do you want?' Violet said to the crofter, louder than she meant to.

The elderly man's eyes grew wide. He took a quick step back and held out his mug with a shaky hand.

'I'm sorry. I'm sorry.' She filled his tankard and handed it back to him. 'This one is on the house as well.'

He gave a toothless grin, mumbled his thanks and scuttled off to join the men in the corner playing skittles.

Violet looked over at the annoying stranger who had agitated her so. He raised his tankard at her in a toast, so she sent him her most severe look, letting him know that not all women were susceptible to his supposed charms and his seductive smile had no effect on her whatsoever.

Herbert had lured him up to Norfolk for the weekend because he believed there wasn't a woman alive that Jake couldn't charm. But Herbert had clearly not met the pretty young woman sneering at him from behind the bar. She alone would prove the falsehood of Herbert's exaggerated claim. As Jake always did with women, he had flirted. He had smiled. He'd tried to be charming, and she'd reacted as if he was the devil incarnate. This did not bode well for the task ahead.

He could only hope that Lady Violet Maidstone was more amenable than that scowling vixen. Although, if she was only half as comely as the barmaid, the weekend would not be an entirely unpleasant one.

He took a sip of his beer, unable to look away. She certainly was a beauty. Or, at least, she would be if her brow wasn't creased in a frown of disapproval. And those full lips would be decidedly luscious if they weren't pulled down at the edges in a grimace. Something had made that woman so bad-tempered and caused her to be ill-disposed towards men.

Her accent was not that of a country lass, but one of an educated woman. Was she a gentlewoman who had fallen on hard times? Was that why she was working as a barmaid? And was that why she was so angry? As tempting as it was to find out, that was not why he was here in this village. Once he left the tavern, he would have to put all thoughts of the intriguing barmaid out of his mind.

But for now, he could enjoy his drink and enjoy watching her at work. The moment he'd finished his drink, it would be all business. He would have to spend a boring weekend at Maidstone House trying to charm an old maid, his only compensation being he was helping his friend in his quest to find true love.

The barmaid threw one more disdainful look in his direction, letting him know that his admiring glances were as welcome as his attempts to flirt.

Reluctantly, he turned to the man sharing his table, who was staring down at the full tankard in front of him, as if unsure what to do with it.

'Cheers,' Jake said, raising his mug. 'At least the beer at this house is more convivial than the barmaid.'

The sullen man raised his head and glared at Jake. 'Don't talk about my Betsy like that. I know she's done wrong, but I loves her. For me, there will never be no one other than my Betsy.'

Jake stared at him. Had he heard correctly? This man was in love? And with the barmaid? Really? The poor, hunched wretch looked more like someone who had just been told the world was about to end than one who was in love. But then, what did Jake know of love? He'd never experienced it himself and, looking at the pathetic husk in front of him, was pleased he never had. Not when it turned a man into a miserable wreck.

'No offence intended.' Jake took another sip of his beer and looked over at 'my Betsy'. Despite his cynicism towards love, he could see why a man might be besotted with her and he wondered what it was she had done wrong. She didn't seem like the sort to stray, more's the pity. The way she was banging the tankards down on the bar in front of her customers could never be described as coquettish behaviour. This was one young woman who did not want the attention or admiration of men.

'She's quite the firebrand, isn't she?' he said as much to himself as to the love-struck man.

'My Betsy? No, never. She's the sweetest woman you could ever meet. She might not be much of a looker, but what she lacks in beauty, she makes up for in her gentle, friendly manner.' Tears sprang to his eyes and he looked back down at the untouched tankard. 'A bit too friendly, that's the problem, see. That's why I never saw what was happening, right under my very nose.'

Jake looked from the man crying into his beer and back up to 'my Betsy'. It never failed to amaze him how love could make men blind. Usually they saw the love of their life as more beautiful than was the case, but not this man. How could he not see that his Betsy was a beauty? With a mass of rich chestnut-brown hair, those flashing brown eyes and those full, pouting lips, she was stunning. Looking at her, it was all but impossible not to wonder what she would look like when that long, thick hair was set free, to drape over her lovely, curvaceous body, or to imagine what she could do with those luscious lips.

He coughed to clear his throat and sipped his beer. No, the man was completely deluded. And as for gentle and friendly? That was not how he'd describe 'my Betsy'. There was nothing gentle about how she had spoken to him and he doubted he'd ever met a less friendly woman, or one less suited for the role of barmaid.

And as much as he would like to know what 'my Betsy' had done right under this man's nose, and with whom, he had delayed his real reason for being in this village long enough.

'Well, you're lucky to have such a woman in your life.' Jake drained his tankard. 'Luckier than me, that's for sure. I'm about to spend the weekend up at Maidstone House. That's why I needed some fortification before doing so. I hear Lady Violet is quite an old dragon.'

The man raised his head, looked up at him, his eyes enormous, then he flicked a fearful look towards 'my Betsy' as if the wrath of the gods was about to descend on them. 'I wouldn't know about that,' he murmured, then lowered his head. 'Keep to myself, I do. Mind my own business. Don't know nothing about what happens up at the big house.'

Once again, the hunched man stared down at his untouched beer, making it clear he wanted no more conversation.

Jake placed a few coins beside his empty mug as an additional tip and departed, hoping that 'my Betsy' and the crying patron weren't typical of the people who lived in this village and their strange behaviour was not a harbinger of a difficult weekend to come.

Chapter Three

He had gone. Good. She looked towards the door through which he had just left. Violet had enough to think about without letting some annoying man disturb her equilibrium. As the lady of the house, she should be getting home so she could greet the guests. Not that her presence was really necessary. Greeting people and making them feel welcome was something Bianca was more than capable of doing. In fact, Bianca's friends would most likely prefer it if she were not present.

Tom entered the tavern, along with a young woman aged about eighteen.

'This here is my daughter, Rosie,' Tom said. Rosie gave a low curtsy then smiled at Violet, revealing dimples in each appropriately rosy cheek.

'Have you worked in a bar before?' Violet asked her.

'Oh, yes. I can pull a pint, know the prices of all the drinks and know my sums, so I can take and give change. I used to help out Betsy when she was…' Rosie paused and looked to her father for help.

'When she was otherwise occupied,' Tom said, keeping his face expressionless. All three flicked quick looks in the direction of the tavern keeper.

'Can you start now?' Violet asked.

Rosie's smile grew bigger and her dimples deeper. She clapped her hands together, lifted the bar opening and instantly started taking orders. While she pulled pints, she chatted away with the customers as if they were all good friends. In response, the men laughed and joked with her in an easy, friendly manner. That was presumably how the handsome stranger had expected Violet to behave. No wonder he was taken aback when she gave him a stern telling off for daring to flirt with her. Well, it was no more than he deserved, and she would devote no more time to even thinking about him. She had too much still to do to waste time in such an idle manner.

'Have your wife and her sister agreed to cook for us this weekend?' she asked Tom.

'Aye, they have. They've already gone up to the house to see what food you have in and what they can make for tonight's meal.'

'Then I had better get going so I can help them get organised.'

'And arrange for their wages. They'll be wanting payment in advance,' Tom added as she rushed out the bar.

Violet ran through the village, then up the gravel path leading to Maidstone House. Carriages were parked outside the entrance and cases and trunks were piled up, waiting for footmen to carry them to the assigned rooms.

Palmer, the butler, rushed out before she had even made it up the stairs. Palmer never rushed and he never looked harried. But he was now.

'Oh, Lady Violet. Thank goodness you are here. Apparently there's to be a house party this weekend. No one informed myself or the housekeeper. Rooms are yet to be prepared or assigned and Cook is away for the weekend.'

'Yes, I'm so sorry, Palmer. I've only just found out myself. I should have let you know before I…' She pointed towards the village, then decided it would only waste more time explaining all that had happened. 'But I've organised some women from the village to cook this weekend. You'll just have to do your best regarding the rooms.'

'I must warn you, Mrs Hampton is not happy.'

Violet was not surprised. The housekeeper prided herself on her ability to run all aspects of the house like clockwork. She did not like surprises or to appear any thing less than completely competent. Fortunately, she adored Bianca and, once she discovered this was all due to Bianca's impetuousness, then all would be forgiven.

'Thank you, Palmer. The guests are only here for the weekend and as they're Bianca's friends, they probably don't mind a bit of chaos. But I must get on. I have to make sure the cooks are settled.'

She rushed round the side of the house and accessed the kitchen through the servants' entrance, hoping to find two women hard at work preparing the evening meal. But it seemed that such a straightforward solution to her second problem was too much to ask.

* * *

Jake delayed his arrival at Maidstone House for as long as he possibly could. He took a leisurely stroll along the tranquil river, then sauntered across the estate, taking in the surrounding rolling green hills, the groves of trees and the well-tended fields. It was rather pleasant to be out of London for a few days, just unfortunate that he would be spending those days at a dull house party. Eventually, he turned and walked up the winding, tree-lined gravel path towards the stately three-storey cream stone house. He could delay the inevitable no longer.

He noted that his luggage had arrived before him and his trunk was being carried inside by a footman.

And there was something else he also noted, something unexpected and intriguing. A flustered Betsy running around the side of the house, one lock of hair flying loose from her bun. She disappeared into the house through the servants' entrance. Did she work in this house as well as in the tavern? He hoped not. The last thing he needed was the distraction of the lovely Betsy when he was supposed to be dedicating his time to distracting the gruesome Lady Violet.

But if she did work in the house, she would be hidden away downstairs and he was unlikely to see her, which was something to be both pleased and disappointed about.

Perhaps she was delivering an order of wine and brandy, although there was no sign of a delivery cart. Whatever it was, it was no business of his. He paused for a moment longer, staring in the direction in which she had gone, then turned to the house and wandered up the stone stairs towards the entranceway.

Inside he found a hive of confused activity, with footmen running every which way. A frowning butler was shouting orders, while an older woman, presumably the housekeeper, was giving instructions to a flotilla of maids. When the butler saw Jake leaning against a marble pillar at the entrance, his face immediately took on the impassive expression of a well-trained servant. He walked towards him, as if oblivious to the mayhem.

'May I be of assistance, sir?' he asked.

'Yes, I'm Lord Jake Rosemont, a friend of the Honourable Herbert Fortescue. I've been invited to spend the weekend.'

'Very good, my lord. All the guests have gathered in the blue drawing room. I'm afraid there has been a spot of confusion and the rooms are not yet ready, but that will be put to rights presently. If you'll join the others, we will let you know when you can retire to your rooms to freshen up.'

'Thank you.'

Jake followed the butler down the corridor and entered the drawing room, where twenty or so people were already helping themselves to drinks, greeting each other enthusiastically, chatting and laughing loudly. Obviously, whatever confusion had upset the butler and the other servants was not affecting the guests.

'Jake.' Herbert's voice bellowed out from across the room. 'You made it.'

He joined his friend and scanned the room, expecting to see a woman sitting in the corner with her book or her knitting, or something else that would mark her out as the old maid.

'Lady Violet isn't here yet,' Herbert said more quietly. 'Hopefully she'll stay wherever she is all weekend and you can spend your time with the other lovelies that Bianca has invited.'

Jake doubted that. The 'lovelies' were all quite obviously debutantes, and debutantes were only ever after one thing: a husband. They were best avoided at all costs.

Herbert led him across the room and introduced him to Bianca, and Jake could see why his friend had been caught, hook, line and sinker. She was a pretty blonde with a bubbly laugh and, from her wide smile, he suspected, an equally bubbly personality.

'Isn't this fun?' he said, thrusting a glass of champagne into his hand. 'I've got ever so much organised for this weekend, games, picnics and lots and lots of champagne, so no matter what else happens we'll never go thirsty.'

Could that explain Betsy's presence? Was she delivering champagne? No, he doubted that. Local taverns might have plenty of barrels of beer to quench the thirst of a platoon of farmhands and other workers, but the patrons' tastes and pockets rarely ran to French champagne.

'And to add to the fun, we're going to have to rough it a bit,' Herbert said, smiling at Lady Bianca as if the thought of roughing it was the best news he'd had all week. 'Slight problem with the rooms. We might even have to dine in our travelling clothes if the servants don't get things organised in time.'

'I suppose we'll just have to struggle on under such adversity,' Jake said, taking a drink of his champagne.

'That's the spirit,' Herbert said, not catching the sarcastic note in Jake's voice.

Herbert and Bianca introduced him to the other guests, and the assembled party began discussing the usual topics at society events: the latest gossip, the plans for the Season and, that old standby, the weather. Ennui descended on Jake like a shroud, as it always did at such gatherings. No wonder he was driven to gambling. It was usually the only source of excitement available and he wondered if Lady Bianca's weekend fun would include a round or two of baccarat or a few hands of poker.

He wandered over to the window and looked out at the gardens, at the trees bearing their pink and white blossom and the spring flowers bobbing about in the gentle breeze.

He half expected to see Betsy marching off down the pathway. Perhaps she was still in the house. Perhaps she *was* a servant. But servants worked long, hard hours. Why would one also work at the local tavern? Was that the reason she was so short-tempered? Exhaustion?

It wouldn't hurt to find out, would it? Perhaps he might be of some assistance. If she was in straitened circumstances, he could have a word to Herbert, who could pass it on to Lady Bianca. Then all her problems could be solved and maybe he could put a smile on Betsy's stern face.

And saving Betsy would at least provide him with a

momentary distraction while he waited for Lady Violet to arrive. Then he could begin his task of charming the old maid.

He looked over at Herbert, who was staring at Lady Bianca as if she was an angelic vision who had descended from on high. Neither would notice his momentary absence.

Discreetly leaving the drawing room, he retraced his steps through the still-bustling entranceway, around the footmen and the scurrying maids, and out into the garden, then breathed in deeply, filling his lungs with the fresh country air. Society events always had a stifling effect on him, as if he was being forced into a cage that was too small for him. Making small talk with the debutantes was not only tedious, but he always wanted to inform them they were wasting their time. He was not in search of a wife, and their precious husband-hunting time was better spent pursuing another, more willing victim.

He strolled casually to the side of the house, as if he was merely stretching his legs. When he passed the servants' entrance, the sound of raised female voices assaulted him.

What they were arguing about was none of his business. He should keep on walking. He stopped and listened to the shrill voices and shrugged. Perhaps he could be of some service. After all, smoothing ruffled feminine feathers was another one of his limited skills, so he entered the kitchen.

Feathers did indeed fill the air and two women were staring at each other, daggers in their eyes, while a crumpled Betsy sat at the kitchen table, her head in her hands. All three were oblivious to his presence.

'I've been plucking chickens since I was a girl and you don't do it like that,' one woman said, ripping out a few more feathers and adding them to the snowstorm of feathers floating in the kitchen.

'Yes, and that's why your chickens are always as tough as old boots. That's not how our ma showed us. If you'd been paying attention instead of chasing after every boy in the village, you would—'

'How dare you say that? I was always a good girl. You know that. It was you who couldn't keep her drawers—'

'Ladies, ladies, what seems to be the problem here?' Jake said, cutting through the argument before the cooks revealed more about their wayward youth than they should.

The two arguing women turned to him, their faces still pinched, then they smiled at him and bobbed quick curtsies. This was the reaction Jake usually got from women, young and old, but he wasn't getting the same reaction from Betsy.

She hadn't even bothered to stand and certainly hadn't curtsied, but at least she had lowered her hands from her head, although was now glowering at him from her seat at the table.

'It's just me and my sister having a bit of a to-do about the dinner. Nothing to worry about, sir.'

'I see. I'm sure the to-do can be easily set to rights,' Jake said, as if sorting out cooking problems was something he did every day. 'Perhaps you...' He indicated the woman in the green apron who had addressed him. 'Sorry, young lady, what is your name?'

'Myrtle,' the woman said with another quick bob and a little smile.

'What a lovely name. Myrtle, it suits you. Perhaps you could prepare the chickens.'

She nodded her agreement and he turned to her sister.

'And what's your name, young lady?'

'Beryl, sir,' she said with a smile.

'Beryl, perhaps you could turn your fair hands to…' He looked around the kitchen, wondering what else went into preparing a meal.

'I could do the vegetables, sir.'

'The vegetables, excellent idea, Beryl. Clever as well as pretty, a rare combination.'

For that compliment, he got the expected blush and light giggle. The two women exchanged little grins, then went about their assigned tasks.

He had no idea what Betsy did in the kitchen, apart from glaring up at him, and he didn't dare suggest a task for her.

'And I, for one, am looking forward to savouring all that you have to offer,' he said, turning back to the cooks and giving them a smile which many a woman had described as suggestive.

The two women laughed louder and nudged each other, but continued with their work.

'Guests are not welcome in the kitchen,' Betsy said, cutting through their laughter. 'Go back out that door.' She pointed to the kitchen door. 'Go round to the front of the house and Palmer will show you to your room.'

It was an unexpected reaction from a servant, but nothing less than he would expect from Betsy. He tipped an imaginary hat at the busy cooks and departed to the sound of girlish giggling from the middle-aged sisters.

'Well, I never,' Myrtle said, expressing exactly what Violet was thinking herself. That man was the limit. Who did he think he was, barging into the kitchen, taking over, throwing his weight about and giving orders to her staff?

It was now obvious he was one of Bianca's guests. No surprise there. Bianca said she had invited a group of her closest friends, along with some eligible men. No doubt he would spend the weekend charming the debutantes with that seductive smile and teasing manner. Well, she just hoped Bianca's friends were not gullible enough to fall under his spell. Violet knew from bitter experience that when it came to men, the more charming they were, the less substance there was to their character. She also knew that they did not reserve their charm for the women they were courting, but spread it wide and far, and were not averse to going further than a bit of flirtation.

Lucky she was now completely immune to charming men and that man more than most.

'Savouring what we have to offer. The cheek of him,' Beryl said, her laughter suggesting that, unlike Violet, she did not object to such cheek. 'I'd happily let him savour what I've got to offer any time and anywhere he wants.'

This comment caused Myrtle to laugh louder. 'I

know who I'll be thinking about the next time my Tom gets a bit frisky,' she said, wiping away a tear of laughter from her eye. 'My, oh, my, a real toe curler that one is.'

Her comment elicited further ribald laughter from her sister. Then they both looked at Violet and their laughter stopped abruptly. 'Begging your pardon, my lady,' they both murmured, but continued smiling as they went about their work.

He might be annoying, but at least he had solved the problem of the warring cooks, who were now talking quietly, apparently united in their appreciation of his obvious attractive qualities. Qualities that were *far too* obvious, Violet would say, if anyone wanted her opinion. But she had no time to fritter, contemplating that irritating man. With two problems solved, she still had to endure a house full of guests, the tedium of two days with Bianca's inane friends, and find a manager to run the estate.

She retraced her steps and passed through the entrance way, which was mercifully now clear of luggage and frantic servants. Mrs Hampton informed her stiffly that the rooms had been prepared and the guests had retired to dress for dinner.

Violet thanked the housekeeper warmly and went upstairs to try to undo the damage that her hectic day had caused to her usually robust composure.

The sight that greeted her in her dressing room mirror was worse than she expected. Her hair was in complete disarray. Long tendrils had escaped from what had started off as a tight bun at the nape of her neck and were now strewn haphazardly down her back and around her shoulders. Her flushed face showed clearly how she had spent the day. Not seated idly in a drawing room making polite conversation, as most women of her class would, but working in a stuffy bar, running to and from the village and trying and failing to mediate an argument between the cooks.

Her disordered appearance must have given that annoying man such a good laugh at her expense. Violet released an exasperated sigh. Well, she would not give him another opportunity to mock her further.

She pulled out her hairpins and threw them on the dressing table. Normally, she did not care one fig about her appearance, but she did not like to be laughed at, especially by men who thought they were irresistible.

She summoned her lady's maid, who rushed in carrying a pitcher of warm water and a bowl for Violet to wash in, there being no time to fill a bath.

'I think I'll wear the cream gown with the gold embroidery tonight, Agatha.'

Her lady's maid's eyes momentarily grew wide, then she composed her face and removed the gown from the wardrobe. She looked at it and frowned. 'This will need ironing, my lady. It's been a while since you've worn it.'

She held up the gown for Violet's inspection. The dress was somewhat dated, having been made for Violet's first Season, eight years ago. At the time, Violet had loved wearing it. She had adored the soft silk fabric and the way the train swirled around her legs as she walked. Everyone had commented on how elegant it was and how the colour contrasted dramatically with her dark eyes and hair.

'Thank you, Agatha, just do your best in the time

available.' She turned to the mirror and began brushing her hair, remembering how she had looked during her Season. Not only did she have countless dresses in the latest fashions, she had also almost achieved the fashionably pale skin expected of every young debutante. Now, after years of not caring if she caught the sun, her skin was tanned and her cheeks had taken on a ruddy appearance.

Well, there was nothing to be done about it and she most certainly would not attempt to make it pale with the application of lemon juice or any other concoction that women used out of desperation to make their skin porcelain white.

She ran her fingers lightly over her skin, then noticed just how rough her hands had become and dropped them to her side.

This was ridiculous. Why should she care what any of Bianca's guests thought of her? None of them were even likely to notice a woman of her advanced age. They'd be too busy flirting with each other to pay her the slightest bit of attention.

While she waited for her lady's maid to return, she washed and changed into a clean chemise and corset. Her lady's maid rushed back in, the gown draped over her arm.

'Perhaps we should tighten your corset laces, my lady,' Agatha said, looking at Violet's waistline. She knew what the lady's maid was thinking, something that had crossed her mind as well. Would she still fit into a gown she had worn when she was eighteen?

'Do your best, Agatha.' She turned her back and winced as her lady's maid gave the laces a firm tug.

She lifted her arms as Agatha lowered the gown and held her breath as she closed the line of buttons down the back of the gown.

When she released her breath, she was pleased to discover the gown still fit her perfectly.

'Perhaps you can restyle my hair as well, Agatha. Do it in that manner that Bianca wears.' She twirled her hands around the top of her head. 'All puffy and piled up on top.'

Surprise once again briefly flicked across Agatha's face, before she gave a polite, 'Yes, my lady.'

She then commenced to brush out the locks, back-comb them, divide them into sections, wind them round the end of her comb, plait them and do heaven knows what else, to achieve an intricate, voluminous creation that young ladies currently favoured.

When she was finished, Violet had to admit it was flattering. Her dress might be behind the latest fashion, but at least now no one would laugh at her hairstyle.

'You look beautiful, my lady,' Agatha said, admiring her work. 'You'll be the envy of all those other young women.'

'Thank you, Agatha. That will be all,' Violet said, more harshly than she intended.

Her lady's maid bobbed a quick curtsy and departed.

Violet continued to stare at herself in the mirror. What on earth had she been thinking? She was an old maid of six and twenty, dressed in a gown that was eight years out of fashion, and trying to look like a sweet young debutante of eighteen. She was determined that she would not be laughed at, but in dressing like this, wasn't she making herself an even greater source of fun?

Perhaps she should change into something plain and more fitting for her age and position and undo Agatha's ornate hairstyle, but she had already spent enough time away from the guests and had neglected her role of chaperon to her young sister for far too long. Too much time had been wasted on such fripperies. She needed to get down to the drawing room to make sure none of those eligible young men were paying Bianca undue attention.

Her little sister was so susceptible, even more than Violet had been at her age. She was open and naive and still thought all men were honourable and trustworthy. Violet had learnt the hard way that men were not always what they seemed, that they could be deceptive, false-hearted and unbelievably selfish.

It would break Violet's heart if any man treated her lovely sister the way Randolph had treated her. No one had protected Violet from that deceitful scoundrel, but she would do everything in her power to protect her sister, so she didn't make the same mistake as her older sister and fall hopelessly for an unsuitable man.

That would be her focus for this weekend, and indeed the entire Season, and nothing and no one would distract her from that purpose.

Chapter Four

While Jake had been sorting out the problem with the servants, his valet had unpacked his bags and set the room up just as Jake liked it. After he had shaved, his valet helped him into his dinner suit and brushed it down until it reached the high standard acceptable to the valet's well-trained eye, while Jake mentally prepared himself for what was expected of him.

He was to woo the wallflower, charm the crone, dally with the dragon—in other words, keep the shrewish sister busy while Herbert found true love.

It was all going to be tedious beyond belief, but was in a good cause. His friend was captivated by the delightful Lady Bianca. Spending time in that young woman's company would either cure Herbert of this unfortunate condition, or it would be true love and his friend would go the way of many a good man, bound by the ties of matrimony.

He descended the stairs, paused at the drawing room door, put on his most charming smile and entered. He scanned the room for his intended target, but instead of seeing a wallflower hidden away in a corner, he saw Betsy, standing by the mantelpiece, looking bored but beautiful. Her hair was no longer bedraggled, but styled immaculately, and she was wearing a gown that exposed her shoulders and a tempting hint of cleavage. While she still looked stunning, he had to admit he preferred her tousled and disordered, with a flush of exertion on her cheeks.

But it begged the question, what on earth was she doing here and why was she dressed like a guest? Shouldn't she be pulling pints back at the tavern, or failing to control the servants down in the kitchen? This woman became more and more intriguing every time he saw her.

Herbert bustled up to him, his shoulders sloping, his brow crinkled. 'Thank goodness you're here, Jake. She's already interfering. She really is a nightmare. Lady Bianca and I were getting on so well before she turned up. You'll have to use all your charm and keep her out of my way.'

'Right, you'd better introduce me to the harridan.' He looked around the room, which only contained bright young women twittering and flirting with the assembled men. Not one of those smiling ladies looked capable of reducing any man, even Herbert, to a gibbering wreck.

Herbert moved tentatively across the room, as if approaching a wild animal, and stopped in front of Betsy.

'Lady Violet, may I present my friend, Lord Jake Rosemont.'

Betsy looked him up and down and Jake fought hard to just smile politely and keep the laughter bubbling up inside him from bursting out. The beauteous Betsy was his harridan, his old maid, his crone, the shrewish sister he had come to charm. This weekend party had just become a lot more interesting.

'Lady Violet and I have already met,' he said, taking her gloved hand and bowing. 'But we are yet to be formally introduced.'

'You have?' Herbert looked confused. 'How, where, when?'

Jake knew what he was thinking. They hardly moved in the same circles and, if they'd met before, why had he not informed Herbert?

'It hardly matters, does it?' Betsy, now known as Lady Violet, snapped, causing Herbert almost to jump back. 'It is something I do not wish to discuss and which you do not need to know.'

'Right oh,' Herbert mumbled, looking around for an escape. 'I'll leave you two to reacquaint yourselves, then, shall I? While I…yes…'

He quickly rushed across the room and joined the smiling Lady Bianca, who took his hand in a reassuring manner and stroked it gently, as if soothing a frightened child.

'Herbert Fortescue is a capital fellow,' Jake said, starting his job of selling Herbert as a potential suitor for Lady Violet's sister.

'A good friend of yours, is he?' Her disapproving gaze moved from Herbert and back to him. And from the stern look on her face, it was obvious that being a friend of Jake's was no recommendation at all.

'Yes, we are friends. We first met when we were members of the same church choir.' It wasn't entirely a lie. They had both been choir boys at school. Although their friendship had really begun when the vicar inadvertently forgot to lock the communion wine away in the cabinet. That night, they discovered the joy of overindulgence and had never looked back. As their friendship progressed, that overindulgence had moved on from illicit wine to various other vices, but always revolved around having as much fun as possible.

'*You* are in a church choir?'

'I was. Name any hymn you like and I could belt it out. Not as well as Herbert Fortescue, of course. He's got a voice that could make the angels weep.' Weep because of the pain he was causing to their ears, Jake could add, but didn't.

'I suppose everyone must have one accomplishment.' They glanced over at Herbert, who was gazing at Bianca as if she was an angel and her beauty was about to make him weep.

'His singing voice is just one of his many good qualities.'

She frowned at him, her expression unconvinced. 'Oh, and what other qualities does he possess?'

Jake racked his brains. 'Well, he's loyal to a fault.'

Whenever Jake was ejected from a gambling house, Herbert always followed him. That was loyalty, wasn't it?

'And he's generous and honest.'

In other words, he always settled his gambling debts on time.

'And he's humble.'

Or, to put it another way, he didn't object when he inevitably lost.

'I hear he has a gambling problem.'

'What? Herbert Fortescue? No, never.'

That did rather depend on what one considered a problem. Yes, Herbert gambled quite a lot, but he never saw it as a problem. It was just something he could well afford and enjoyed doing. If he didn't see it as a problem, there was no reason why anyone else should. 'Did you solve the ruckus in the kitchen? Has everything settled down with the cooks?' Jake asked, pulling the conversation away from gambling.

'I suppose we're about to find out when dinner is served.'

He waited for her to explain. She didn't. Instead, she stared over at Lady Bianca and Herbert.

'I'm sure it will all be splendid,' he said. 'And if you need my help with the servants again, you only have to ask.'

Her angry gaze turned on him. 'I don't and I won't. And I didn't ask for your help in the first place.'

'No, but I'm always happy to be of assistance.'

'Happy to interfere where you're not wanted. I'm certain things would have settled down without you. Eventually.'

He was tempted to say that neither Beryl nor Myrtle seemed to object to his interference, but decided her difficulties in managing the servants were perhaps another area best avoided if he was to succeed in his quest to charm her to distraction.

'And will you be working in the tavern again? You seem to be quite at home pulling pints.' He smiled to let her know that he was teasing, but he was still curious to know why the lady of the house also took on the work of a barmaid.

Her lips pinched together. 'One of the local girls has now agreed to work as the barmaid.' Once again, she looked him up and down disdainfully. 'And you'll be pleased to know she is a young woman who doesn't mind being called darling, or men acting as if buying a pint of beer gives them the right to talk to her in an overly familiar manner.'

'Oh, yes, about that. Sorry, obviously I didn't know who you were.' Jake sent her what he hoped was his most contrite smile, one that had gained him forgiveness from countless women in the past.

'Don't be sorry. Just don't do it again. And it should not have mattered who I was. All women deserve respect, whether they're a barmaid, a servant, a debutante or a titled lady.'

Jake fought to keep smiling through these unfounded accusations. 'I always respect women,' he said, pleased that his words did not expose the irritation rising inside him.

Her eyes narrowed as if she didn't believe him. 'Do you even know what respect is when it comes to women?'

Images of all the women who had moved through his life, and his bed, came to mind. Every one of them, he was sure, would say he'd treated them with the utmost respect and always made their needs and their pleasure a priority.

'I would like to think I always respect women and aim to make them happy.' He raised his eyebrows in a suggestive manner that usually caused women of all ages to blush and giggle girlishly.

Instead, she sniffed her disapproval and he swallowed his frustration. This was not going well. He *was* keeping Lady Violet distracted, but his instructions had been to charm her, not to argue with her or offend her. Another approach was needed.

'The tavern keeper seemed rather upset about losing his Betsy.' If Jake knew women, and he prided himself that he did, there was nothing they enjoyed better than a good gossip, particularly when the gossip involved lovesick men.

'Mr Armstrong has had some disappointments in his life, but it's hardly something to look so gleeful about.'

Jake's smile froze. It was supposed to be a flirtatious smile, not a gleeful one. He instantly adopted a more serious expression. 'You're quite right, Lady Violet. I did my best to console poor Mr Armstrong when I was at the tavern The poor man.' He shook his head dolefully.

'Oh, for goodness' sake. Do you take me for a half-wit?'

'No, of course...'

'Believe me, I am not one, Lord Jake. Your interest in Mr Armstrong is as genuine as your claim to respect women. Now, if you'll excuse me, I need to rescue my sister from your loyal, generous and humble friend.'

She pushed past him and joined Lady Bianca and Herbert. Herbert looked at him over the heads of the two sisters, his eyes appealing to be saved. Jake could only shrug his shoulders in a helpless response.

He had tried, but had already failed, and the weekend had only just begun. Lady Violet was not a woman to be charmed. She did not like to be flirted with and was uninterested in gossip.

That made her unlike any woman he had ever met, and his usual bag of tricks was not working. Somehow, he had to prove to her he was a man for whom she would happily neglect her duty as chaperon. To do that, it was essential he find out more about this disarming woman and modify his behaviour to suit. A task which, surprisingly, he had no objection to undertaking.

Violet should have known. Not only was Lord Jake one of Bianca's eligible young men, but he was a friend of Herbert Fortescue. Violet and Bianca had met that buffoon when paying a visit to his mother. It had been patently obvious he had seen Bianca as a good catch, as indeed she was, and now his friend was trying to convince her that the man had hitherto unknown fine qualities.

Well, she was not an imbecile. She was fully aware that Mr Fortescue wanted to court Bianca for exactly the same reason as Randolph had courted her. Bianca's wedding settlement was a sizeable one, big enough to satisfy even the most inveterate gambler. But history was certainly not about to repeat itself and she would do everything in her power to protect her sister from the snares of fortune hunters.

She joined her sister and the mooning Mr Fortescue. He was telling Bianca a story, which was causing her to titter behind her gloved hand, but he stopped immediately when Violet joined them and looked over at Lord Jake, like a drowning man, watching the last lifeboat sail off without him.

Violet could not decide who was more annoying, Mr Fortescue or Lord Jake. No, she suspected Lord Jake was more annoying. At least Mr Fortescue was rightfully wary of her.

But Lord Jake appeared to be afraid of nothing, as if he could just laugh, smile and charm his way through all of life's adversities. Well, that's what happened when you were privileged, handsome and a man. Nothing or no one ever caused you any genuine grief. That was another reason the man irritated her. He could do what he wanted, treat women however he wanted, and no one would ever think any less of him. It was all so easy for men.

And how could he possibly say he respected women? The nerve of the man. He probably only respected them when they were swooning over him and falling gratefully at his feet just because he'd shown them some attention.

Well, he had better not expect such a reaction from her. She would not be tittering like Myrtle and Beryl or making bawdy speculations about what they'd like to do with him if given half a chance.

Heat rushed to her cheeks as she remembered their comments about letting him have them anywhere, any time, and she wondered what they meant by him being a real toe curler. Whatever it was, it was something she did not need to know about.

To underline just how much she did not care about their comments, she sent him another scowl of disapproval. Big mistake. Instead of seeing it as the intended rebuff, he smiled and walked across the room.

Her annoyance must be the reason her heartbeat was

increasing its tempo as he sauntered towards her in that casual, relaxed manner. It was anger and irritation that were causing her temperature to rise and her stomach to flutter as if it was a long time since she had dined.

'May I have a quiet word with you, Lady Violet?' he said, taking her gently by the elbow and leading her away as if she had no say in the matter. And in her disconcerted state, she allowed herself to be led.

'Well, what is it?' she asked, trying to ignore the way her arm was still tingling where he had touched it.

'It seems I have made a poor impression on you.'

He had no argument from her on that score.

'I just hope you are too sensible to let first impressions cloud your judgement. Surely you are not the sort of woman who would dismiss a man before giving him a chance to show you just what he is like?'

'And what are you like, Lord Jake?' She wondered whether he was the type to hear the disdain dripping off every one of her words.

'That is what this weekend is for. It is a chance for you to find out just what your guests are like. We've got two days together. Hopefully, by the end of that time, you will see that I am a man you can respect, maybe even admire, and that we have many things in common.'

Violet fought not to impolitely roll her eyes. 'I'm afraid you will see little of me this weekend. I have a household to run and a sister to chaperon.' She looked across the room to Bianca, who was giggling while Mr Fortescue whispered something in her ear.

'Surely you are too young for such responsibilities. Can't your father chaperon your sister? And can't the housekeeper manage the house? Isn't that what they're for? Then you can enjoy yourself with your guests.'

'They're not *my* guests. They are all friends of Bianca's. And the housekeeper has enough to do. Bianca sprang this party on her with no warning while the cook was on holiday and my father...' They both looked around for her father, who was nowhere to be seen. He had been present when Violet first arrived in the drawing room, but after greeting the guests he had no doubt retreated to his study, where he would most likely remain for the rest of the weekend. 'My father leaves the task of chaperon to me.'

'But that can't be right,' he said, giving her another of those smiles that were presumably supposed to be endearing. 'Shouldn't someone be chaperoning you as well?'

This time she didn't let politeness stand in her way and she did roll her eyes. He must know as well as anyone that she was past the marriageable age and past the age when preserving her virtue was anyone's concern but her own. 'I do not need a chaperon. I'm perfectly capable of looking after myself.'

His smile slowly grew wider as he stared into her eyes. 'Are you sure about that?' he murmured.

Despite her determination not to, her gaze moved from his eyes and lingered on those smiling lips. Her body flushed and her heart and stomach quivered as an unbidden image entered her mind. One which involved Lord Jake smiling down at her, just before those lips touched hers.

Where on earth had that come from?

She shook her head as if flinging that image away.

Her gaze flicked back to his eyes. She would not be undermined by him. That was not who she was. She was a strong, capable woman with responsibilities.

To prove just how capable she was and how nothing he did or said would ever disconcert her, she stared back at him, adopting a challenging expression that had caused many a man to wither and scuttle away.

He held her gaze. She would not let him rattle her. Maybe once she had been susceptible to attractive, self-assured men, but not any more. Since her guard came up eight years ago, she had never once been tempted to lower it. And she wasn't about to start now. Lord Jake needed to know that she was unaffected by his attentions.

To that end, she continued to stare into his brown eyes. Eyes so dark, so deep, they seemed to draw in the light and draw her in along with it.

His smile faded, but he held her gaze. This had gone on for too long to be acceptable. She should look away. She wanted to look away, yet she couldn't. Her heart was pounding hard in her chest and invisible vines seemed to have wound themselves around her, holding her in place. Why she was gazing into his eyes, she no longer knew. All she knew was that she wanted to drown in those dark eyes, to surrender to the intense sensations swelling up inside her and let them take her where they willed.

The resounding sound of the dinner gong halted all conversation. Violet had never been more grateful to hear that noise. Not just because it meant that the cooks had managed to organise a meal to feed the guests, but because it freed her from this silent war of wills she no longer knew how she had got into. As if emerging from a trance, she looked around the room. Conversation erupted once more as couples paired up for the parade to the dining room.

'Would you do me the honour?' he said quietly.

She looked down at his extended arm, reluctant to take it. But what excuse could she use? She could hardly say, *I don't want you to escort me into dinner because I'm disconcerted by the way you make me feel. I prefer to be totally in control at all times and being close to you unravels that control in a manner that is unsettling and confusing.*

No, she would not say that. She'd rather not even think it. Instead, she put her discomfort down to the trying day she had endured, which had left her unnerved, shattered and unable to think clearly.

Yes, that had to be it. Nothing else could have caused her to so easily forget all the lessons she had so painfully learnt.

He was just a man, and no man would ever affect her again. She was no longer that naive, trusting debutante she had once been. Life had taught her how to keep men firmly at bay. They now saw her as a terrifying virago, a woman best avoided at all costs, and that was how she liked it. Herbert Fortescue had quickly learnt to fear her. She now just had to find a way to teach Lord Jake Rosemont that he, too, should see her as a woman to be wary of.

With that firmly in mind, she took his arm, raised her head and allowed him to escort her down the corridor to the dining room.

Chapter Five

Violet stared at the dining table. This was a disaster. She had wanted Bianca to take more responsibility. Now she wished she had organised every facet of this weekend party herself and left nothing to her little sister.

The table did look beautiful, but that was due to the expertise of the household servants. Even with such little notice, they had created a magnificent centrepiece of spring flowers, and the delightful scent of hyacinths and freesias filled the air. The silver was all highly polished, so it glittered in the light of the candelabras, and the sparkling glassware was lined up with military precision.

But it was still a disaster. Violet looked at each table setting, bearing a card with Bianca's beautiful scrolling handwriting denoting where everyone was to sit. Bianca was next to Mr Fortescue, at one end of the table, as far away from Violet as it was possible to get. And she was seated at the other end, next to Lord Jake.

It was tempting to grab all the cards and quickly

rearrange them, so Bianca was at one end of the table, Mr Fortescue at the other, and Violet was in a position where she could watch both of them. How was she supposed to chaperon her sister if she was so far away? And how was she supposed to focus on that task when she had the distraction of Lord Jake sitting right beside her?

But it was only one meal. It would be over soon. And for the remainder of the weekend, she would keep that Mr Fortescue and Bianca constantly under her vigilant gaze.

With much laughter and loud talking, the rest of the guests entered the drawing room and stood by the chairs assigned to them. Lord Jake pulled out her chair, as did the other gentlemen for the women beside them, and with much rustling of silk and satin gowns, the other ladies sat down.

Violet kept a close eye on Bianca, who continued smiling at Mr Fortescue as she took her seat. Lord Jake gave a discreet cough. She looked at him to see what his problem was and he tilted his head towards the chair he was holding out for her. She was the only woman still standing. There was nothing for it. She didn't like it, but she would have to stay where she was. She could hardly pick up her chair, move it to the other end of the table and place herself between Mr Fortescue and Bianca, as tempting as such an action was.

Taking her seat, she tried to ignore how close Lord Jake was as he leant over her and pushed in her chair. But she failed to ignore that now unfamiliar but still unforgettable musky scent of a man and the underlying hint of something fresh and enticing that was uniquely

Lord Jake's. His shaving soap, perhaps. What was that scent? Sandalwood, bergamot, cardamom? Whatever it was, it was captivating. Violet took in another deep breath and briefly closed her eyes.

As if caught doing something unforgivable, her eyes snapped open. She rang the silver handbell fiercely to summon the footmen. They entered carrying soup terrines and, with the tension once again gripping her shoulders, she watched them move around the table, serving the creamy liquid into each bowl.

She had no idea whether Beryl and Myrtle could cook, but she was about to find out. She looked along the table at Bianca. These people were her sister's friends, but she seemed not the slightest bit concerned over the quality of the food she was about to feed them. Instead, she was talking animatedly with Mr Fortescue and the other young people surrounding her.

'I'm sure the soup will be a triumph,' Lord Jake said. 'And if it's not, I doubt anyone will care. I don't think it is the food that brought these people to your home.'

She looked up and down the table. Everyone was doing the same as Bianca, laughing, talking, flirting, drinking and having a good time.

'Yes, perhaps you're right,' she said, not entirely convinced.

Violet lowered her spoon and took a tentative sip. Potato soup. It was not what she would have placed on the menu if she'd had time, preferring more fashionable French cuisine for a dinner party, but she had to admit it was rather tasty.

'Delicious,' Lord Jake said and smiled at her. 'My

compliments to Beryl and Myrtle and to you for finding such superb cooks at short notice.'

She looked along the table. Everyone was still talking and laughing as before, but they were also eating their soup and she could see no signs of complaint.

'Is Lady Bianca now forgiven for inviting guests to the house without informing you first?' Lord Jake asked.

'I wouldn't go that far. Only a ninny would hold a weekend party when the cook was absent.'

He frowned slightly at the insult.

'Oh, all right. I shouldn't call Bianca a ninny. It's just sometimes her behaviour does worry me. Since our mother died ten years ago I've had to take on the responsibility of caring for her and, when she acts in such an impetuous manner, it makes me wonder what other, more serious mistakes she is going to make in life.'

Such as falling for the first man who shows her any attention, just like I did.

They both looked towards the other end of the table. Bianca smiled at them and raised her glass as if the success of the soup proved that Violet had been unduly worried.

'It can't have been easy taking on that responsibility at such a young age,' Lord Jake said quietly, then smiled. 'But Lady Bianca strikes me as a sensible young woman who just likes to enjoy herself. She might not be adept at organising house parties, but perhaps her skills lie elsewhere.'

'Unlike your friend Mr Fortescue, Bianca is not much of a hymn singer.'

He laughed lightly and warmth radiated through her. It was rather nice to make a man laugh.

'I'd never describe Herbert as a ninny, but I would have to admit he is not an intellectual giant. But then, not every woman wants an intellectual giant for a husband and not all intellectual giants make good husbands.'

'Hmm, perhaps.' Her father was an intelligent man, but had neglected his wife, who'd had no interest in academic pursuits. Her poor mother. She must have been so lonely. Like Bianca, she'd loved parties and nothing had made her happier than a good gossip with her friends, but her husband had no interest in such things. He preferred to be alone in his study, and when he did socialise it was with other academics, men with whom her mother had nothing in common.

She looked at Mr Fortescue and wondered, *would* he make a good husband for Bianca? Then just as quickly, dismissed this idea. 'Bianca doesn't have to pursue an intellectual giant, but there has to be someone more suitable than Mr Fortescue.'

'Suitable for whom? You or Bianca?' he said quietly, causing her to scowl at him.

The footmen removed the soup bowls and Violet used that time to try to think of a response which would explain why she was a better judge of the sort of man Bianca should marry than her sister would ever be. She knew what men were like. Her sister didn't. She knew that men were often not what they seemed, while her sister thought the best of everyone she met. Unlike Violet, Bianca did not know that men could say one thing and mean another, they could pretend to love you when what they really loved was your marriage settlement.

No, she was definitely better placed to find a suitable husband for her sister than Bianca ever would be. That was what she should say to Lord Jake, but there was no reason she should have to explain herself to him or anyone else. Bianca was her responsibility and that was the end of the matter.

'Lord Jake, what an unexpected pleasure to see you here,' Lady Alice Smithers said from across the table, interrupting Violet's thoughts.

She saw Lord Jake take a quick glance at the place name before answering, 'And you, too, Lady Alice. Lovely to see you again.'

Lady Alice smiled sheepishly, as if the two were on very familiar terms, but it was obvious Lord Jake had no idea who she was. One of his conquests, perhaps. Lady Alice had always struck Violet as a rather silly young woman, even if she was very pretty. No doubt she was exactly the sort of woman to appeal to Lord Jake. Mindless, frivolous and flirtatious. Thank goodness Violet had none of those qualities.

'You made such an impression on all the debutantes at the first of the Rosemont balls last Season,' Lady Alice continued. 'First impressions are so important, don't you think, Lady Violet? I believe one can tell the character of a man right from that very first meeting.'

'For Lord Jake's sake, I hope you are incorrect.' Her response was intended as an insult, but caused Lord Jake to laugh as if at their own private joke.

Lady Alice tilted her head in a coquettish manner. One that was presumably meant to be enchanting. 'Well, you certainly made a good first impression on me, Lord Jake.'

Violet looked at Lord Jake, expecting him to make some wry comment that only she would understand, but instead he was smiling at Lady Alice as if her coquettishness was indeed enchanting him. Or did he look at all women like that, including her? And did all women react to him the way Lady Alice was, with smiles and simpers? Including her?

'I so enjoyed our little chat,' Lady Alice continued, gently running her finger around the rim of her glass as she batted her long eyelashes. 'You really were so entertaining.'

'Was he?' Violet said, feigning innocence. 'And what did you talk about that was so entertaining?' If he couldn't remember Lady Alice's name, Violet was confident he wouldn't remember their conversation either.

'Oh, this and that,' he said vaguely.

'This and that what?' She was not about to let him off the hook that easily.

'Oh, you know, the sort of things one talks about at a ball.'

'No, I don't know. I haven't been to a ball in many years and when I do, it will be in my role as chaperon. I won't be indulging in entertaining talk with men.'

'Then perhaps you should.'

'Well, if I do I will first need to know what *this and that* they talk about, won't I?' She suppressed a smile as she watched him squirm. 'So, what did you talk about with Lady Alice that was so entertaining?'

They stared at each other, both knowing that she was trying to make things as awkward for him as she possibly could. His brow briefly furrowed, then he turned to Lady Alice and smiled. 'Perhaps Lady Alice would like to tell us. After all, she, too, was particularly entertaining that evening.'

Lady Alice fluttered her eyelashes once more, while Lord Jake smiled back as if he knew exactly what their conversation had been about and they were both enjoying the recollection.

'Well, I don't want to sound immodest,' Lady Alice said, her chest thrust out, her head held high, in a way that was anything but modest. 'But you told me I was the prettiest young lady in the room and if you weren't being called away on urgent business, nothing would give you more pleasure than to dance the night away with me.'

Violet couldn't stop a low groan from escaping. He had charmed this woman while actually rejecting her and she still felt he had paid her a compliment. The man really was insufferable.

'Yes, it was unfortunate I had to leave,' Lord Jake said, still smiling at the simpering Lady Alice.

'So what was the urgent business?' Violet tried to keep any hint of pique out of her voice.

'Urgent *private* business.'

She sent him a look that she hoped conveyed her disbelief.

'But you were a very naughty man,' Lady Alice continued. 'I didn't see you again until the final Rosemont ball at the end of the Season. And then you only danced with me once.'

'Ah, well, with all that happened that night I, along with the rest of the family, was otherwise preoccupied.'

'Oh, yes, Ethan's proposal.' Lady Alice placed her hands over her heart. 'Everyone was hoping the Duke would choose a bride last Season and we were all so disappointed when he didn't. But your other brother made up for it with that romantic proposal. Right in the middle of the dance floor, it was so beautiful.' She blinked her eyes so rapidly Violet was unsure whether this was a further coquettish gesture or she had dust in her eyes. She assumed the first, but hoped for the latter.

'Perhaps you'll also make the same romantic gesture when you propose.' Lady Alice sent Lord Jake another simpering smile. 'But you're here now, all weekend, so we can finally have that dance you promised me.'

'I don't believe there will be any dancing this weekend, will there, Lady Violet?'

Violet was tempted to make him feel even more uncomfortable, to punish him for charming Lady Alice and for every other young woman who had fallen under his spell so easily and so hopelessly. 'No, there will be no dancing,' she said instead. Bianca had suggested dancing and, while Violet could no doubt organise some local musicians to perform, if need be, for some reason she did not want Lord Jake to dance the weekend away with Lady Alice.

Not that she was jealous. It must be because she had some sort of protective feelings towards Lady Alice. That must be it. She did not want him giving false hope to a woman he quite obviously had no honourable intentions towards.

Although why she should see her role as protecting the virtue of a debutante who meant nothing to her, Violet was unsure. There was only one debutante she was trying to protect. She leant forward so she could see what Bianca was doing. She was actually holding Mr Fortescue's hand, their fingers interlaced as they looked at each other in a highly suggestive manner.

She had allowed her attention to be once again diverted away from her task, and by something as trivial as a flirtation between Lady Alice and Lord Jake. What on earth was wrong with her? She had to focus on the most important task of this weekend. To chaperon Bianca. And from now onwards, that was exactly what she would do.

Lady Alice was exactly the reason why Jake had been reluctant to attend this weekend party. He avoided society events as much as he could, particularly during the Season. For the last six years the Rosemont ball had opened and closed each Season, and they were two events he could not get out of. His mother hosted the balls, with the intention of finding a suitable wife and future Duchess for her eldest son. Most husband-hunting mothers and their debutante daughters set their sights firmly on the Duke, but some, unfortunately, saw the second son as an equally attractive option.

Lady Alice obviously fell into this category. Jake could but hope she was the only one like that present this weekend. Nothing was more tedious than having to make small talk while a very young woman attempted to pique your interest with fluttering eyelashes, coquettish fan gestures and flirtatious chit-chat.

And it was particularly unwanted if it took his attention away from his assigned task of distracting Lady Violet, a woman who could never be described as a

coquette and was anything but tedious, let alone flirtatious.

Footmen served the second course of roast chicken
and, thankfully, the man sitting next to Lady Alice
engaged her in conversation, allowing Jake to turn his
full attention back to Lady Violet.

'It appears Myrtle and Beryl put aside their differ-
ences on how to pluck a chicken. This looks wonderful,'
he said, keeping his voice light and friendly.

She merely huffed, while continuing to stare at her
sister and Herbert. It seemed complimenting the food
would not work. Time to try yet another approach.

'Will you be coming down to London for the Season
this year?' It was a familiar topic of conversation and
one he usually avoided, but he had to keep her talking.
She was taking far too much interest in the goings-on
at the other end of the table.

'Yes,' she murmured, not taking her eyes off her
sister. 'It will·be Bianca's coming out, so I will attend
as her chaperon.'

He was definitely losing her attention, so it was time
to turn to that old standby. Flattery. It worked on most
women. It was a bit of a long shot, but perhaps it would
work on Lady Violet as well.

So what could he say? He could tell her she had the
most beautiful hair he had ever seen. It wasn't chest-
nut, as he had first thought, but contained strands of
red and gold, which caught the light as she moved. Or
he could say he had never before seen eyes like hers?
They were as much gold as they were brown. Each time
she looked at him, he thought of flickering flames,
which was so apt. There was a fire burning within her.

Unfortunately, that fire usually burned in anger, but it showed she was a passionate woman who experienced emotions intensely.

That's what he should say to Lady Violet. But he couldn't. Those words weren't just flattery, designed to make a woman feel well disposed towards him. It was how he really felt about her, and for some reason, he couldn't comment on her appearance in a casual, offhand manner.

But he had to say something to take her attention away from Herbert's attempt to woo Lady Bianca.

'Will I be seeing you at my family's ball? The Rosemont ball traditionally starts off the Season.' It was a feeble attempt, but it was the best he could come up with.

Her head tilted higher, a flicker of flame in her eyes. 'Won't you be too busy dancing the night away with Lady Alice?'

'Why, Lady Violet, that almost sounded like jealousy.' He was teasing, but it certainly did his masculine pride the world of good to think that a woman as formidable as Lady Violet might be jealous that another was showing interest in him.

And it did the trick. He now had her full attention. The fire in her eyes went from flickering to a raging inferno and her chin lifted high as she prepared to give him what for. 'Don't be ridiculous,' she said, loud enough to draw the attention of several guests seated nearby, and she grimaced. 'Don't be ridiculous,' she repeated, her voice much lower, but still seething.

He continued to smile while she continued to glare.

'You didn't answer my question,' he said, unable to keep the amusement out of his voice.

'I did. I am not jealous. I couldn't care less who you talk to, flirt with or dance the night away with.' Her clenched jaw made a lie of her claim not to care. That was interesting.

'That wasn't the question I was referring to. I mean, will you be attending my family ball?'

She released a long, slow sigh, as if his question was the most exasperating one she had ever been asked. 'Bianca will be attending. I will be present, but as her chaperon.'

'Then I will look forward to seeing you there.'

'Why? So we can talk about this and that? Or so you can make some excuse to avoid dancing with me?'

'I would never do that.' It was a polite, flippant remark, but it had some truth. He had agreed to spend the weekend diverting Lady Violet, but the more time he spent with her, the less of a chore it became. She was decidedly diverting. He never thought he'd enjoy arguing with a woman, but Jake was actually enjoying himself. When had he ever been able to say that about a society event? Never, was the simple answer to that question.

'It hardly matters anyway,' she said. 'I will not be dancing. Nor will I be indulging in mindless chatter on this and that. My role will be to chaperon Bianca.' As if remembering that role, she returned once more to observing her sister. Like Lady Violet, Lady Bianca had hardly touched her meal, but unlike Lady Violet, it was because she was enjoying herself too much flirting with Herbert to bother eating.

'Herbert Fortescue really isn't as bad as you think he is,' Jake said.

She turned back to face him. 'And I suppose that's your unbiased opinion, is it?'

'I've known him since we were in short trousers. Yes, he has his faults, as do we all, but he's a good, kind man, and his intentions towards your sister would never be anything other than honourable.'

She rolled her eyes. 'The man's a wastrel and a gambler. That hardly makes him an ideal husband.'

Jake winced. She could be describing him, but then, he had no intentions of becoming anyone's husband, so what did it matter if he was a wastrel or a gambler? 'Like many members of our class, Herbert does sometimes fritter away his time and, yes, he has been known to play a game or two of cards, but that is merely because he has time on his hands he needs to fill. I know that when he marries, his wife and his children would become the focus of his life.'

'In my experience, men never change.' For a brief moment, an unfamiliar expression flitted across her features, then quickly disappeared, to be replaced by a look of annoyance. It was as if, for a fleeting second, he had glimpsed the woman beneath the stern exterior, the woman she hid from the world.

What was she hiding? What was it she did not want him or anyone else to see?

'Mr Fortescue *is* a wastrel,' she continued, her lips once again pinched. 'He always has been, always will be, and my sister can do much better than him.'

Her words were defiant, almost like a declaration of war against mankind itself.

'And what sort of man do you think your sister *should* marry?'

Her furrowed brow tightened, as if she had never considered that such a man could exist. 'Well, he should be someone who can occupy his time in a better way than gambling, for a start.'

Jake had to agree with that and that was another reason why he would never make a good husband. *Or a good man*, he heard a little voice at the back of his mind whisper, a voice that sounded remarkably like his father's. A voice he mentally swatted away, like an annoying fly.

'What else do you expect from Lady Bianca's future husband?'

'He should be honest, with no artifice or trickery. Bianca should know that the man she is courting is exactly the man she will be married to, rather than one who pretends to be something he is not just to get her up the aisle and his hands on her marriage settlement.'

Once more he saw that flicker of sadness, the one that suggested there was a more vulnerable side to Lady Violet, one she had buried deep behind her protective armour of angry words and caustic comments.

'They are all eminently sensible qualities to look for in a potential husband,' he said. 'And qualities I can assure you Herbert Fortescue possesses.'

She hmphed out her disagreement.

'Look, I'm not trying to say that he is perfect. He's a man, after all, and we all come with imperfections, but I know he is not someone to toy with a woman's heart.'

'I believe that is for me to decide, not you, Lord Jake.' That vulnerable side, if it really did exist, had disappeared once again. 'You are hardly an impartial judge of his character, or indeed of any man's.'

Her implication was clear. She had already summed him up as a man of low character. What had caused it? Had his reputation preceded him? Was it because he'd flirted with her when he'd thought she was a barmaid? Was it Lady Alice's comments? Whatever it was, surely it didn't matter. He wasn't here to impress Lady Violet with his upstanding character and fine qualities. And thank goodness for that. If he was, he really would have his work cut out for him.

'And what about you? Are you an impartial judge? Or do you distrust all men and has that clouded your judgement on who would be suitable for your sister?'

Her jaw clenched tightly. Her nostrils flared. He braced himself for the onslaught of her wrath. 'That's not fair,' she murmured instead, the pain in her words affecting him more than her wrath ever could.

Chapter Six

He was wrong. Wasn't he? All she wanted was for her sister to not repeat her mistakes. Yes, perhaps she did distrust men, but hadn't she good reason for doing so? She would hate for her loving, happy sister to go through what she had. There was nothing wrong with that.

She, too, had once been like her sister, but Randolph had destroyed all that. Randolph had made her see what men could really be like under the charming exterior.

No, Lord Jake was wrong. Bianca needed to be protected and there was no one other than she who would do it.

She shook off her doubts and sat up straighter.

It was so easy for him. He was a man. No one would ever break his heart or humiliate him. Instead, he was able to live his life in that free and easy manner, while women like Lady Alice, a woman whose name he couldn't even remember, vied for his attention.

She sent him what she hoped was a withering look. Instead of withering as he was supposed to, he smiled

back at her. Did she detect pity in that smile? That was
something she would not stand for. She much preferred
to be feared, even despised, than to be pitied.

The third course was served. Violet cringed. It was
the dessert course already. It seemed that three courses
was to be their lot tonight. If Cook had been in residence Bianca's guests would have been served at least
seven courses, maybe as many as fourteen. Instead,
they had to make do with this paltry fare. She sent her
sister a look of remonstrance, to say, this is what you
get when you invite your friends for the weekend without thinking about how they will be fed.

But Bianca was oblivious to her censure, so she
looked down at the dessert plate in front of her.

Jam roly-poly. Again, it was something that Violet
would never have put on a dinner menu, but the guests
started eating it with great enthusiasm.

'Reminds me of school,' she heard one man say,
causing Violet to cringe again.

'Yes, lovely,' a young woman added. 'Nanny used
to serve this and I haven't had it for years.'

'It seems Myrtle and Beryl's simple food continues
to be a success,' Lord Jake said.

'Hmm,' Violet responded, not wanting him to think
she had forgiven him, although she was no longer sure
what he needed forgiveness for.

She was saved from continuing to make strained
conversation when Lady Cynthia, the woman sitting
to his left, started talking to him in an animated manner. What they said was of no interest to her whatsoever and she tried to not pay them any attention. Why
should she care whether they were flirting? It did not

matter one fig if she was another young woman like
Lady Alice to whom he had promised to dance the night
away. Perhaps they were meeting for the first time, but
they did seem rather familiar with each other for people
who had no history.

She leant a little closer. *The weather.* They were discussing the weather. She almost snorted with laughter.
He must be bored senseless. Lady Cynthia was smiling, fluttering her eyes and acting as if they were having the most riveting conversation. *About the weather.*

She was no threat whatsoever. Violet almost choked
on her pudding. Where on earth had that come from?
Of course that young lady was no threat, because Violet did not care if Lord Jake became enamoured with
any of the debutantes at the party. He could run off
with Lady Alice, or the one giving the weather fore-
cast, or whoever he wanted. She did not care. And it
would be much better if he did. Then he would stop
bothering her.

Despite that, she couldn't help but continue to eaves-
drop. Once again the conversation had turned to the
romance of the last Rosemont ball and once again the
young lady was hinting that maybe he, too, would make
a similarly romantic gesture when he proposed.

Lord Jake was laughing it off. Couldn't Lady Cynthia see what was so obvious to Violet? He was merely
playing with her. She was seeing him as a potential
husband and he was seeing her as little more than a
passing diversion.

Men, they were all the same. Randolph had also
flirted, he had charmed and, just like Lord Jake, every
woman he'd met had adored him. Adored him far too

much. Her breath caught in her throat as the full extent of Randolph's treachery crashed down on her. While he was courting her, he was doing much more than just flirting with other women. How he must have laughed at her. While she'd denied him even the most chaste of kisses, saying it must be saved for their wedding night, he was taking his pleasure with other women. If he hadn't been caught in flagrante by one debutante's father and forced to do the honourable thing, he would have married Violet, just so he could get his hands on her money, with no intention of stopping his philandering ways.

The footmen removed their bowls. Lady Cynthia continued to monopolise Lord Jake's attention. Laughing at something he said, she actually placed her hand on his arm in an overly intimate manner. Violet looked along the table. Bianca was doing the same. Staring at Mr Fortescue as if besotted and tittering at everything he had to say.

This was outrageous. This dinner party was descending into something resembling a bacchanal. What were the other chaperons thinking, letting young ladies behave like this? It was up to Violet to put a stop to this overfamiliarity before they all came to regret it.

She stood up, signalling to the ladies that it was time to leave the men to their brandy and cigars. Several stood, but most lingered in their seats, including Bianca and Lady Cynthia, who had still not removed her hand from Lord Jake's arm. Violet picked up her silver bell and rung it vigorously. The little bell merely tinkled, hardly enough to be heard above the excessive laughter and chatter.

'Ladies,' she called out in her loudest voice. 'Ladies,' she repeated, even louder, her throat straining. Finally, voices stilled and with much rustling of skirts and a few groans of annoyance, the remaining young women rose. They formed a somewhat less than orderly file, but at least they all followed Violet out of the dining room.

As soon as the dining room door closed behind them, Bianca took her arm. 'You and Lord Jake seem to be getting on very well.' Before Violet could counter her claim, Bianca sighed with contentment. 'He's so handsome, almost as handsome as Mr Fortescue.'

'I hadn't noticed,' Violet responded, unsure why she was lying. How could she say she had not noticed that Lord Jake was handsome? It was the first thing she had noticed about him and, every time she looked at him, it was the one thing she could not deny. He was possibly— no, probably—no, definitely the most handsome man she had ever met. And handsome men were top of her list of those one could never trust, along with men who were trying to get their hands on a generous marriage settlement. Men, no doubt, like Mr Fortescue.

'Yes, you've made quite the conquest there and are going to be the envy of every other woman present,' Bianca continued. 'Except me. I have no interest in him, but I have heard that he's quite the lady's man, with a bit of a naughty reputation.' She giggled, as if a naughty reputation was something to be admired rather than disapproved of.

'I have no wish to discuss Lord Jake.'

'As much of a catch as he is, I think Mr Fortescue has more finer qualities.'

With every word that came out of her mouth, Bianca

was proving just how much she needed Violet's guidance. How could she possibly think that a man with a *naughty* reputation was a catch? And how could she use the words *finer qualities* when discussing either Lord Jake or Mr Fortescue?

She needed to ignore the churning in her stomach that mention of Lord Jake's success with the ladies evoked and concentrate on curtailing Bianca's over-exuberance. 'As I said, I have no desire to discuss Lord Jake, but as for Mr Fortescue, all I can say is that you are paying him far too much attention.' Violet's voice was suitably stern. 'You should be attending to your other guests, not billing and cooing with Mr Fortescue.'

Bianca laughed. 'Oh, can't you relax a little, Violet?' She patted her hand. 'Everyone's enjoying themselves, and isn't that what this party is supposed to be about?'

Violet grasped at a reply. In her opinion, they were enjoying themselves way too much. There was far too much familiarity going on, what with young ladies touching men's arms, flirting, fluttering eyelashes and so on.

'And tomorrow we're all going on a picnic.' Bianca gripped her hand tighter in excitement.

Violet stared at her sister. Surely she was jesting?

'Don't look at me like that. It will be such fun and the weather will be simply divine. I just know it.'

'And have you told Beryl and Myrtle? They'll need to organise food.'

'Oh, stop fretting. You worried about tonight's dinner and it all went off perfectly well. It will be just the same with the picnic.'

'Not if the cooks have not been informed that a picnic lunch is required. I suppose I'm going to have to sort that out now while you continue to enjoy yourself.'

'Thank you. And tell them Mr Fortescue particularly likes salmon sandwiches.'

'Bianca, I'm warning you, be careful. You're giving far too much encouragement to that man and he's not good enough for you.'

'I'm paying no more attention to him than you are to Lord Jake.'

Violet opened her mouth to counter her smiling sister's accusation, but could think of no response. Instead, she turned and strode off down the corridor towards the kitchen to sort out her sister's latest impetuous decision, while the other ladies retired to the drawing room.

As she entered the kitchen, where Beryl, Myrtle and the scullery maids were cleaning up, Bianca's words continued to ring in her ears. She wished her sister was wrong, but knew she was right. She had spent more than enough time with Lord Jake, but that was hardly her fault. Violet hadn't invited him this weekend. She hadn't asked him to visit the tavern and she most certainly hadn't placed him beside her at dinner. All these things were beyond her control. But no more. From now onwards she would take back control. Control of events and control of herself. At least, she would from tomorrow. Right now, she had an unexpected picnic to organise.

'Well done, old chap.' Herbert laughed as he sat down next to Jake and banged him heartily on the back. 'You're keeping the harpy busy, just as you promised.'

'I would hardly describe Lady Violet as a harpy.' Jake bristled. 'She's actually entertaining company.'

'Yes, yes, quite right.' Herbert winked at him as if they had shared a private joke, looked around at the other men sitting back and enjoying their cigars, then leant in closer. 'Wouldn't want anyone to know what we're up to. Might get back to her and ruin everything.'

Herbert sat up straighter. 'Yes, Lady Violet is a delightful woman,' he said loudly, causing Jake to shake his head in disbelief. A career on the stage was certainly not something his friend should be considering.

'So, tomorrow, my darling Bianca has organised a picnic. We plan to make our escape early. If you can keep her sister busy for as long as possible, I'll be eternally grateful.'

'Perfectly happy to do so.' A statement that was surprisingly true.

'But do be careful.' Herbert once again leant in close as if to impart some worldly wisdom. 'Apparently, she was engaged once, so she's not completely averse to men and marriage. You wouldn't want her dragging you to the altar.' Herbert gave a hearty laugh at the impossibility of such a notion.

'Who? Why? What happened?'

Herbert raised his hands, palms upwards, to signal he had no idea, and even if he did, it was of little concern to him. 'Don't know the details. My sister mentioned something about it when I informed her we were coming up here for the weekend. You know how women like to gossip. Just thought I should give you a word of warning, old chap.'

'Right,' Jake said, somewhat amused by Herbert's

attempt at a man-to-man talk, but also curious to know what sort of man would have captured Lady Violet's heart and why she had decided not to go ahead with the nuptials.

The brandy carafe was passed around the table yet again, and each man served himself a generous glass. As they downed their drinks, the men relaxed more, the voices grew louder, and that was the end of any possibility of private conversations.

Herbert went back to singing Lady Bianca's praises. Not that anyone was listening and not that Herbert cared whether or not they were.

As Jake sipped his drink, he contemplated Herbert's words. His friend was worrying needlessly and was wrong about everything when it came to Lady Violet. She was anything but a harridan. She might frighten Herbert, but fear was most definitely not what Jake felt in her company. In fact, he found being with her invigorating and could not remember a time when a woman's company had been so stimulating, in more ways than one.

And as for the likelihood of her ever expecting a marriage proposal from him—that was laughable. She had made her opinion of him very clear. He was the last man on earth she would see as a potential husband. Well, perhaps the second to last man on earth. Her opinion of Herbert was even lower than her opinion of him.

No, the only thing Herbert needed to worry about was getting Lady Violet to change her mind about him. He looked over at his friend, who had managed to monopolise the attentions of one of the guests and was regaling him with the many amusing things Lady Bianca had said over dinner. Herbert was oblivious to the man's obvious boredom, but then, at the moment, he was oblivious to everything except the woman he loved.

Tomorrow, Jake would do his best to convince Lady Violet that she should put up no obstacles to Herbert's courtship of her sister, and he most certainly would give no further thought to Herbert's irrational fear that the lady might harbour aspirations of her own in that direction.

Chapter Seven

The next day, Violet readied herself for that unwanted picnic. Another day in the company of Bianca's tedious friends. Another day of playing the chaperon to a sister who didn't want her help or advice. *Another day with Lord Jake.*

But before she could fritter away more time on pointless picnics, she still had work to do. She'd spent the early morning going over the estate manager's accounts, but could make no sense of them. When she'd asked her father for his help, he'd merely waved his hand in dismissal and told her she was much better at such things than him and he was far too busy.

She'd informed him she couldn't go through the accounts while at the same time chaperoning Bianca. That, too, had been met with a wave of the hand along with a claim that Bianca didn't need chaperoning and Violet should let her sister have some fun with her friends.

Her father even had the audacity to tell Violet she was in danger of becoming an old stick in the mud if she wasn't careful and she should stop worrying so much. She had been tempted to inform her father that someone needed to worry or the entire estate would fall into ruin, along with his younger daughter. She'd also wanted to add that if anyone had bothered to worry about her during her first Season it might not have ended so catastrophically. But there was no point reminding her father of that.

Instead, she put aside the estate's accounts for now and dressed for more sitting about, more unwanted socialising and more time-wasting.

She picked up her straw hat, pushed it on to her head and gave herself a quick inspection in the mirror. The dove grey skirt and white blouse with the high lace collar were perfect for a picnic. Sensible and flattering. Not that flattering mattered. She wasn't trying to impress anyone, and especially not Lord Jake, but she wouldn't want to embarrass Bianca in front of her fashionable friends. She did a small twirl in front of the mirror to see how the outfit looked from behind, then strode out of her bedroom.

Laughter greeted her the moment she left the house. The guests had already gathered beside the river. The women were dressed in an array of pastel shades, their lacy parasols twirling in their hands, while the men were all attired in tweed and checked suits. While the young ladies were seated on the picnic rugs, many of the men were lying down. Picnic hampers had been thrown open, but few were eating, preferring to sip champagne and make mindless chatter.

But one thing was painfully clear. Bianca was nowhere in sight, nor was Mr Fortescue.

Panic rising within her, Violet pushed through the revellers to where Lord Jake was seated. Once again, Lady Alice was vying for his attention and was gazing adoringly at him over her champagne flute. Violet had no time to consider that or her irritated reaction, not when Bianca's virtue was at stake.

'Where are they?' she demanded in a fierce whisper, not caring that she had interrupted Lady Alice's flirtation.

'I assume you mean Herbert Fortescue and Lady Bianca,' he said quietly as he rose to his feet.

'Of course I do. Where are they?'

'They took a boat out on to the river.'

'What? When?' Violet looked at the slowly flowing river, as if it would reveal where they had gone and what they were up to.

'Don't worry. She won't come to any harm with Herbert. The man rowed for his university.'

Violet scowled at him. How could he possibly think that Bianca's safety on the river was her only concern? But now was not the time to enlighten him on that particular matter. Instead, she rushed off down the path towards the boat shed.

Two boats were usually hanging against the wall, but one had been removed. Violet's hands covered her eyes as if she didn't want to see the evidence of her sister's wanton disregard for propriety.

Oh, Bianca, you foolish, foolish girl. If Mr Fortescue ruins your reputation, you will have to marry the man. Can't you see what he's up to? Can't you see that all he wants is your dowry?

Her heart pounding, her stomach clenching, she

raced to the edge of the boat ramp and looked up and down the river. They were nowhere in sight. This was a disaster.

'All is not lost, Lady Violet.' Lord Jake joined her at the bottom of the boat ramp, where the water licked at the wooden planks as if its gentle calmness was mocking Violet's agitated state.

'Yes, it is. They've gone and I have no idea where to and no way of finding them.'

'I didn't have time to tell you before you rushed off, but Herbert informed me as to where they were going. He said they'd go upstream and find a pleasant spot for a picnic, so it would make the return journey much easier if they were tired.'

If they were tired? A pleasant spot to be alone together? No, no, no.

She leant over and looked as far up the river as she could.

'And I, too, rowed for my university,' he added with a laugh, as if such a thing was an amusing joke. 'So if I may be of service?'

'Yes. Hurry up. Get going. We have to stop them.' She continued to look up the river as she waved her hand towards a second boat.

'Perhaps you'd like to accept my offer graciously rather than barking out commands.'

She turned and stared at him, hardly able to take in his words. He could not be serious. They were in the midst of a crisis and he had the audacity to think he had the right to give her a lesson in manners. He waited as she continued to glare at him. Slowly, she exhaled. This man really was the limit, but she had no time to argue with him. Her sister's virtue and reputation were at stake. 'Thank you, Lord Jake. Yes, I would be most grateful for your assistance in finding my sister.'

Before your friend ruins her reputation and her chance of making a decent marriage.

'Certainly, my lady.' He sent her another annoying smile and pulled his forelock as if he was an obedient serf. But at least he did as she asked. He lifted the boat and carried it down the ramp.

While he did so, she paced up and down the ramp and tried not to notice how easily he had hoisted the boat above his head. He must be rather strong. She wondered what his muscles would look like under his shirt and jacket. And for one unforgivable moment, she imagined him as a workman, toiling in the fields, his shirt off, his muscular skin sweat slicked.

She averted her gaze and guilt ripped through her. How could she think of such things when her sister was in peril? Bianca had been taken away by a man who was right this moment doing heaven knew what with her and she was thinking about Lord Jake without his shirt on.

'Get a move on, can't you?' she all but shouted as he lowered the boat into the river.

Once again, he pulled on his forelock. 'Yes, m'lady. Moving as quick as I can, m'lady.'

He climbed into the boat and reached out his hand towards her.

She hesitated, then took his outstretched hand. A shiver raced up her arm and lodged itself in the centre of her chest. Why on earth did she have to react in that way to this man, a man she didn't even like, a man who was far too handsome, far too charming, far too flirtatious for his own good?

Letting go of his hand as soon as she was in the boat, she quickly plonked herself down on the wooden seat, causing them to rock in the water.

He removed his jacket and rolled up his sleeves. Violet had wondered about his muscles, but she would not look as he exposed his forearms. She didn't care, really, she didn't, and she most certainly did not want any telltale blushes suggesting otherwise.

He placed the oars in the oarlocks, leant back and began stroking the water. Under different circumstances, this might be a pleasant way to spend a day. Being rowed along a calm river, edged with weeping willows bearing their light green spring foliage, the water slapping gently against the side of the boat, the birds flitting between the branches. If she was a different woman it might be pleasant. If she did not have endless responsibilities, did not have to chase after errant sisters who should know better, she could enjoy wasting her time on frivolous pastimes.

Despite her resolve not to, she watched as he pulled back on the oars. The swish of the oars cutting through the water and the movement of his arms was almost hypnotic. His rolled-up shirtsleeves did indeed expose his powerful forearms and a hint of bicep. With each stroke, the muscles contracted and then relaxed, and Violet was unable to look away as the bands of muscles moved against each other. There was beauty in those sculptured muscles and the temptation to lean over and run her hand up his arm, to know what they felt like, pulled at her. Her gaze moved to the hint of bicep, flexing and bulging, and her fingers itched to feel that movement under her hands.

'Herbert won't have gone far,' he said, his words breaking through to her addled brain. 'We'll catch him soon.'

'So you rowed for your university, did you? I didn't know you had a degree.' Her questions were asked more as a means to divert her attention from speculating about his muscles than from any genuine curiosity about his sporting prowess or academic pursuits.

'I said I attended university and I rowed. I'm afraid I didn't do terribly much studying. Then I got sent down for taking far too much money off the other students at the card table.'

Her lips pinched together in disapproval.

'Don't look like that. No one was forced to gamble and I can hardly be blamed for winning.'

'You had the opportunity to go to university and you squandered it?'

He gave an annoying shrug of his shoulders as if such things were neither here nor there. 'It didn't seem like much of an opportunity to me. Sending me off to university was more about my father getting me out of the way, and he never expected me to actually achieve anything.'

His smile had disappeared and for a moment she could detect uncharacteristic rancour in his voice, before that familiar smile returned. 'Which was fine by me. I never could see the point in studying ancient Greek and Latin.'

'Do you know how many people would love to have that opportunity and will never have it because of their lack of money or because they happened to be born the wrong sex?' Violet refused to show him any undeserved pity.

'Does that include you, Lady Violet?' He slowly looked her up and down. 'Were you born the wrong sex? It certainly doesn't look that way from where I'm seated.'

She turned her head and looked back up the river, her cheeks burning. Hopefully, he would assume her consternation was caused by her anger at his flippancy or her concern at her sister's absence and not due to any reaction to how he had looked at her.

'Can't you go any faster?' she snapped. 'Or were you as much a failure as a rower at university as you were an academic?'

He gave a low laugh, obviously not offended by her insults. 'Yes, but if we take our time, it will give us a chance to get to know each other better.'

She sent him her most caustic look. 'I believe I know enough about you already. So, please, go faster.'

'I'll go as fast or as slow as you desire,' he said, smiling at her as if she'd said something witty. 'I had assumed you'd prefer a slower, more refined pace. It seems I've learnt something about you already. You like it fast.'

She was certain he was teasing her and that there was some inappropriate innuendo contained in his words, something that would make Myrtle and Beryl chortle with ribald laughter, but at least he had done what she asked. They were now pulling through the water at a swifter rate.

Despite that, there was still no sign of Bianca and Mr Fortescue.

She looked back down the river. 'I do hope you're telling me the truth, Lord Jake, and this is the direction in which they went.'

'You have my word as a gentleman.'

She turned back to him and raised her eyebrows in disbelief, which merely caused him to laugh.

But this was no joking matter and she wished he would appreciate that. 'You don't seem to understand just how precarious a situation in which this has placed Bianca. If anything happens between her and Mr Fortescue, or even if word gets around that they were alone together, her reputation will be ruined. She will be unable to find a husband.'

'I think she has already found the husband she wants.'

'Mr Fortescue?' she scoffed. 'Mr Fortescue has nothing to offer Bianca.'

'He has his love. I would have thought it was every woman's dream to marry a man who adores her. If you put aside your prejudices and actually looked at the man, you'd see that Herbert worships your sister. He will do everything in his power to make her happy.'

She scoffed again. 'Mr Fortescue's powers are very limited.'

'So what is it you actually want for your sister if it's not marriage to a man like Herbert Fortescue?'

'I do want her to marry, but I want her to make a *good* marriage to a *sensible* man. That is not too much to ask, is it?'

'A good marriage? That usually means a socially advantageous one. As the eldest son of a viscount, Herbert's place in society is assured and his background is impeccable.'

'I don't care about that.' Randolph had also had a high place in society, but that did not make him a good man.

'Well, are you then after a financially advantageous marriage for your sister? If that is what you want for Lady Bianca, then I can promise you that the Honourable Herbert Fortescue is financially sound.'

She merely hmphed a reply. Randolph had also been reputed to be financially secure, but she now knew that as a gambler who took enormous risks no money would ever be enough to satisfy that particular demon, including her own generous marriage settlement.

'So, you don't care about his position in society, his financial stability, how he feels about your sister or how she feels about him. I believe, Lady Violet, that what you want for your sister is a man whom you yourself could fall in love with and that man is not Herbert Fortescue.'

'Nonsense,' she shot back, rising from her seat as if desperate to escape from his criticisms and causing the boat to rock slightly.

He stopped rowing and waited for her to retake her seat.

'That's nonsense,' she repeated in a more constrained manner. 'But at least I have more sense than to be beguiled by a man who gambles the way Mr Fortescue does. Or a man who thinks frivolous fun is the only purpose to life. I wouldn't fall in love with a man who plays tricks and leads my sister off by herself. Nor would I fall in love with a man who makes crude innu-endos and teases women for his own sport.'

That annoyingly charming smile curled his lips once more. 'I don't believe Herbert has ever teased a young lady, for sport or otherwise. And as for crude innuen-dos, I doubt if he'd know how to make one. Is it really Herbert Fortescue you're objecting to?'

She looked away, ashamed that her cheeks were once again burning.

'As for gambling, that is more my vice than Her-bert's. Yes, he accompanies me to various gambling dens, but I know he'd much rather be spending his time with your sister. As for frivolous entertainment, yes, perhaps you're right. I can see that such behaviour worries you, but can you honestly say it would worry your sister?'

She turned her head further, as if fascinated by the passing trees.

'As I said, I believe you are describing the sort of man you would like to marry, not the man you think would best suit your sister.'

'You're wrong,' she shot back. 'No man would suit me because I don't want to marry anyone.'

He laughed. 'Yes, you're far too sensible for that. Love and marriage might suit other women, but that just shows how frivolous they are.'

She twisted back to staring at the trees, not wanting him to see how his words had cut through her.

'But I don't think your sister sees things that way. She wants to marry Herbert. He wants to marry her, and there seems to be only one impediment stopping them from finding happiness.'

She fought to find a retort to his claim, but none came.

'Or is it happiness in general that you object to? You're not happy so you think anyone who is must lack your intelligence and common sense and be way too frivolous for their own good?'

'How dare you?' she seethed through gritted teeth. 'I am perfectly happy.'

Her claim merely caused him to tilt back his head and laugh loudly. 'If this is what you look like when you're happy, I can hardly imagine what you look like when you're angry.'

He was right. She was angry. Angry at him.

'Just row, will you,' she said, hating that he was right. It *was* a long time since she had felt happy. And even worse, when she had been happy, it had been because she had been deluded into thinking she was in love. That just showed how deceptive love and happiness could be, but she wasn't going to tell him that.

Chapter Eight

He had seen it again. It was so fleeting he might have missed it if he hadn't been looking at her so intently. There was something behind the anger. Something she was hiding. Was she like him and kept past pains buried deep down, although unlike him she buried them under anger, not laughter? That must be why she intrigued him so much—because intrigue him she did. And that had to be the reason he was so drawn to her, as she could never be described as his type. Jake usually liked women who took life no more seriously than he did. Women who enjoyed uncomplicated fun. There was nothing uncomplicated about Lady Violet Maidstone.

'There's the boat,' she cried out, standing up and pointing up the river, causing their boat to rock once again.

'You might want to sit down if you don't want to put us both in the river.'

'And you might want to hurry up. Hopefully, we're not too late and no harm will have been done.'

He looked over his shoulder to where the boat was

moored under a tree, gently swaying in the current. He'd done his best to give Herbert and Lady Bianca as much time alone together as he could. Hopefully Herbert had been able to woo his lady, plight his troth or whatever it was he so desperately wanted to do. If the two had found the time to declare their everlasting affection for each other, agree to marry and live happily ever after, then he would be freed from his commitment to distract Lady Violet.

He looked back at the lady in question, who had sat back down but was leaning forward as if that would make the boat go faster.

He had to admit, distracting her was not such an arduous task as he had first imagined. If nothing else, Lady Violet was entertaining, and she was certainly a lot more attractive than Herbert had led him to believe. And right now, bathed in the gentle sunlight, attractive didn't do her justice. She was simply beautiful.

It was as if she burned with an inner light. Each time she moved her head, the sunlight caught the burnished copper, red and warm gold threads in her hair, making it seem alive. And whenever he said something she objected to, which was more or less every word that came out of his mouth, those brown eyes flashed with gold, like sparks from a fire.

He smiled to himself. A fire did burn inside Lady Violet. It was just a shame it always ignited in anger, directed against the entire world, including him. She deserved to be happy and he would love to be the man to show her how to relax and enjoy herself.

And if he was being completely honest, he'd also like to be the man who transformed her from a woman who burned with anger to one who burned with passion. He closed his eyes briefly, savouring an image of Lady Violet's long, dark hair spread out over a white pillow, of her looking up at him, those golden eyes sparking with desire, those plump red lips parted in invitation, her voluptuous body…

'What's wrong? Why have you stopped?'

They had drifted to a halt, the still oars suspended over the water.

'My apologies, Lady Violet.' He leaned back, pulling hard on the oars and directing the boat through the water towards the bank where Herbert's boat was moored. What on earth had come over him? Who cared whether or not Lady Violet was passionate? Not him. Once this weekend was over, he would never see her again. He did not need a complicated woman like her in his life, no matter how intriguing she was or how tempting her lips might be.

He grabbed an overhead branch and pulled their boat close to the bank.

'I can't see them anywhere,' she said, once again standing up and looking around. 'I hope they haven't wandered off. Oh, this really is a disaster.' She scowled at him as if he was somehow responsible.

'Let me just tie up the boat and we can set off to find them. They won't have gone far.'

'How can you possibly know? They could be anywhere. Can't you hurry up?'

'I know Herbert, and he's not one for long walks. They'll be somewhere nearby.'

She continued to look around, her hand above her

squinting eyes, agitation crinkling her brow, like a sailor seeking a sign of land after many months at sea.

'We will find them, I promise. And I also promise your sister will be perfectly safe with Herbert.'

She glared down at him as if his promises meant nothing to her.

'But it will be best if you sit down while I climb off the boat, then I can help you out,' he said, pointing towards the wooden seat.

She ignored his suggestion, leant forward and placed one foot on the bank.

'Don't stand in the middle of the boat or you'll—'

Capsize it, he was about to say, his words cut off as the boat pulled away. With one foot on the bank, one still in the drifting boat, her position became more precarious and, dare he admit it, more comical.

Stifling his laughter, he grabbed her around the waist and pulled her back towards him, attempting to keep her upright as he did so. She pulled against him, as if she'd rather take a dunking than accept his help.

Her actions set the boat rocking. She leant forward, reaching out for the bank with flailing arms. There was nothing for it. He tightened his grip and pulled her hard. They tumbled backwards, fortunately landing in the bottom of the boat and not in the river.

While he laughed, she continued her wriggling, trying to untangle the jumble of limbs, but succeeding only in rocking the boat more vigorously.

'Stay still,' he said into her ear. 'Just wait till it stops moving, then let me help you out of the boat. You wanted to go fast before, Lady Violet, but now you need to take things slowly, gently.'

With his arms still around her waist, his lips close to her cheek, Jake was content to remain this way for as long as it took for her to calm down, but Lady Violet had different ideas.

'Just let me go, will you?' She fought to free herself, the boat rocking more violently with her movements.

'I will once you settle down and be a good girl. You're risking the two of us getting a drenching. And while a dunking might be just what you need to cool your temper, I have no desire to end up in the river.'

She continued in her attempt to stand up. He tightened the grip on her waist. 'Just relax,' he murmured in her ear. 'I'm not going to let you go until you do.'

She mumbled her annoyance, but her body did finally relax under his hold. The boat stilled. He didn't move. Nor did she. Instead, they lay together, his arms around her waist, her body lying on his.

'That's better,' he whispered, and he wasn't just referring to the stilling of the boat. There was nothing to stop him from standing now and helping her out, but having her lying on him was more pleasurable than anything he had felt before and he could stay this way for ever.

As if under a will of their own, his fingers drifted over the curve of her waist, then even more slowly to the soft flare of her hip. He suppressed a groan of pleasure. Was there anything more enticing than the area where a woman's waist rounded out to her hips and buttocks? It was definitely one of the parts of a woman's body that was Jake's weak spot, along with the small of her back, the inside of her thigh, the...

'What are you doing?' a curious voice said, interrupting his inappropriate thoughts.

Jake looked up. A woman's silhouette was leaning over the boat, the sun behind her. It had to be Lady Bianca. They both sat up immediately, but that did nothing to improve their situation. Lady Violet was now sitting on his lap.

She squirmed to free herself, wriggling and scrambling in what would be an undignified manner for any woman, but even more so for one as proud as Lady Violet. He quickly took hold of her waist once again and lifted her off him, then stood up and smiled at Lady Bianca and Herbert as if nothing untoward had happened.

'There you are. We were looking for you, weren't we, Lady Violet?'

Instead of leaping to her own defence, Violet kept her eyes lowered, her cheeks flushed. In other words, the epitome of guilt.

'Well, you've found us, but you haven't answered my question,' Lady Bianca repeated, amusement in her voice. 'What were you doing in the bottom of that boat?'

'We weren't doing anything,' Lady Violet said defiantly, her momentary lapse in composure gone.

'That's not how it appeared to us, is it, Mr Fortescue?' She turned to her smiling accomplice, who nodded vigorously. 'I believe, dear sister, this is what one would describe as being found in a compromising position with a man. You're lucky it is only Mr Fortescue and I who are here to witness your indiscretion. Heaven only knows what damage this would do to your reputation.'

'I fell. I was anxious to find you and I fell trying to get out of the boat. That is all. And Lord Jake was kind enough to...to...stop me from falling into the river.'

Lady Bianca raised her eyebrows in a knowing manner. 'Yes, sister. It would be terrible if you had become a fallen woman. And should anyone find out what you were up to, then that is exactly what we will all say. Lord Jake was just helping you out of the boat. Won't we, Mr Fortescue?'

'Indeed, we will. Your secret is safe with us.'

'There is no secret, nothing to keep safe,' she almost shouted, her cheeks and neck turning deep red as she attempted to scramble to her feet.

As much as *he* enjoyed teasing Lady Violet, he hated to see her going through this agony and he needed to put an end to her torture as quickly as possible.

He jumped to the bank and offered her his hand. 'Let's do this properly this time, shall we?'

She paused, stared at his hand and, for a moment, he thought they were about to go through the same ordeal. While he had no objections to once again having Lady Violet fall on him, he doubted her dignity could take any further assault. She, too, seemed to have come to that conclusion and she tentatively placed her hand in his, then carefully stepped on to the bank.

'There you go, safe and sound. Isn't it better when you accept people's help?'

She mumbled her thanks, then turned to face her sister and sent her one of her most blazing looks. But Lady Bianca was uncontrite and continued to smile at her sister, presumably aware that she had gained the upper hand.

'Now that you two have finished whatever it was you were up to in the bottom of that boat, you might like to share our picnic.' Lady Bianca indicated a tree, behind which a blanket and picnic hamper had been discreetly placed.

'No, we do not want to eat,' Lady Violet answered for both of them as she grabbed her sister's arm. 'You and I are going for a walk and we need to have a talk. Now.'

'We'll be back soon,' Lady Bianca called over her shoulder as Lady Violet strode off, all but dragging her smiling sister along. 'Don't drink all the champagne while we're gone.'

'I'm sorry about that,' Jake said as soon as the two young ladies disappeared over the small hill. 'I took as long as I could, but Lady Violet is rather a difficult woman to hold back when she sets her mind to something.'

'Not to worry, old chap. Bianca and I made the most of the time we had alone together. I plan to propose tonight, and I'm certain she'll say yes.'

They continued to look in the direction the two women had gone.

'But I'll need some more time alone with Bianca.' Herbert sent Jake his most doleful look. 'I want to do it properly, bended knee and all that. Perhaps you can keep Lady Violet busy again this evening? You know, give her some of that smooth talk the ladies love so much.'

'I'll do my best, but I'm afraid Lady Violet is rather impervious to my so-called charms.'

'Perhaps you can tackle her to the ground the way you did when you arrived. Bianca and I watched the whole thing. It took all my self-control not to burst into laughter. What sort of woman doesn't wait for a man to help her out of a boat? Quite unnatural. It would have served her right if you'd just let her take a dunking. Isn't that what they used to do with witches?'

Jake bristled. 'She was in a hurry because she was anxious about her sister. That's why she was impatient to get off the boat. She only wants what's best for Lady Bianca.'

Horror distorted Herbert's face. 'But *I'm* what's best for Bianca. Haven't you told her that?'

'Don't worry. I'm doing my best to convince her you are the perfect husband for her sister.'

'Good chap.' Herbert slapped him on the back, and a twinge of guilt gripped him. He might be doing his best to convince Lady Violet, but he suspected his best would never be good enough for her. She had dismissed him as a wastrel and rightly so. A man who only cared about having fun, the sort of man a woman like Lady Violet could never take seriously. And poor Herbert was being tainted by association.

'So, tonight, you can exercise that famous charm of yours on Lady Violet and keep her busy while I propose to Bianca.' Herbert rubbed his hands together in happy expectation. 'I know she'll say yes, and Lady Violet will be so bedazzled with you that you'll be able to convince her to put up no objections when I ask Bianca's father for her hand. It's a perfect scheme.'

Jake cringed. 'I don't believe it is going to be quite that easy.'

'Nonsense. From where I was standing, it looked like you were doing a splendid job. The woman is besotted with you.'

Jake doubted that and suspected Herbert was seeing what he wanted to see.

'But if she's not responding to your charms, then perhaps you need to try another tack.' Herbert frowned, a sure sign that he had been thinking hard. 'Perhaps you should pretend to be interested in the things she's interested in.'

It was a thought that had occurred to Jake, too, but so far all Lady Violet seemed to be interested in was protecting her sister and criticising him.

Herbert leaned forward, as if about to impart some words of wisdom. 'I asked Bianca what sort of things she likes to do. Apparently, she enjoys reading books.'

Jake waited for him to explain further.

'She's quite the bluestocking, apparently. If you could let her think you read books as well, then she's certain to fall under your spell and hang on your every word throughout the remainder of the weekend.'

'Did Lady Bianca say what she likes to read? There are rather a lot of types of books.'

'Yes, she did. Serious ones, apparently,' Herbert said, frowning, as if that explained everything.

Jake waved his hand in a circle to show he needed Herbert to be a bit more precise.

'Really serious ones. Bianca said the books she reads are so boring that they'd send any normal person to sleep before they'd got through the first page. If she sees you reading the most boring books in the library, that should do the trick.'

Jake wasn't completely convinced, but it was worth a try. After all, nothing else was working and he still had to distract Lady Violet for one more evening.

While they waited for the ladies to return, they opened the untouched picnic hamper, made a grab for the chicken legs and lay back to enjoy the sunshine. While Herbert no doubt contemplated his future proposal, Jake considered all the ways he'd really like to distract Lady Violet and none of them involved reading really boring books.

Chapter Nine

Bianca halted the moment they crested the hill, grabbed both Violet's arms and beamed at her. 'I'm so happy for you, Violet. I was right, wasn't I? Oh, the way Lord Jake was looking at you, it was so romantic.'

Violet stared at her sister as if she had lost all sense of reason. 'Don't talk such nonsense. The only reason Lord Jake is here is because he was helping me find the two of you. The only thing I care about is your reputation, Bianca. I certainly care nothing for Lord Jake.'

'Oh, you can't fool me.' Her sister continued to smile in that frustrating manner. 'I also saw the way you were looking at him, as if he's the most handsome man in the world and you can't get enough of him. It's just so exciting when people's feelings for each other are mutual.' Bianca placed her hands over her heart, closed her eyes and sighed.

'You do not know what you are talking about. There are no feelings, mutual or otherwise.' Heat rushed to Violet's face, and she could almost feel his hands around her waist, holding her tight. When his hand had moved to her hip, a feverish sensation had erupted deep inside her. It had been unlike anything she had experienced before and had left her completely disorientated.

She coughed to drive away that memory before she once again became distracted from what she was supposed to be doing. Bianca was not taking this situation seriously enough. Her reputation was at stake. That should be the only thing they were discussing.

'Bianca, you really cannot afford to ruin your reputation before the Season has even begun and especially not over a man like Mr Fortescue. You must not be alone with him ever again. Surely you must realise that.'

Bianca shrugged, picked off a long blade of grass and ran it slowly through her fingers. 'I knew you would find me eventually and none of my friends will give a fig how long we were missing or say anything about it, so no harm has been done.'

'No harm?' Violet could hardly believe what she was hearing.

'Nothing happened between us.' That impish smile returned. 'And we certainly didn't roll around together in the bottom of a boat. What an entrance you made, Vi. It was all so dramatic.' Her hands returned to her heart. 'Oh, and the way his hands encircled your waist as he caught you and saved you from ending up in the river. It was so romantic. But then you ruined it by tripping over and falling into the bottom of the boat.' Bianca tilted her head in question. 'Or was that deliberate? Did you want to end up with your arms and legs entangled, lying on top of him, with his hands on you?'

'I most certainly did not,' Violet said, louder than

she intended. 'I was just desperate to get to land to stop you from ruining your reputation.'

'You certainly looked desperate for something.' Bianca giggled. 'But I don't blame you. Who wouldn't fall for a man like him? And in your case quite literally.' She nudged Violet as if they were co-conspirators. 'He really has swept you off your feet, hasn't he? Again, quite literally.'

Violet placed her hands firmly on her hips. 'He has not.'

Bianca merely smiled.

'And anyway, that is not the issue. The issue is you should not be alone with Mr Fortescue. Bianca, will you promise me not to be alone with that man for the rest of the weekend?'

Bianca shrugged.

'Promise me.'

'Oh, all right.'

'Good. That's all I needed to say to you. Now, let's get this picnic over and done with.'

'Missing Lord Jake already, are you?'

Violet seethed inside, but she would not rise to the bait.

They retraced their steps to where the men were lying stretched out on the picnic rugs. Bianca and Violet paused at the top of the hillock and looked down at them. Her sister was unfortunately correct. Lord Jake was such a handsome man. With his eyes closed, she took the opportunity to observe the outline of the lean muscles of his long legs under his grey trousers, his flat stomach and the breadth of his chest.

She had felt his hard muscles up against her when

she had been lying on him in the boat. That disturbing, exciting shiver rippled through her again, the one she had experienced when his hands had gone round her waist, then stroked their way to her hips. For one irrational moment, she had longed for his hands to move from her hips, to explore more of her body. It had been as if he was bringing her back to life, and she had been incapable of moving away from him.

Violet shook her head as if to force out that memory. Yes, she had momentarily lost herself, and fallen at Lord Jake's feet, as Bianca said, quite literally. It seemed despite everything that had happened to her, every humiliation she had experienced, she was still not immune to being charmed by a handsome man. Just as she had warned Bianca not to be alone with Mr Fortescue, she needed to heed her own advice. In the future, she should be careful not to be alone with Lord Jake.

'Let's join our menfolk, shall we?' Bianca said.

Before she'd had a chance to say, they are not *our* menfolk, Bianca had skipped off down the hill and sat down on the picnic rug next to Mr Fortescue. He rose from his prone position and looked at Bianca with adoration. Pain gripped Violet's chest. No man had ever looked at her like that. Even when he had proposed, Randolph had not looked at her in that manner, as if she was the only woman in existence. Was that what real love looked like? No, of course not. It was just a man looking at a pretty young woman who came with a substantial marriage settlement.

She strode down the hill, ignoring that knot in her chest. 'We should get back,' she blurted out, standing beside the rug. 'You're neglecting your guests, Bianca, and I have much to do back at the house.'

'We haven't finished the picnic food,' Bianca said, removing wine glasses from the hamper and passing a bottle of champagne to Mr Fortescue to open. 'Your cooks went to so much trouble, it would be rude to return the hamper without eating all the food.' Bianca looked up at her, her face all sweetness and innocence. A look that did not fool Violet for one moment. When had Bianca ever cared about inconveniencing the servants? But what choice did she have? She could hardly take off in one of the boats and leave Bianca alone with these two men.

Instead, she sat down on the edge of the rug and took a glass of wine from the shaking hand of Mr Fortescue. The moment she took it, his hand quickly withdrew as if he feared getting burnt if it stayed too long.

She looked into the hamper, packed with sandwiches, chicken legs, pies and cakes. Enough to feed a battalion. It looked as though she was going to be stuck beside this gently flowing river, in the shade of this tree, drinking champagne and eating delicacies for quite some time.

Lord Jake rolled over on to his side, once again drawing her gaze to his long legs before she quickly looked away and out to the river.

'A toast,' he said, raising his champagne flute. 'To being lucky enough to enjoy lazy days beside the river and to sharing such days with good friends.'

'Hear, hear,' Herbert added, as he and Bianca raised their glasses.

'Some of us have more important things to do,' Violet said, refusing to take a sip.

'And some of us should learn to appreciate what we've got,' Lord Jake responded. 'Wasn't that what you said to me about having the opportunity to go to university? That it was something not available to everyone and I should have been grateful. Well, the world is full of people who would love to be lying beside a river, enjoying good food, good wine and good company.' He raised his glass to all three and the other two raised their glasses in response. 'So perhaps we should all appreciate how lucky we are.'

Violet did not like the implied reprimand, but she had no choice but to raise her glass and take a sip. The bubbles tickled her nose. She fought not to smile, then gave in to it and smiled slightly.

She watched the others enjoying themselves. They were drinking, eating and chatting quietly together, as if aware that loud noises would disturb the tranquillity. They found it so easy to relax and enjoy themselves. So why couldn't she?

Lord Jake passed her a plate of sandwiches and she sent him a smile of thanks. Was he right? Would it not be easier just to appreciate what she had and not always be at war with herself and at war with the world?

Perhaps he *was* right. They *were* lucky and she should appreciate what she had.

When she had finished her food, she lay back down on the rug and watched the way the light coming through the leaves sent a lacy pattern flickering over her dress. It was almost hypnotic, as if she were drifting off to sleep while still awake.

She closed her eyes. It was so still, the only sounds being the gentle rustle of the breeze in the trees and the chirping of the birds. It had been a long time since she had been on a picnic. She had almost forgotten such enjoyments, or how being beside a river could soothe one's nerves.

Still in a dreamlike state, she pulled herself up on to her elbows and looked at the others. Lord Jake was also lying on his back, his eyes closed, his handsome face calm and relaxed. Bianca was lying on her stomach beside Mr Fortescue, tickling his ear with a blade of grass, which was causing him to smile like a contented cat. They looked the very picture of an adoring couple. One could almost forget that this tableau of young love was that good-for-nothing Mr Fortescue and her beloved sister.

Violet sat up and jumped to her feet so quickly she felt dizzy. It *was* her beloved sister and that good-for-nothing. This had all gone on long enough.

'Right, it's time we got back to the house. I have a lot of work to do in preparation for tonight's dinner.'

Bianca rolled over to face her, the blade of grass still suspended over Mr Fortescue. 'Oh, you and Lord Jake go back. We'll follow along shortly.'

Violet placed her hands on her hips and exhaled loudly. 'We need to return to your guests. Now. It's rude to abandon them.'

'Oh, all right.' Bianca pulled herself into a seated position. 'I suppose another boat trip will be fun.'

Mr Fortescue stood up and offered his hand to

Bianca. She took it with a coquettish smile and he pulled her gracefully to her feet. They continued to stare mindlessly into each other's eyes, still holding hands, as if planning to remain that way for an eternity.

'Oh, for goodness' sake.' Violet started shoving plates, glasses and empty bottles into the picnic hamper, then bundled up the rug. Lord Jake lifted them up and placed them into a boat. Once the work had been done, Mr Fortescue and Bianca sauntered down to the bank, still holding hands. Mr Fortescue climbed into the boat and offered his hand to Bianca. She stepped lightly into the middle of the boat and sat down.

Violet stood at the side of their boat, waiting for Mr Fortescue to do the same to her.

'There's no more room,' Bianca said, spreading her skirt out over the wooden seat, which was obviously capable of accommodating two. 'You and Lord Jake will have to share the other boat.'

Before Violet had time to argue, Bianca flicked her hands at Mr Fortescue, who quickly untied the boat and pushed it out into the river where the current caught it. In great haste, he rowed away, as if suddenly they had an urgency to return to the house, leaving an outraged Violet standing at the side of the river.

'I think you've been outmanoeuvred, once again,' Lord Jake said, as they both watched the boat depart at a swift pace around a curve in the river.

'Hurry up, we have to catch them.'

He climbed into the boat and held out his hand to help her in. She hesitated, reluctant to touch him again and risk setting off those unsettling and confusing reactions in her body.

He raised his eyebrow, his question obvious. If she was in such a hurry, why was she still waiting on the side of the bank? She took his hand. A tingling sensation shot up her arm. Forcing herself to remain calm, she stepped into the boat. Think of Bianca, think of her reputation, she reminded herself as she took her seat.

'Right, get going. Quickly.'

'As you command, m'lady,' he replied as he pulled out into the water.

They rounded the curve in the river and there they were. After such a rapid departure, they were now drifting along, as if they had all the time in the world.

'What are they doing now? Don't they realise we have to get back home? I have a dinner to supervise.'

Lord Jake looked over his shoulder. 'It appears that you're going to have to make a choice. Either supervise dinner or supervise your sister, because I don't believe Herbert and Lady Bianca are in any hurry.'

Why did people have to make things so difficult for her? 'Well, if dinner is a disaster, it will be their fault entirely.'

'By the look of those two, dinner is the last thing they care about.'

They quickly caught up with the other boat and, when they did, it was worse than Violet had feared. Mr Fortescue and Bianca were leaning forward, their eyes fixed on each other, their heads almost touching. Had they been kissing? Violet hoped and prayed they had not been.

'Perhaps you should just sit back and enjoy the journey,' Lord Jake said soothingly. 'There's not much they can do in a boat.' He let go of the oars, allowing their boat to also drift. 'If they get too amorous, they'll over-turn their boat. If you don't believe me, we can do an experiment, and see how long it is before we end up in the drink.'

She knew he was teasing, but that didn't stop that annoying blush from heating her cheeks.

'Hurry up, you two,' she shouted out instead. 'We haven't got all day.'

Mr Fortescue jumped in surprise, grabbed the oars and commenced rowing, although not as swiftly as Violet would have liked. After what seemed like the longest boat ride along the shortest river that Violet had ever experienced, they finally arrived back at the boat ramp.

While the men stored the boats in the boathouse, Violet took Bianca's arm and tried to get her to walk at a brisker pace back to the house, but her languid sister was in no hurry.

The other guests had finished their own picnic. Some were strolling around the grounds, others had presumably retired inside and the more sensible ones were hopefully now preparing to dress for dinner. Whatever her guests were doing, Bianca did not seem in the slightest bit concerned whether their needs were being met. She was more interested in looking over her shoulder and waiting for Mr Fortescue to catch up with them.

'Go and see to your guests, while I see to dinner,' Violet said when they reached the house. She suspected that once again Bianca would not follow her instructions, but at least she was no longer alone with Mr Fortescue.

Violet entered the kitchen to once again find the

two cooks in mid-argument. What was wrong with these two women? They were sisters. Why couldn't they get along?

Beryl was glaring at Myrtle over a table piled high with untouched vegetables and meat, her chin raised, her hands on her hips, while Myrtle stared back at her, a soup ladle raised in a threatening manner. This was the last thing Violet needed.

Mirroring Beryl's stance, Violet placed her hands on her hips and lifted her chin. Some firm discipline was what these women needed. They weren't in their own homes now. They were in service and they should act appropriately. She was paying them a more than generous wage. She deserved a bit of loyalty.

'You women need to stop all this—'

'Ladies, I just had to come and thank you for the delicious picnic hamper and to say that last night's meal was simply outstanding,' a familiar male voice said all too charmingly behind her before she had managed to get out her words of reprimand.

The belligerent cooks immediately turned towards the door and bobbed curtsies, smiles replacing glares of anger.

'Thank you, sir,' the sisters said in unison, both bobbing another curtsy.

'You should have heard the compliments,' he continued, causing them to smile even brighter.

'Whoever said too many cooks spoil the broth didn't know what he was talking about. You two young ladies obviously work together in perfect harmony and it shows in your cooking.'

'Thank you, sir,' they both repeated, with yet more

curtsies. How many curtsies did these women think they had to perform? They were bobbing up and down like corks in the ocean.

'And I'm sure tonight's meal will be as much of a triumph as last night's.' He held out his arm to Violet. She frowned at him. She was not about to leave. She still needed to discuss tonight's menu with Beryl and Myrtle.

'I believe Lady Violet and I should let you get on with what you do best and not take any more of your precious time.'

Both women bobbed further curtsies at Lord Jake and went back to their preparations, as if whatever argument they had been in the midst of had never happened.

'Lady Violet? Shall we?'

Reluctantly, she took his arm, and he led her out of the kitchen.

'I could have managed that situation myself, you know.'

'I saw that look on your face when you stormed off and it was not the look of a diplomat. If you'd angered those women any further, no meal would have been prepared and you possibly would have had a mutiny on your hands. There is a saying, Lady Violet, you catch more flies with honey than with vinegar.'

That was easy for him to say. Compliments just oozed out of him like honey.

'But smoothing over another cooking crisis wasn't why I was in the kitchen. I was looking for you, Lady Violet.'

'Why? I'd have thought you had seen enough of me today.'

He smiled and she didn't know whether or not that was in agreement. 'When I arrived, no one showed me where the library was. I'm desperate for something to read.'

'I'm afraid we don't have any Penny Dreadfuls. You might be able to purchase some in town.'

He laughed as if she had made a delightful joke. 'I had heard you have an impressive collection of medieval poetry and a wide selection of books and pamphlets on political and philosophical discourses.'

She looked to see if he was joking. 'You read medieval poetry and books on politics and philosophy?'

'Yes, all the time. There's nothing I like better than burying myself in some really serious reading. The more serious the better.'

It seemed unlikely, but if he wanted boring books, their library was well stocked with them, and at least if he was reading, he would not be getting in her way.

'All right then. Follow me and I'll find you some really serious reading material.'

They entered the library and Jake inhaled the scent of the leather-bound books lining the walls, along with the lingering smell of cigars from countless generations of men who had used the room as a masculine retreat. For many men, their library provided somewhere to enjoy a brandy and cigar in undisturbed peace, away from the women in the household. The books were often little more than camouflage. They gave the impression the man was involved in the serious activity of improving his mind, without him actually having to do anything.

Although, in Jake's case, he was involved in the serious activity of convincing Lady Violet that he was a studious man, one she would happily spend all her time with, perhaps discussing poetry, politics or philosophy. The fact that these were three topics about which Jake knew very little would hopefully not present a stumbling block.

'Here you are.' She pulled a dusty book from the shelf and handed it to him with a sly grin.

He looked at the cover with its unpronounceable title and looked to her for an explanation.

'That's the book of medieval poetry you were so eager to read.'

'Ah, yes, delightful.' Jake flicked through a few pages and boredom hit him like a physical blow. It seemed he had already reached his first stumbling block.

'Now let's see if I can find you a suitable book on philosophy, or a book of political discourses, or better still, a book which discourses on political philosophy.'

Jake forced himself to keep smiling as she ran her fingers along the spines of the books. This was a big mistake. Why did he listen to Herbert? His friend was even less successful with women than he was with cards, Lady Bianca being the unique exception. He was the last man in the world to give good advice on how to attract a woman's attention.

Lady Violet placed a large pile of books on the table and sent him a malicious grin. 'These should keep you busy for a while.'

'Wonderful.' He picked up the book on top of the pile. 'Yes, Kierkegaard's *Concluding Unscientific Postscript to Philosophical Fragments*. I've been wanting to read this for some time.'

'While you're entertaining yourself with that—' she frowned at the tome in his hand '—I'm going to busy myself with trying to make some sense of the estate's accounts.'

She turned to leave the room.

Jake dropped the book on to the table and followed her out. After all, there was no point pretending to be clever if he didn't have an audience. 'Accounts? Perhaps I can help you with them.'

She continued walking down the corridor at an accelerated pace. 'I don't think so.'

'I believe I can. I'm even better at sums than I am at rowing.'

She stopped and turned to him. 'Oh, and I suppose you're going to tell me you took mathematics at university.'

'No, I'm afraid not, but it was my best subject at school. Father wouldn't let me take it at university. As he pointed out, it was not exactly much value to a man who would never have to work for a living.'

Jake tried to force down the unwanted memory of his father's condemning words. He had been so proud of getting the top mark in mathematics at school and had hoped it would make up for his father's obvious disappointment in him. A disappointment that had resulted in Jake being dragged around their home to view the portraits of his ancestors and listen to a recitation on the sterling characters and accomplishments of each, so Jake would know what was expected of him.

When he had joked that the Duke in a wig looked like a lady and laughed at the Tudor Duke wearing bulging bloomers and stockings, his father had been outraged. He had shaken Jake until his teeth rattled, then dispatched him off to school, as if no longer able to bear the sight of his second son.

Jake had hoped his success in maths would make up for that transgression, but his father had merely said, 'What use is that? You're not a tradesman. Thank goodness you're merely the second son, and let's hope a wastrel like you never becomes the Duke.'

'As I said, I didn't take mathematics at university.' He forced himself to adopt a more jovial tone. 'But you can't be a good gambler without being able to figure out the odds quickly and, if nothing else, I am an extremely good gambler.'

'I don't want anyone gambling with the estate accounts.' She pointed back at the library. 'Just stay in the library and read your unscientific postscript thing.'

'Do you need help with the accounts?'

She shrugged her shoulders. 'Yes.'

'Then it wouldn't hurt to let me look at them, would it?'

She hesitated, her face wary. 'Oh, I suppose it won't hurt if you have a quick look at my figures.'

He fought hard not to smile and even harder not to tease her about how much pleasure looking at her figure would give him.

'Lord knows, I can't make head nor tail of them.' She rushed off down the corridor and he paused briefly.

After all, she had given him permission to have a look at her figure. Yes, very nice, with all the curves in the right places, was his assessment.

'Are you coming?' she said over her shoulder. 'I haven't got all day.'

He caught up with her and they entered the study. She pulled a leather-bound ledger off the shelf and placed it on the desk. He opened it to the last entry and quickly scanned down the numbers. Then he took a closer look.

This can't be right.

He sat down and ran his finger slowly down the figures, then flicked back to previous entries.

He slammed shut the ledger and placed it on the desk. 'Where's your estate manager? I'd like to have a word with him.'

'That's the problem. He's not here.'

'When will he be back?'

'I don't believe he is coming back.'

That explained a lot. 'Do you know where he is? How he can be contacted?'

'No.' She collapsed into the nearby chair. 'He ran off with the tavern keeper's wife. Betsy used to be the barmaid at the Golden Fleece. That was why I was in the tavern when you arrived. Mr Armstrong was so upset about it he was refusing to open the tavern and the villagers were threatening to riot.'

Jake nodded slowly as he digested this information. 'The tavern keeper's wife wasn't the only thing your estate manager ran off with. It looks like he's taken rather a substantial amount of your income as well.'

'What?' She stood up, opened the ledger and stared at the estate manager's tidy handwriting.

He stood behind her. 'These don't add up.' He ran his finger down the line of numbers, pausing each time there was a discrepancy. 'Plus, according to these figures, he's been buying at highly inflated prices and selling produce from your farm at absurdly low prices. I suspect somewhere there is another set of account books that have the accurate numbers that will show exactly how much he's taken.'

Her hand covered her mouth as she scanned the shelves, as if expecting the authentic accounts to present themselves.

'And I also suspect that your former estate manager has either already disposed of those account books or has taken them with him.'

She collapsed back into her chair. 'No wonder he was always so happy. I'd assumed he just enjoyed his job. He would have known his crimes would never be discovered. At least, not by me. I'm hopeless at figures and Father takes no interest whatsoever, and as for Bianca...' She waved her hand in the air as if that explained everything. 'I suppose we were ripe for the picking.'

'I also suspect with the amount that he's taken, he and his barmaid will be long gone, probably to the colonies or the Americas and are now living a rather high life on your money.'

She looked down at her tightly clenched hands. 'What can we do? Should we hire someone to find them? Drag them back here, make them pay for what they've done and try to get our money back?'

'You could,' he said quietly. 'But you might just be wasting more money. They probably travelled under assumed names and could be anywhere in the world by now.'

She cocked her head, her brow furrowed. 'So, how do you know so much about the return one gets on farm produce?'

'Whenever I visit our Somerset estate, I always have a look over the figures.'

'Don't you trust your estate manager, either? Are they all rogues?'

'Our estate manager keeps impeccable figures and has been with the family all his life. His father was the estate manager before him. No, I just like numbers. Always have. Not that it's of much use to me, except at the card table.'

'Perhaps we should hire you as the estate manager.'

He knew she had said that in jest, but it was something that in different circumstances would have given him immense satisfaction. It was just a shame that as the second son of a wealthy duke, he was not expected to find honest employment. His father would turn in his grave if a son of his took such a position. Although, that in itself was tempting enough to take her up on the offer, just to show his father how low he had sunk.

'I'll ask our estate manager if he can recommend anyone,' he said. 'But there's nothing we can do about it tonight. In the meantime, we have dinner to dress for. You have guests to entertain and a sister to chaperon.' The last on that list was something he was supposed to be distracting her from, but right now, distracting her from her worries was of more importance.

Her face remained despondent and she did not rise from her chair.

'You don't need to worry too much, Lady Violet. From what I could see, the estate is still a productive one and any losses I'm sure will be redeemed.' *Eventually*, he could add, but doubted that would make her feel better.

'Yes, I suppose,' she murmured, stood up and walked to the door. Then turned back towards him.

'Thank you, Lord Jake,' she said before departing, leaving Jake feeling strangely pleased that he could, for once, be of some help. He turned to the shelves and pulled out several more ledgers to see just how much had been stolen from the Maidstone estate.

Chapter Ten

How was Violet ever going to tell Bianca? Her sister always thought they had endless amounts of money to spend on countless gowns and extravagant entertaining and that her marriage settlement was so substantial it would be the envy of all other debutantes.

Violet released a loud sigh as she sat down in front of the dressing room table so her lady's maid could style her hair. This was not what Violet had expected from the house party. Once the problem of the missing estate agent was solved, she had thought her only worry would be supervising her impetuous young sister.

But at least there was a silver lining to this particularly dark cloud. A drop in the estate's income would solve the problem of Mr Fortescue. If he really was a fortune hunter, once he heard Bianca was not worth as much as he expected, his affections would surely move on to another young lady. Violet hated the thought that Bianca might be hurt, but she was young and pretty and her first Season hadn't yet begun. She was certain to attract the attentions of a much more suitable man, one who loved her for herself and not her dowry. And Violet was determined to provide the guidance of a caring sister to make sure that happened.

'Shall I style your hair in the way I did last night?' her lady's maid asked.

'Yes, fine.' Violet's thoughts were on other matters, but there was no harm in making an effort tonight, as it might be the last time they entertained at Maidstone House.

Tonight, perhaps she also could try to be a bit more accommodating to Bianca's guests. They might be annoying and frivolous, but they were Bianca's friends and she deserved to have fun with them one last time. Once Bianca heard they were going to have to cut back on their spending, she would be heartbroken. Fortunately, they had already paid for Bianca's gowns for this Season, and there was a strong likelihood that a young woman as delightful as Bianca would be married before the Season was over, tempting dowry or not. Her sister might never have to know that the estate's income had been affected.

This might not be as bad as she feared. Violet and her father were more than capable of living a quiet, frugal existence. In fact, that was exactly how they did live.

Her thoughts returned once again to Lord Jake. Fancy a wastrel being the one to expose the estate manager's chicanery. Perhaps the unflattering description of him was a tad unfair, as there was really much more to the man than she had first thought.

Tonight would also be the last time she was likely to be in his company. That should not concern her, but being with him was not entirely unpleasant and she had perhaps been a bit harsh in her initial judgement of him. Yes, he was handsome and charming like Randolph, but she could never imagine Randolph scanning through the estate's accounts, unless it was to see how much he could skim off for himself. No, in that respect at least Lord Jake was not like Randolph. But he was still a womaniser, a gambler, a man who thought only of having a good time. Not that it really mattered. After all, she wasn't interested in Lord Jake, or any other man.

Violet discovered she had slumped down on the bench in front of her dressing table and her reflection had taken on a despondent appearance. This would not do. She stood up and turned to her lady's maid.

'Make haste, Agatha. I've much to do.'

Agatha's eyes grew wider and Violet knew what she was thinking. The only person delaying her dressing was Violet, who had spent far too much time in pointless contemplation. But like the good lady's maid she was, she said nothing and removed the gown from the wardrobe.

Violet's breath caught in her throat as Agatha brushed down her pale green dress with the dark green embroidery. She had worn that gown the night Randolph had proposed. Usually, the very sight of that dress would have caused a warring tumult of emotions to erupt within her, with anger, shame and self-pity fighting for dominance. Slowly, she drew in a breath and waited to be assaulted by those devastating emotions. Nothing happened. Instead, all she saw was a rather pretty gown that had been designed to flatter her figure and her colouring.

It was hard to even remember the girl she had been when she had last worn that gown. She had been happy, carefree and looking forward to her future with the most charming, attentive man imaginable. That now seemed like a lifetime ago.

Agatha helped her into her gown. She stood in front of the mirror and observed her reflection, waiting for that familiar agony to grip her. It didn't. What was happening? Had enough time passed so she was no longer affected by the memory of Randolph and the humiliation he had inflicted on her?

And yet, only yesterday she had reeled when her father had mentioned being left at the altar. What had changed? Could it be Lord Jake? Violet quickly turned from the mirror and picked up her gloves. She had neither the time nor the desire to ponder why this gown no longer affected her. She had too much to do, too much else to worry about than a silly dress.

She entered the drawing room to find Bianca and her friends already enjoying a pre-dinner drink. And from the florid complexions of some of the men, and the loud laughter of the young ladies, Violet suspected many of them had enjoyed more than just one drink.

Lord Jake was standing by the unlit fireplace, leaning on the mantelpiece as several of the women vied for his attention, including Lady Alice and Lady Cynthia. A small thrill caused her body to tingle as he excused himself and crossed the room, his brown eyes fixed on hers.

'You look lovely tonight, Lady Violet,' he said with a bow.

Only a few days ago, she would have dismissed such

flattery as insincere, but the look in his eye suggested he meant every word. But she had no time for that now. She had much she needed to discuss with him, so she took his arm and led him to a quiet corner of the drawing room, away from the noisy crowd.

'Please, say nothing to anyone about what you discovered in the account books,' she said, keeping her voice low. 'I particularly do not wish for Bianca to find out. Her first Season is about to start and I want it to be special for her.'

'You have my word. And after further investigation, I don't believe the damage is too bad. I took the liberty of looking through past account books. It seems the estate manager's criminal activity only started last year. There appears to be no lasting damage.'

Relief flooded through her. 'Oh, that is good news. Thank you, so much.' She smiled and placed a grateful hand on his arm. He smiled back, causing her to become aware of her overly familiar gesture. She removed her hand and adopted a sterner countenance. 'Although I would not object if you dropped a few hints to Mr Fortescue that Bianca's marriage settlement might not be quite as generous as he expects.'

'I have already told you that Herbert does not care about such things as marriage settlements. He has no need of money and it is obvious to anyone that when he looks at your sister, money is the last thing he is considering.'

'I believe your friendship for Mr Fortescue has blinded you.'

'And I believe you are blinded by—'

Whatever he was going to say was drowned out by

the resounding boom of the dinner gong, which cut across all conversation.

The couples paraded to the dining room. Once again, Bianca had placed herself next to Mr Fortescue and Violet next to Lord Jake. Violet had intended to check the seating arrangements so this would not happen again but had been so distracted by the news of the estate agent she had forgotten to do so. But there was nothing to be done about that now.

Once again, dinner was an unexpected triumph. The cooks had provided simple but tasty fare and each course elicited surprising oohs and aahs from the guests, who had been used to the finest their entire lives. Nor did anyone seem put out that once again there were only three courses of beef broth, lamb shanks and an assortment of flavoured jellies.

Violet had intended to suggest that Beryl and Myrtle serve an additional fish course tonight, maybe some game, perhaps platters of cheeses and pâtés, but their argument had put an end to that idea. But no one seemed to mind. Perhaps Bianca's friends did deserve some credit for their ability to adapt to circumstances.

'I must go down and compliment the cooks again,' Lord Jake said when the dessert plates were removed.

Violet knew just how those women would react. They'd primp and preen, in a manner in which women usually responded to him. Although, she had to admit, that was something else for which she should be grateful. If it wasn't for Lord Jake, the cooks might be still arguing and the guests would all be left sitting staring at their empty plates. She could see that he had the potential to make someone a good husband and could certainly run the estate better than she or her father ever could.

Violet coughed and spluttered, almost choking on her wine at the absurdity of such a thought. He might be good with staff and with numbers, but that was the only way in which he would make a good husband. And he most certainly would never make a good husband for a woman like her. Far too frivolous, far too charming and far too handsome for his own good.

'Are you all right, Lady Violet?' he asked, handing her his napkin.

She tried to speak, but could only cough. She took his napkin and dabbed her lips with as much dignity as she could.

'Perfectly fine,' she said with a strangled voice.

What on earth was happening to her? Had she lost all sense of reason? The words Lord Jake and husband should never occur in the same sentence, unless she was thinking what a terrible husband Lord Jake would make some poor, unfortunate woman.

To stop her mind from dwelling on that perilous subject, she stood up to inform the ladies that it was time to retire to the drawing room and leave the men to their brandy. Before the words were out, Bianca jumped to her feet and tapped her glass to get everyone's attention.

'Let's all go to the drawing room and play parlour games,' she said, her eyes sparkling with excitement.

A cheer of hurrah went up from her friends, chairs were scraped back in haste and, forgetting all about protocol, they all rushed off down the corridor, leaving only Violet and Lord Jake to follow on behind at a more dignified pace.

'Good, everyone's here,' Bianca said when they entered the drawing room. She was holding up a man's white silk scarf and staring straight at Violet, a glint in her eye that looked almost evil. 'The first game we will play is blind man's buff. And I propose my sister goes first.'

Violet took a series of quick paces backwards towards the door. Several male guests took her by the arms, blocking her escape, and, laughing, led her into the centre of the room. She was blindfolded by Bianca, then spun around and around until completely disorientated.

Her hands out in front of her, she took a few tentative steps forward. The rustling of a woman's silk gown and a familiar quiet laugh alerted her she was close to Bianca. She took a decisive step forward, her arms reaching out to grab her sister, but her arms flailed at empty air. Bianca's stifled giggle and the guffaw of a man, Mr Fortescue, made it clear they were toying with her.

Well, she would not let them do that. She turned around and, as if she could see perfectly well, she stepped forward until she grabbed the nearest person.

'You have to tell us who it is,' Bianca said, her voice so high-pitched with excitement she was almost squealing.

It was a man. That much was obvious from the dinner jacket lapels she had hold of. She reached up. It was a strong, fit man. The breadth of his chest made that clear. Her hands moved up to his face, and she ran her fingers over a firm jawline, the slight stubble rough under her fingers.

It was Lord Jake. She'd recognise his scent anywhere. That masculine mix of musk and the spicy tang of his cologne were unmistakable. She was tempted to lean in and inhale deeply, and only the sound of a woman's stifled giggle stopped her from doing so.

She knew who it was. It was time to announce it to the group and get this foolishness over and done with. But she didn't. Her fingers continued to explore his face. She ran them lightly over his cheeks, across the high cheekbones, then up to his hair. Her fingers tunnelled into the locks, that thick hair she knew to be dark brown, almost black. Her hand traced back down his face. She stopped, then as if with a will of their own, her fingers moved to his lips and her breath caught in her throat as she felt their softness under the pad of her thumb.

'Who have you caught, Lady Violet?' a man's voice called out.

'Come on. If you don't know, you can take a guess,' a woman added.

'It's Lord Jake,' Violet said, then cursed her voice for coming out as a purr.

The guests clapped loudly and several shouted out well done. The scarf was lifted from her eyes and she looked up at Lord Jake. He was gazing down at her, not smiling like the other guests, but staring at her with an unsettling intensity. She hoped the way she had traced her fingers over his face with more fervour than was entirely necessary for such a childish game had not offended him. Hopefully, he would think it was because she did not like to get things wrong and would have to make certain she was right before taking a guess.

He continued to stare at her, the white scarf dangling from his hand.

'Come on, Jake,' Mr Fortescue called out. 'Your turn now.'

Lady Alice rushed forward and nudged Violet out of the way. She stood on a footrest and tied the scarf around Lord Jake's eyes. Then Mr Fortescue spun him around. He walked forward a few steps. Lady Alice and several other ladies deliberately stepped in his way. Weren't you supposed to try to avoid being caught?

Violet was tempted to stomp out of the room, but she would not give the others the satisfaction of thinking that she cared one bit who Lord Jake caught.

Not surprisingly, he took hold of Lady Alice and almost immediately guessed correctly. How did he know? Was he that familiar with her body that one light touch would reveal her identity to him?

Instead of looking pleased, Lady Alice seemed disappointed. Had she hoped that Lord Jake would explore her face the way Violet had explored his? Heat rushed to Violet's face.

Had she embarrassed herself by doing so? Or, even worse, caused the other guests to think that she was in some way interested in Lord Jake? Or worse even than that, was that the impression she had given him?

He tied the scarf around Lady Alice's eyes, turned her around then stepped back. Giggling, she swung her arms around, trying to grab hold of one of the guests. She neared one man, then turned off in a different direction. She was seeking out Lord Jake. That much was plain to see. But he was standing well back. Violet suppressed a smile as she took hold of Mr Fortescue's jacket.

Mr Fortescue laughed loudly, making it impossible not to know who Lady Alice had captured.

'Mr Fortescue,' she said, not bothering to hide her disappointment and ripping the scarf off her eyes.

Mr Fortescue took his turn and headed straight for Bianca. Could he see through his scarf, or had they devised some scheme so that he would find her?

Just as she had done with Lord Jake, Mr Fortescue ran his hands lightly over Bianca's face. Bianca giggled. How could he not know who she was? Mr Fortescue traced his fingers over Bianca's lips, which she parted in a suggestive manner.

This had gone on too long and gone too far. Violet took a step forward. It had to stop. Lord Jake took her arm, halting her progress. 'It's just a bit of fun, nothing more than some harmless flirtation,' he whispered in her ear. 'They're in a room full of people, all of whom are friends,' he continued. 'No harm can be done to your sister's reputation.'

She pulled against his arm.

'Or do you think exploring another's face like that should be interpreted as some sort of attraction, maybe even an invitation?'

She froze, closed her eyes and swallowed. 'No,' she responded, her voice an embarrassed squeak.

'Good, then let them enjoy themselves.'

Eventually, after what seemed like an agonisingly long period of time, Mr Fortescue whispered, 'Skin so soft could only belong to the beautiful Lady Bianca.'

Bianca smiled, reached up, gently removed the scarf

and lightly kissed him on the lips, causing Violet to gasp in outrage.

'And that is your reward, Mr Fortescue,' Bianca said. 'For being such a clever, clever man.'

Violet shrugged off Lord Jake's arm. 'I think we've had enough of that game,' she said and pulled the scarf out of her sister's hands.

'Quite right.' Bianca clapped her hands together, not in the slightest bit put out by Violet's terse tone. 'Let's play sardines instead.'

Violet groaned, but at least with sardines she could monitor where her sister went and who she was with.

Bianca looked at her, that wicked glint once again in her eye. 'As Violet was the first to play blind man's buff, she should be the one to hide first. Find somewhere with plenty of room, won't you, as we're all going to have to squeeze into the same hidey-hole and I just know you won't want us to get too close to each other.'

'I don't see why I should have to...'

Violet's objections could not be heard over the sound of twenty guests, all counting loudly to one hundred. With a huff of annoyance that no one heard, she turned and stormed out of the room. It was ridiculous. She would not be looking for a hidey-hole anywhere in the house, not when there were much more productive ways to use this time. While the others scoured the house, she would escape from all this nonsense and get some work done.

To that end, she strode down the corridor and entered the study. Lord Jake had said that only last year's accounts were inaccurate. Perhaps she could have a look at previous years to try to work out the discrepancy and see just how much money the estate manager had stolen from them.

She pulled several account ledgers off the shelves and laid them side by side to make a comparison. The figures seemed to swim before her eyes, making no sense at all. How could they? She had no idea how much bales of wool should cost, did not know what all the categories for different ages of sheep could possibly mean and what the going rate would be for them at different times of the season.

She sank into a nearby chair. It was hardly her fault. Her father had never seen the point of educating his daughters. That was something it seemed she had in common with Lord Jake. He obviously had a natural aptitude for mathematics and yet his father had stifled such talent. Was that why he was such a wastrel? Because he never had the opportunity to do what he was good at and what he enjoyed.

Perhaps she was as wrong about him as she was about the estate manager. And she had certainly been wrong about the estate manager. He had been cheating them right under their very noses, just as he had been having an affair with Betsy right under the tavern keeper's nose.

How he must have laughed at her. Violet had believed she was taking care of everything on the estate, that she was so much more responsible than her flibbertigibbet sister or her absent-minded father. She was supposed to be the serious, diligent one, but it had taken the decidedly unserious, undiligent Lord Jake to point out that she was as incompetent as both her sister and her father.

The door opened slowly and the very man entered. He quietly shut the door behind him.

'I thought you'd be here,' he whispered. 'I don't think you've quite grasped the idea of sardines. You're supposed to find somewhere to hide.' He looked around the room, which held nowhere suitable for one person to hide, never mind a party of twenty. 'Somewhere like that.'

He pointed under the desk in the middle of the room.

'There's hardly enough…'

He placed his finger on his lips and she lowered her voice.

'There's hardly enough room for the entire party to fit in there.'

'That is part of the fun. You find somewhere that not everyone can fit, then there's much hilarity as they all try to squeeze in.'

She looked at him, waiting for him to explain just how that was actually funny.

'You wouldn't want your guests to think you were trying to ruin their fun, would you? After going to all that trouble to ensure they had a good dinner, it would be a shame to put a damper on things by ruining their game.'

Violet still did not move. The last thing she wanted to do was to climb under a desk, and she most certainly did not want to do so with Lord Jake.

He smiled, the glint in his eye having a remarkable similarity to Bianca's wicked look. 'If you crawl in under the desk, once this game is over, I'll explain how those accounts work so you'll never be cheated again.'

She looked at the open ledgers, then down at the

small space under the desk, then back up at Lord Jake. It was the strangest bargain she had ever heard of.

He waited.

'Oh, all right.' It was all foolishness, but if that was what it took so she could manage the estate properly in the future, it would be but a small sacrifice. Gathering up her skirt, she crawled under the desk and wedged herself into the corner, folding her legs under her in the most decorous manner possible in the confined space, then tucked her skirt around her. He crawled in after her and sat with his legs crossed in front of him.

'That's much better. Now you're entering into the spirit of things,' he said approvingly.

'What do we do now?'

'We wait until the others find us and the last one who does is "it". Then they have to hide and we have to find them.'

Violet shook her head in disbelief, although why she should be surprised at the ways people wasted their time, she did not know. 'How long is this likely to take?'

'Well, you haven't exactly picked a difficult hiding place, so it shouldn't take long.'

'Good.'

Violet placed her hands in her lap and tried to remain perfectly still. She hoped, prayed, they would find them soon and not just because this was a waste of time. Remaining still did nothing to slow her heartbeat, which was pounding loudly in her chest. So loudly, it must be reverberating through the confined space. She wriggled further into the corner. That didn't help. They were still almost touching. His chest was mere inches from hers. His thighs were actually right up against hers. And worse than that, the warmth of his body wrapped around her and there was no way she could ignore his unmistakably masculine scent, nor the smell of his cologne. What was that scent? She was yet to fully identify it. Lemon verbena with a hint of allspice? Whatever it was, it had taken possession of her senses, making her fully aware that she was alone with him.

Alone and hidden away from prying eyes. There was absolutely nothing to stop him from taking advantage of this situation.

'This is just silly,' she muttered again, her voice hoarse and constricted as she wondered whether he would indeed take advantage of the situation, and whether that was something she would object to or indeed something she secretly wanted.

'I've got far too many things to concern myself with than childish games,' she added, with a defiance that made it clear it was most definitely not what she wanted.

Chapter Eleven

'You've got nothing to worry about.'

That was easy for him to say. He probably found himself in confined spaces, pressed up against women, on a regular basis, but this was a novel experience for Violet. One that was decidedly unsettling.

'The estate is still making a profit. The farm is productive, and you're getting a good rate of return on all the buildings you own in the village. The estate manager sold off some of your farm machinery, which you'll have to replace, but it should not take more than a season or two for the estate to recover completely.'

Violet almost laughed at her stupidity. While she had been worried that he might take advantage of her, all he wanted to do was talk business.

'I'm such an imbecile.'

He turned towards her, which in the confined space meant he came even more disturbingly close.

She had not meant to say that out loud.

'That's not true,' he said, his voice consoling. 'You're not an imbecile. You were just too trusting.'

This time she did laugh, a harsh, disparaging laugh. When she called herself an imbecile, she hadn't been talking about the estate agent tricking her. And as for being too trusting of men, that was the last thing she would expect anyone to accuse her of.

His eyebrows drew together as he waited for an explanation.

'How much longer are they going to take?' He did not need to know why she had laughed and she certainly had no intention of telling him.

'I take it you don't enjoy playing parlour games?'

'No, I think they should be played by children, not adults.'

'So did you play like a child when you were a child, or were you always this serious?'

She tried to move further into the corner, not liking the direction in which his questions were going.

'What's wrong?' he asked, his voice gentle.

'Nothing.'

'It's not nothing. Something has upset you?'

'Oh, all right. There was a time I enjoyed playing parlour games. During my first Season, I acted the fool and indulged in all the usual frivolities, just like all the other debutantes.'

He waited for her to continue, but that was all he was going to get out of her on that subject. She did not need to relive those painful years, or, at least, how those years had come to a painful end.

'I can't imagine you playing the fool.'

'And you can't imagine me having fun either, can you?'

'We're having fun now, aren't we?'

She shrugged, unsure what her answer should be.

'Does that mean you did all the things a debutante does, had a coming out and attended all the events of the Season?'

'Yes.'

He waited, but she said no more.

'But only one Season?'

'Yes.'

Once again, he waited, but she would reveal no more to him. She did not want him to think any less of her than he already did. Did not want him to know that in her first Season she had been so naive that she had let a charming cad deceive and humiliate her.

'Why not?' he asked quietly.

She sat up straighter, or at least as straight as the confined space would allow. 'Unless you're trying to find a marriage partner, I can't see the point of the Season and I am not in search of a husband.'

'On that, we are in complete agreement. I, too, avoid the Season.'

'But it's different for a man,' she snapped, revealing more of her annoyance than she wished. 'If you don't attend the Season, it's assumed you're off somewhere having a good time, sowing your wild oats. For a woman, you're classed as a bluestocking or a wallflower. Neither of which are particularly flattering descriptions.'

'And neither of which apply to you.'

She looked at him to see if he was teasing, but he was not smiling. She almost wished he was. Instead, he was looking at her with...with what? She would almost say desire, but knew that to be ridiculous. Men like him did not desire women like her.

His gaze drifted from her eyes to her hairline, down to her lips, then back up to her eyes. 'You are an intelligent woman, but that doesn't make you a bluestocking. You don't like frivolity and abhor the Season. That doesn't make you a wallflower.'

The gentleness in his voice had a more powerful effect than if he had been mocking her. A lump formed in her throat and she looked down at her hands, clasped tightly together in her lap. When she was young, she would not have expected to one day become such a serious woman who scorned fun and frivolity as a pointless waste of time. But that was a role forced on her when she was rejected and ridiculed.

When she had been stranded at the altar, she had decided to never allow any man to treat her like that again. Being lonely on occasion was better than having your heart ripped out of your chest. It was better to have no dreams than to have them destroyed and in such a cavalier manner as if your feelings mattered not one jot. No, she was much better off on her own.

'Well, no matter what you say, at six and twenty I'm officially an old maid.' She gave a little laugh, as if to suggest that such a description did not hurt.

'Again, it's not a description that could ever be attributed to you. And I'm also six and twenty—that hardly makes me over the hill.' He smiled, as if the thought of such a thing was almost too silly to contemplate.

'And I could say, again, it's different for a man.'

He shrugged as if he could not see why such a thing should matter.

'And anyway, I don't care what people call me, old maid, wallflower or bluestocking, it makes no difference to me.'

'None of those titles apply to you,' he whispered and held her gaze. 'What I see when I look at you is a beautiful, intelligent woman who knows her own mind.'

She gasped, not just because of his words but because his gaze had once again moved slowly from her eyes to her lips. He reached over and pushed an escaped lock of hair behind her ear, his hand gently stroking her forehead and her cheek. 'You have the most beautiful hair I have ever seen,' he murmured, as if talking to himself.

He blinked, coughed lightly and looked away, as if those words had never been said, as if he hadn't touched her in such a gentle manner. 'And yet you attended one Season. Why only one? Does that mean you once had thoughts of marriage?'

Still staring at his handsome face, now in profile, she considered telling him the truth. His question had been asked in such a manner that he seemed to care, to not want to mock her, or worse, pity her.

Then she, too, coughed to clear her constricted throat and looked back down at her lap. It was safer to stick to the lie she told everyone, a lie that she had told so many times she was beginning to believe it herself.

'After one Season, I realised what a load of nonsense it was. I decided I was much better off, much happier, on my own than I would ever be with a man.

And thank goodness I came to that conclusion before I made a terrible mistake.'

'Once again proving what a sensible woman you are. So many society marriages are nothing but miserable.' He gave a harsh laugh. 'My parents' marriage being the perfect example. They married because their families could see it was advantageous to combine two such wealthy and noble families. No one cared that they were so ill-suited.'

'Is that why you haven't married?'

'Maybe.' He laughed again, but she could still hear pain behind the laughter. 'Or perhaps it's because I've enough decency to know that no woman should be burdened with a wastrel like me for a husband.'

'You're not a wastrel.' She was tempted to place her hand on his arm in reassurance, but forced herself not to succumb. Touching him would be wrong, not just because of propriety, but because she did not know if she could stop at just touching his arm. Like a physical memory, her fingers could almost feel what it was like when she had run her hands over his cheeks, could remember the hardness of his jaw and the softness of his lips.

She gripped her hands together more tightly. 'A wastrel wouldn't have spotted the discrepancies in the account books or know what prices farm produce should be sold for.' She breathed out, pleased they were once more back to discussing the business of the estate.

He shrugged. 'They're hardly necessary accomplishments for a second son of a duke. I'll never have an estate to manage, so it's all pointless, really. Just like my life.'

Then she did place her hand on his arm, just in consolation, nothing more.

He patted her hand lightly and smiled. 'It looks like tonight is a night for baring our souls,' he said as that familiar slow smile crept over his lips. 'So, I need to bare a bit more of my soul and make a confession.'

Her hand shot back from his arm and she braced herself. What on earth could this man have to confess to her? She already knew that women found him attractive, that he could probably have anyone he wanted, and she suspected he often took what was offered. Hadn't Bianca said he had a naughty reputation? She did not need to hear any of that.

'You don't need to tell me anything about your past. I don't indulge in gossip, so will hear nothing untoward about you. You don't have to confess any of your antics.'

I don't want to hear about the other women. It doesn't matter to me, but I still don't want to hear about them.

He laughed. 'That's not the sort of confession I meant. I have to confess that I don't really read books on political philosophy. Nor am I interested in poetry written in old English. Lady Bianca told Herbert that you like to read really boring books. I was trying to impress you so I asked for the most boring books I could think of and tried to act as if they fascinated me.'

It was her turn to laugh, in relief as much as humour. 'You didn't have to try so hard. Bianca thinks all books are boring, but you really selected the worst ones in the library. Even I'd draw the line at poetry in old English.' She stopped laughing when the other part of what he had said rang through. 'Why would you want to impress me?'

His laughter stopped. His gaze lingered. Time stretched out as he stared deeply into her eyes, making her grateful that the light from the lamps did not fully illuminate the space under the table, so he could not see her blushing. 'Why would a beautiful, intelligent woman ever need to ask a man why he wants to impress her? That's what men do. We have no choice in the matter.'

She swallowed and hoped he couldn't hear the lump moving down her throat.

'You think I am beautiful?'

'I know you are beautiful and so should you. Everything about you is beautiful—your lovely hair that shimmers when it catches the light, your sparkling brown eyes that at times appear to be on fire, your skin that looks so soft and pure, and your lips.' His gaze lowered to her lips, causing Violet's heart to seemingly jump inside her chest.

'What about my lips?'

'Do you really want to know?'

Violet wasn't sure, but she nodded anyway.

'The moment I saw you, I thought those full, red lips were just waiting to be kissed and the man that you give your kisses to will be privileged indeed. He will be a man that all other men will envy.'

She tried to laugh off his compliments, but the laugh became stuck in her throat and came out as a small gasp.

'If you really wanted to make a confession, I believe you should have confessed that you are a man who likes to charm women,' she said, forcing her voice to stay even. 'But I'm afraid your attempt at being charming is wasted on me.'

'I wasn't trying to be charming. You asked me a question, and I merely answered with the truth. You are a beautiful woman. A woman I would like to kiss.'

Her hand shot to cover her mouth. Then she slowly lowered it and placed it on her chest, where the drumbeat of her heart pounded to an increasingly rapid tempo. His gaze remained fixed on her lips. She swallowed to relieve her dry throat and fought to draw in a breath.

'May I kiss you?' he said so quietly she could barely hear him.

Say no. Say no. You have to say no. She nodded her head.

His gaze held hers, so intently she felt incapable of moving, incapable of thinking. She nervously raked her teeth along her bottom lip as his hand took her chin and gently, slowly tilted up her head. The pounding of her heart moved from her chest to throb throughout her body. As if pulled by an invisible thread, against which she had no resistance, she leant in towards him. He lowered his head. Then his lips were on hers. He really *was* kissing her. This handsome, intoxicating, exciting man was kissing her.

She closed her eyes and moaned softly. His touch was gentle, feather-light, as if she was made of delicate porcelain and he was afraid of breaking her. But she was not delicate, nor was she made of porcelain. She was a woman and she wanted him to kiss her properly.

She edged herself closer. Her hand stroked his cheek,

loving the feel of the rough stubble under her fingers. His lips pressed more firmly against hers. Was he responding to her caresses? Had that been seen as an invitation? Her fingers wove through his thick hair, cupping the back of his head, and she parted her lips. Was that enough of an invitation? Would that let him know she wanted more, much more?

Yes. The pressure of his lips intensified. Tilting back her head, she parted her lips further and was rewarded with his tongue lightly stroking her sensitive bottom lip. Excitement surged within her. Every inch of her body came alive, hot and aching for him. She should not be doing this. Deep down, she knew that. But she was and, now that she had his kiss, she wanted so much more, wanted him to consume her, to relieve her pounding, insistent need for him.

His lips withdrew from hers and he smiled down at her, his hand still holding her chin. 'That was not the kiss of a bluestocking, wallflower or an old maid.' He gently kissed her waiting lips once again. 'Perhaps it is you that needs chaperoning, not your sister.'

'Stop talking,' she murmured, her lips finding him and kissing him again with a fervour that revealed how much she needed him. She drank him in, loving the touch of him, the smell of him, but it still wasn't enough. She had to have more, had to get out of this confined space so his arms could surround her, so she could feel his entire body hard up against hers.

He lightly kissed her neck, nuzzling it softly. She tilted back her head, her breath becoming quick, panting gasps. 'We should…we should…' She could hardly talk, could hardly breathe.

'We should what?' he murmured, his lips so close his breath lightly caressed her cheek.

She pulled in a deep, steadying breath to give herself courage.

'We should go somewhere where we can—'

A loud bang drew his attention away from her and he looked at the opening under the desk. It was the sound of the door being thrown open in haste. Then the room filled with the familiar sound of Bianca's giggles.

Violet's hands sprung back from his head, where they had unaccountably become entangled in his hair. 'Oh, no, that's...'

He placed his finger lightly over her lips to stop her talking and whispered, 'Shh.'

Violet's heart continued to pound frantically against the wall of her chest as her mind fought its way out of a fog of desire.

Closing her eyes, she slowly drew in a series of deep breaths. Bianca would soon find them. She needed to be composed, needed to show her sister that she was merely playing her childish game. Nothing else had happened. Bianca most certainly did not need to know that she had just been kissed in a manner that had caused her to lose herself and forget all sense of propriety. After all, wasn't she supposed to be setting an example for her impressionable little sister?

She opened her eyes and waited for Bianca to look under the table. It was the only place in the study that anyone could possibly hide. Surely she would at least check to see if that was Violet's hiding place?

Lord Jake looked at her and raised his eyebrows in

question. She turned her palms upwards to indicate she, too, did not know why her sister was taking so long.

Bianca giggled again. What on earth did she have to laugh at? Then she sighed. Then there were strange noises that sounded like sucking and licking, and what almost sounded like a man grunting. It was obvious why Bianca had not looked under the table. She was with that Mr Fortescue and he was kissing her. This had to stop.

'This is outrageous,' she hissed, attempting to push past Lord Jake, but he remained where he was, blocking her exit. 'I need to…'

He placed his hand lightly on her mouth to stop her words.

'We're supposed to be hiding,' he whispered.

She pushed his hand away. 'Yes, but they're…' She signalled towards the noise, which was now turning into low moans.

'Doing what we just did.'

Violet frowned in disapproval, hoping that would stop her cheeks from blushing. 'But it's Bianca.' She paused. 'And Mr Fortescue is…' She gave a little shudder.

'By the sound of things, Lady Bianca doesn't think Mr Fortescue is…' He imitated her shudder.

The sighs and gentle moans turned into loud groans. That was enough. Violet could put up with this no longer. If Lord Jake would not get out of her way, then she would just have to crawl over him. She had to save her sister before this went too far.

Reaching over him, she grabbed the edges of the desk and tried to pull herself out.

'Will you please move?' she demanded, her chest against his.

'I don't believe I can,' he whispered, a hint of laughter in his voice. 'You appear to have me pinned down.'

'I have not. Now move.' She pulled herself further forward, sliding more along his body. 'You're doing this deliberately, aren't you?'

'I believe it was you that climbed on top of me and trapped me in place.'

'I did not climb on top of you. I'm trying to get out. It was your stupid idea for us to climb under this desk in the first place. The least you can do is help me.' She pulled one leg forward and angled it over him. Then tried to drag the other leg with it. She was nearly there. Just a bit further and she would be free.

Two heads appeared under the desk.

She looked towards them, then back at Lord Jake, the man she was now straddling. Bianca placed her hand over her mouth. 'Again? Violet, you seem to be making a habit of being found in compromising positions with Lord Jake.'

'So sorry to interrupt,' Mr Fortescue said with a grin. 'We'll leave you alone to get on with whatever it is that you are doing.'

The two heads disappeared.

'Do not go anywhere,' she shouted. 'Help me out of here. Can't you see I'm stuck?'

The heads reappeared, their smiles even bigger.

'But we're supposed to climb in with you,' Bianca said, giggling. 'If you can bring yourself to climb off Lord Jake's lap and make some room, we'll join you.'

'You stay exactly where you are, Bianca Maidstone. And you, Mr Fortescue, and you, Lord Jake, help me out.'

Mr Fortescue looked at Bianca and she nodded.

'Certainly, Lady Violet,' Mr Fortescue said, taking her hands and giving an ineffective pull, as if he were frightened of hurting her.

'With pleasure,' Lord Jake added, placing his hands on her backside and pushing, causing Bianca to giggle even louder. Violet had experienced nothing so undignified in her life. And what was worse, both Bianca and Mr Fortescue presumably thought she had deliberately got herself into this embarrassing predicament.

The door creaked open and several chattering guests entered the room.

'We've found Violet. She's stuck on top of Lord Jake,' Bianca said, turning to the guests.

'I am not stuck on top of Lord Jake. I'm stuck under this desk,' Violet shouted out, hoping they could hear her.

'Yes, she's stuck under the desk on top of Lord Jake,' Bianca added, as if further explanation were needed.

One by one, each guest poked their head under the desk to see the undignified sight, and what remained of Violet's dignity was further shredded.

'Please,' she said, appealing to Lord Jake.

He pushed harder, while Mr Fortescue pulled, and she was finally dragged out from under the desk. Brushing down her rumpled gown, and with as much composure as possible, she stood up, held her head high and tried to pretend nothing untoward had happened.

'So who was the last person to find Lady Violet?'

Lady Cynthia asked, causing the others to look at each other in question.

'It hardly matters, does it?' Violet said. 'This game is now over.'

As one, the other guests oohed their disappointment.

'But it was just getting fun,' Bianca said, looking coyly at Mr Fortescue.

'That was not fun,' Violet blurted out, and everyone looked at her as if they had no idea what she was talking about.

'Getting stuck is all part of the fun,' Bianca said, as if she needed to explain things to her dim-witted sister.

All the guests' heads bobbed up and down rapidly in agreement, causing Violet to wonder what on earth was wrong with them. Did they enjoy losing their dignity? Perhaps they did.

'I do believe that was the funniest thing I've ever seen,' one of the female guests said. 'You really are quite a scream, Lady Violet.'

The others joined in with the laughter, as if it had all been a deliberate part of the game. Violet looked to Lord Jake for an explanation of this absurd behaviour. He merely shrugged his shoulders and smiled, while the guests commenced discussing other amusing antics people had got up to at other house parties.

'I was the last one to come into the room,' Lady Alice called out, her loud voice cutting through the chatter. 'So it's my turn to hide.' She gave Lord Jake a pointed look and mouthed *attic*.

How dare she, Violet wanted to say, but knew she wouldn't and couldn't say such a thing.

'Well, if you're going to continue to play, I must

warn you that the attic is out of bounds,' she said instead. 'We've had woodworm in the floorboards up there and it's rather dangerous.'

'Is it?' Bianca said. 'But we... I mean, I was up there earlier and it all seemed perfectly safe.'

'Well, it's not.'

Everyone stared at Violet. She knew she was being unreasonable, but she felt like being unreasonable.

'Well, then I'll have to find somewhere else to hide, won't I?' Lady Alice simpered. 'I wouldn't want us to all go tumbling through the floorboards.' She mouthed *drawing room cupboard* to Lord Jake.

Violet tried to think of a reason why the drawing room cupboard would also be out of bounds, but nothing came to mind. And anyway, why should she care? If they want to squash themselves in together, it was no concern of hers.

Except she knew it did worry her. After that kiss, it worried her immensely that Lord Jake might be about to do the same with another woman. And that, in itself, increased her indignation. Instead of worrying her, it should remind her how fickle men were, how they could not be trusted, how only a gullible, naive woman would give her heart to a man, any man, and especially a man like Lord Jake.

Not that she had given him her heart. It was absurd to even think such a thing. She had just for a moment, one uncharacteristically foolish moment, forgotten herself. That was all, nothing more. It was just one meaningless kiss during a meaningless childish game and was best forgotten as soon as possible.

Chapter Twelve

The woman he had kissed was gone. The stern, disapproving Lady Violet was back. Her brow furrowed in consternation, she looked around as the other guests counted to one hundred, as loudly as possible and with much joviality. Anyone would think that counting was the funniest thing they had done for some time, but Lady Violet was not amused.

She made her excuses, which no one heard, and headed for the door. After what they had just shared, Jake could not let her get away. He rushed after her, but she was moving at a rapid pace, striding off down the corridor, as if trying to put as much distance between them as possible.

'Lady Violet, don't leave.' It was absurd to be still calling her by her title, but as she had not given him permission to do otherwise, it would be taking a liberty to call her Violet. He smiled at the irony. He had already taken a much greater liberty, but then, her reaction to his kiss had been nothing if not an invitation.

She stopped and turned to him. 'I believe Lady Alice

will be waiting for you in the drawing room cupboard. You don't want to keep her waiting.'

Jake couldn't help his smile from growing. She was jealous. If he was a better man, that would not give him any satisfaction, but it did. He was tempted to tease, to watch her blush the way she had when they had been together under the table. But now was not the time for teasing. He drew his face into a more serious expression.

'You can rest assured, I have no desire to join Lady Alice, nor to continue this game.'

'Why not? Her invitation to you couldn't have been more obvious.'

'It's an invitation I intend to decline. I want to talk to you.'

'I don't believe we have anything to say to each other. So I won't hold you up any longer. I'll let you get back to playing with your friends.'

Jake fought off his exasperation. Why was she being so difficult? And why was he not doing as she wished and returning to the others? He knew the answer to that. When he was with her, he seemed to lose the ability to act in his own best interests. He should not have kissed her, but he had. And now he needed to talk to her. He was unsure what he wanted to say, but they could not part until he had tried to explain himself.

'Lady Violet, we just kissed. I believe that is something we need to talk about.'

'Keep your voice down,' she seethed, stepping towards him.

'I will keep my voice down if you agree to talk to me and not storm off as if nothing happened between us.'

The door to the study swung open. Guests poured out into the corridor. They ran hither and thither in every direction, deliberately bumping into each other, while laughing and shouting out directions on where they thought their prey might have gone.

Lady Violet opened the nearest door, grabbed his arm and pulled him in. He would have laughed at the farcical nature of her behaviour, but just as teasing her about her jealousy was bound to vex her, so, too, would his laughter. Instead, he acted as if it were perfectly normal for a woman to pull him into a drawing room and shut the door behind him.

'Right, now, what do you have to say for yourself?'

That did it. Jake couldn't stop himself from laughing. Her clipped manner reminded him so much of his boyhood days, of countless schoolmasters glaring down at him and saying almost those exact words with the same stern expression. 'Now, young man, what do you have to say for yourself?'

He forced his expression into one that was more serious. 'I believe we should discuss what just happened.'

She flicked her hand in front of her face, either dismissing him, the kiss or the need to discuss it. 'I don't see why. Isn't that what you said people do during those games? They indulge in a bit of flirtation.'

'What happened between us was more than just a bit of a flirtation.'

'Oh, all right. So we kissed. I realise we shouldn't have, but as it meant nothing, we should just forget that it ever happened.'

She could not mean that. He wanted to take hold of her arms and tell her it had meant something to him and he would not be forgetting it any time soon. Jake had long ago lost count of the number of women he had kissed, or even the number he had taken to his bed. But never before had the touch of a woman's lips on his caused such a powerful surge of emotion to well up inside him, like a tidal wave against which he was powerless to fight. Surely she had felt that, too.

'It meant nothing to you,' he said, both a question and a statement.

Her eyes quickly darted up to look at his expression, then just as quickly looked away. 'It *was* just a bit of flirtation, as you said. Best forgotten.'

'And do you make a habit of flirting with men, of kissing them?'

'No, never,' she shot back, her chin lifted, her hands planted on her hips.

'So why did you kiss me?'

'I didn't. *You* kissed me.'

Jake smiled at her odd logic.

'If you're not going to tell me why you kissed me, then perhaps I should tell you why I kissed you.'

'I don't need to hear this.' She took a step towards the door.

He grabbed her arm to prevent her escape. 'Everything I said to you was the truth. I kissed you because I wanted to. Had to. I've wanted to kiss you from the first time I saw you at the Golden Fleece.'

'And now you've achieved your goal, so you can move on to the next woman on your list.'

Jake recoiled as if she had slapped him across the face, although he suspected the sting of her hand would have hurt less. Was that how she saw him? Of course it was. Why wouldn't she? Wasn't that exactly the sort of man he was? The sort that did move on from one woman to the next without a backward glance. But this was different. She had to see that.

'But I have more important things to do than discuss something so trivial,' she continued, each word cutting him more deeply. 'Or do you expect all your women to give you a critique of your performance? Is that what you are after, compliments?'

He took another step backwards. 'No,' he said, hardly able to get that one word out. He dragged in a deep breath to steady himself. 'I did not mean to offend you,' he added with as much composure as he could muster. 'I apologise for taking such unwanted liberties. I hope you will forgive me for my behaviour.'

She blinked rapidly, then looked away, as if suddenly fascinated by something outside the dark window.

She had every right to be angry with him. In the moment he had forgotten who she was. He had wanted to kiss her and so he did. Yes, she had given herself to him readily, had responded with passion and fervour, but that hardly mattered. Her compliance made his behaviour no less unforgivable.

He should never have given in to his desires. He should never have kissed her.

Lady Violet was different. He knew that, yet he had chosen to forget it. The women in his life were always the type who wanted harmless fun, a diversion from their ordinary lives. They were bored wives, adventurous actresses, women who lived outside the rules of so-called polite society. That was not Lady Violet Maidstone.

He had taken advantage of both her inexperience with men and the fact that he had her trapped under the desk. She'd had no way out and when she had tried to escape, he had made fun of her. It was despicable. He was despicable. He had taken what he wanted, what he still wanted.

'I'm sorry,' he repeated. 'My behaviour was unforgivable.'

And yet, despite her innocence, she had responded with such ardour, such passion. Just as he suspected she would. She had put up no objection—quite the reverse. But that did not make what he had done any less reprehensible. She was an inexperienced woman and it was a long time since he could be described as inexperienced. He should have exercised more self-restraint.

'I'm not offended.' She flicked a quick look at him, looked down then stared ahead, her gaze resting somewhere round his shoulder. 'You have nothing to apologise for.'

'Do you mean that?' He wanted her forgiveness, but knew he had no right to it.

'Yes,' she said, lifting her chin and turning towards him. Were there tears in her eyes? Was he that much of a cad that he had made this defiant, remarkable woman cry?

'If I could take back what I did, I would. It was not my intention to hurt you.'

She blinked away her tears. 'Stop apologising. You did not hurt me,' she said in that familiar stern manner. 'I believe we should just pretend that it never happened. Agreed?'

'Agreed,' he murmured, although he knew himself

to be lying. He would never forget what had happened between them. Would never forget the soft feel and honey taste of her lips, or her scent, so feminine, so delicious, so tempting.

'Right, good, now perhaps you should go and find Lady Alice.'

Finding any other woman was the last thing Jake wanted to do, but she wanted him gone and, after his behaviour, he had little choice but to accede to her commands.

'Goodnight, Lady Violet.' He made a formal bow. 'Mr Fortescue and I will be leaving early in the morning to get the train back to London, so I believe this will also be goodbye.'

Instead of curtsying, she shook her head, then nodded. 'Yes, goodbye, Lord Jake.'

He waited. She said no more, so he turned and walked out of the room.

A harmless flirtation. Had a bigger lie ever been told? Yes. She had said it meant nothing to her. That was the bigger lie. Now she had driven him off, probably into the willing arms of Lady Alice. And she only had herself to blame. The temptation to run after him, to tell him it *had* meant something, it had meant everything to her, was all but overwhelming. But humiliation was a painful teacher. She had exposed her heart once before and it had been terribly damaged. She would never do that again.

Instead, she took a few moments to compose herself. It was essential she walk down the corridor with her head held high, looking neither left nor right. She did not want to see what anyone else was up to, especially not Lady Alice. Then she would retire to her bedchamber, away from all this mayhem.

Violet knew she should not leave the party. Bianca needed chaperoning, now more than ever. While she had been kissing Lord Jake under the desk, her sister had been kissing Mr Fortescue above it. Fortunately, no one other than Violet and Lord Jake knew of her young sister's indiscretion. But she could be getting up to much worse right now. If she was, and anyone found out, Bianca's reputation would be in tatters, or, worse than that, Mr Fortescue would be forced to marry Bianca and her lovely sister would be shackled to that fortune hunter for the rest of her life, when she could do so much better.

Yes, she should be taking her duties as chaperon more seriously, but she was tired and emotionally drained. She did not have the energy to follow her sister and that man around the house. What she needed now was a good night's sleep. Everything would look much clearer in the morning and she would be her old self again.

And for the coming Season, she would be vigilant. She would not let Bianca out of her sight or allow herself to be distracted by anyone or anything, and especially not Lord Jake Rosemont.

She took hold of the door handle and gave it a quick, determined turn, then released it and stepped back, needing more time to restore her sense of self-control. It had been such a confusing night, and their conversation in this room had only increased that confusion. He had actually looked hurt when she'd said that his kiss meant nothing to her. But then, perhaps it was just his masculine pride that was hurt. He would expect a woman like her to swoon at the mere thought of kissing a man like him. And to Violet's shame, the thought of kissing him again did make her feel weak.

But he would be gone tomorrow, and she was unlikely to see him ever again. He said he avoided all society events, so there was little danger of him attending any of the balls, soirées or other events to which Bianca had been invited.

She sank into the nearest chair. How had she let this happen? She had avoided men for the last eight years, and tonight she had momentarily let her guard down, had actually kissed a man, and now she was completely disorientated and unsettled. It was as if her world had been spun off its axis and she no longer knew how to think, what she felt or how she was supposed to act.

But at least she had come to her senses before more damage had been done. Her hands covered her mouth as she remembered the words she had almost said to him. She had been about to ask him to leave the underside of the table, to go somewhere with her where they would be able to do more than just kiss.

Her cheeks burnt so hot they were almost painful and she was grateful there was no one to see her mortification. She was such a fraud. What she had said to Lord Jake had been a complete lie. His kisses had affected her so deeply she had lost the ability to reason. The effect of that one kiss could hardly have been more profound. But she could never tell him that.

No, it was so much better that she had lied. If she had told him the truth, how would he have reacted?

Would he have looked at her with horror, backed out of the room and made a run for it? Probably. Or worse, laughed at her.

Yes, she had done the right thing. Repeating that to herself, she stood up, brushed down her skirt and left the drawing room. Ignoring all the mayhem still taking place, the squeals of delight from the young ladies, the loud laughter from the men, she kept on walking up to her bedroom, determined to put all thoughts of the evening behind her.

Chapter Thirteen

The two men sitting side by side in the first-class compartment of the train travelling back to London couldn't have been in more different moods. Anyone observing them would find it hard to believe they had attended the same house party. While Herbert could not contain his excitement, Jake was fighting to hide his despondency.

Under Jake's instructions, they had left as early as possible the next morning. He did not need to see Lady Violet again or be reminded of her determination to dismiss their kisses as a bit of harmless flirtation. Nor did he wish to be confronted with his own inappropriate behaviour.

'Sorry, old chap,' Herbert said, finally ceasing to wax lyrical about Lady Bianca's beauty, her grace and a seemingly endless list of her other attributes. 'Here's me going on and on about what a splendid time Bianca and I had and there's you, miserable because you had to put up with that sister of hers. But cheer up, old chap. You'll soon be back in London, back to all the delights that city has to offer.'

He raised his eyebrows up and down in a manner intended to be comical and suggestive. 'And back to all those women who are a bit more accommodating to a chap's needs than Lady Violet Maidstone ever would be.'

Jake merely nodded.

'I know what will cheer you up and make you forget everything that virago put you through.' Herbert slapped his hands on his knees and leant forward. 'Let's go to the Limelight Theatre tonight. I believe a new play has just started. There's sure to be lots of fresh young chorus girls just dying to show a man a good time. That should put the smile back on your face.'

'Hmm,' he responded without commitment, as the theatre and chorus girls held no appeal.

Herbert leant further forward in his seat and lowered his voice, even though they were alone in the carriage. 'If it makes you feel any better, your sacrifice was not in vain. While you kept Lady Violet busy, I was able to have that serious talk with Bianca. Keep this to yourself, old chap…' he looked around the empty carriage '…but she's agreed to be my wife.'

'Congratulations.' Jake took his friend's hand and gave it a hearty shake.

Herbert puffed himself up with pride. 'Proposed while you were all off playing sardines. Then while you were all searching for Lady Alice, we slipped away and had a word with her father.'

'And?'

'Man said yes, didn't he?' Herbert clapped his hands together, then he leant forward and lowered his voice once more. 'But Bianca wants to keep it secret until the

Season is over. Something about having all the gowns already made or some such. Wanting to enjoy her debut. Never going to have another one, something like that.'

He leant in even closer so the two men's heads were almost touching. 'And she said it was vital that Lady Violet does not get wind of our engagement until the end of the Season. So keep that under your hat, won't you? Not that you'll have to see her again, but Bianca was most insistent that it remain a secret. I'm not even supposed to tell you, but a chap can hardly keep his best friend in the dark, can he? Asking a bit much there.'

'Your secret is safe with me.'

Herbert sat back in his seat. 'Good. Good. So it was a successful weekend all round. I can hardly believe I actually achieved what I set out to do. And it's all because of you. You really went above and beyond the call of duty, I must say. Eternal thanks and all that.' Herbert chuckled. 'Trapping her under that desk, that was pure genius, but you can forget all about her now and get back to enjoying yourself.'

Herbert smiled and went back to listing some more of Lady Bianca's attributes, while Jake stared out the window at the passing countryside. He hoped Herbert was right and he would soon forget all about his time at the Maidstone estate and get back to enjoying his life.

Arriving at his family's London home, Jake found the town house a hive of activity, as footmen and maids ran about in every direction, and the place was alive with a cacophony of tradesmen.

The Season started in one week and, as was tradition, it began with the Rosemont ball.

'Jake, my dear, how was your weekend?' his mother greeted him, breaking from her conversation with a man holding armfuls of flowers, presumably a florist.

'Very pleasant, thank you, Moth—'

'Sorry, dear, the bandleader has just arrived. I need to talk to him about which pieces to perform. Last year they played far too many waltzes and not enough of the lively dances where people mix.'

'But young people enjoy waltzes, it gives them a chance to flirt.'

His mother stopped and turned to face him. 'I believe you're right, Jake. Wasn't it during a waltz that Ethan proposed to Sophia? I believe it was. Yes, I must tell the bandleader to play more waltzes.'

With that, she hurried off down the corridor. Jake had no desire to remain among such mayhem. The moment he had changed out of his travelling clothes, he escaped to his usual haunts, starting at his private club.

Jake ended up once again at the Queen Victoria gambling den in the early hours of the morning.

Entering, he sent a discreet nod to Bill, who scowled in a threatening manner, then gave a quick lift of his chin in greeting.

Hands were dealt, bets were made and a pile of money continued to mount up in front of Jake until the owner had reached the limit of his endurance. Once again, the table was declared closed for the evening and Bill was sent in to escort Jake off the premises.

'Sorry, my lord,' Bill muttered as he grabbed Jake under the armpit and heaved him out of his chair.

'I understand, perfectly,' Jake responded as the two stumbled towards the door.

Once outside, they exchanged the usual pleasantries about their families, then Jake asked him how his new business venture was going.

The burly man was suddenly crestfallen. 'Not so good, my lord. Plenty of punters are attending the gym as there's never a shortage of men wanting to learn how to defend themselves. That's not the problem, but it's all that bleedin' paperwork. Never knew there'd be so much paperwork, accounts and so on. I can't afford to pay no one to look at it and the blighters are bound to rip me off, anyway.'

'I could have a look at your books. I've got a bit of a knack with numbers.'

Bill laughed. 'That you have.' He tipped his shaven head towards the door of the gambling joint. 'That's what gets you thrown out of places like this. You should learn to lose a time or two.'

Jake could only agree. 'But I'm serious. I'd be happy to have a look over your accounts and make sure they're all in order so you don't have any problems with the taxman. After all, I made enough money off you when you were in the ring, it's the least I can do.'

A burden seemed to lift off Bill's shoulders. 'Oh, Lord Jake, I'd be most grateful.'

'Right, I'll come round tomorrow and have a look.'

The two men chatted for a moment longer before Jake wandered off down the dimly lit alleyway, whistling to himself. That warm feeling swept over him, the same one he had experienced when he'd helped Lady

Violet with her accounts. It really was rather good to actually help people. Perhaps he should make a habit of it.

By the night of the ball, the house had been transformed, so that Jake hardly recognised it as his family home. Flowers had appeared on every side table, bureau and sideboard throughout the house. Ferns and foliage filled every nook and cranny. Tables were laden with punchbowls, and a staggering selection of food had been laid out on tables in the drawing room adjoining the ballroom. A band had arrived early, bringing with them an assortment of cases containing heaven only knew what instruments. Maids, footmen and other servants were rushing backwards and forwards, performing an array of unknown tasks, while his mother bustled about shouting out last-minute orders. And a small army of additional footmen had been recruited for the evening. They were all lined up and waiting to jump in immediately to ensure every guest had every need attended to immediately, sometimes before they had even thought about what it was they actually wanted.

His mother seemed to be everywhere at once, a harried expression on her face. Usually, Jake faced the Rosemont ball with a mix of boredom and resignation, but tonight, his mother wasn't the only one who was dealing with a case of nerves.

He raced up the stairs, two at a time, to dress for the evening. What was wrong with him? He had nothing to be nervous about. As his valet helped him into his evening jacket, he laughed at himself. Yes, Lady Violet might be in attendance tonight, but all he had to do was endure one ball. Then, finally, he could put her, and all that had happened at the house party, behind him.

Violet should have made an excuse. It was just one ball. Bianca surely would not have minded missing one ball, even if it was the first of the Season. Violet stood in front of her full-length mirror and frowned at her reflection. Why had she not ordered new gowns for herself instead of simply having the gowns from her first Season altered?

She placed her hands on her fluttering stomach. This was not like her. It was many years since she had felt such jitters. And there was no reason for her to be nervous now. This was not her Season. She was merely attending in the role of chaperon. No one cared what a chaperon wore. No one even looked at a chaperon. And yet she was just as anxious as if this was her coming-out Season.

She had certainly been nervous then. At her first ball, she had been consumed with nervous anticipation, although that had been more due to her excitement about her future and all the fun she was to have.

Violet knew she would have to hide her anxiety from Bianca. Tonight's ball was all about her sister. It was a night for her to shine among the other debutantes. Bianca would be dressed in the latest fashion and in a style that highlighted her beauty. She had more than enough gowns to ensure she was never seen in the same dress twice. That was all that mattered.

While Bianca danced with a succession of eligible young men, Violet would be seated with all the other old maids, married women, mothers and ladies' maids, all keeping an eagle eye on their charges. No one would give her a second glance, nor care whether her gown was of the latest fashion or not.

'I'll wear the garnet necklace and earrings,' she said to her lady's maid. They at least would add a touch of style to her appearance.

Before leaving her room, Violet took a few slow, deep breaths to steady her churning stomach. *You have every reason to be nervous*, she told her reflection. *Tonight is important to Bianca. Those rampaging butterflies have nothing to do with seeing Lord Jake again.* Why should they? She probably wouldn't even see him. He'd probably spend the night dancing with an array of debutantes, maybe even keeping his promise to Lady Alice and dancing the night away with her. He was hardly likely to even notice an ageing chaperon seated away from all the fun.

She joined her sister in the drawing room and her stomach settled somewhat. Bianca looked beautiful. Her pale pastel blue gown was perfect for an innocent young woman. It brought out the brightness of her blue eyes and highlighted her peaches-and-cream complexion. No man would be able to resist her. Bianca was sure to have the pick of the gentlemen and would soon forget all about Mr Fortescue.

Bianca's excitement as their carriage wove its way through the busy London streets was almost palpable. Violet knew she should provide a calming influence, but with her own nerves quivering and twitching the closer they got to the Rosemonts' town house, she was of no help to her little sister.

The carriage pulled up in front of the Mayfair address and Bianca almost jumped out before it had even come to a halt, so excited was she to attend her first ball.

'A bit of decorum,' Violet whispered, taking her impetuous sister's arm and leading her up the path towards the sound of music, laughter and chatter spilling out from the well-lit front door. 'Remember, you are officially no longer a child and have to act like a lady from now onwards.'

They entered the crowded ballroom. Elegant women in an array of brightly coloured ball gowns and men in formal evening dress greeted each other, while debutantes in various pastel shades looked around the room in wonder, each with the same excited expression that Bianca wore.

They all looked so young and so pretty. Had Violet once been like that? It was hard to imagine that she could ever have been so innocent and so trusting. At least Bianca had her older sister to watch out for her. Unlike Violet, she would not be vulnerable to the first Lothario who came her way, promising the world but delivering only heartache.

She looked at the men on offer, hoping she could spot which ones were genuinely looking for a lifelong companion, which were merely seeking a woman with a good dowry to prop up their extravagant lifestyles and which were rakes with conquest on their minds.

She locked eyes with Lord Jake and those butterflies in her stomach gave her a hard kick and, for a moment, the ground seemed unsteady under her feet.

'There he is. There he is,' Bianca said, gripping her arm tightly.

Violet knew exactly where he was and would rather not be reminded.

'And he's coming this way.'

No, he wasn't. He had gone back to talking to a group of elderly gentlemen in the corner.

'Lady Bianca, Lady Violet.'

Violet turned to see Mr Fortescue smiling inanely at her sister.

'May I be the first to place my name on your dance card?'

Bianca thrust her card and pencil at Mr Fortescue. Violet was tempted to object, but reluctantly accepted that it wouldn't hurt if they had one dance together.

He returned the card. Bianca looked at it, then giggled. Violet reached to take the card from her, but before she had a chance to read whatever it was Mr Fortescue had written, he had taken Bianca's hand and led her on to the dance floor.

Violet watched as they took their places for a waltz. Why did it have to be a waltz? If it had been a quadrille, at least they would be with other couples and not exclusively in each other's arms. Or an energetic polka, which provided little time for conversation and did not involve such close physical contact.

But there was nothing to be done now. Violet would retire to the balcony, where she could observe everything that happened between them. She made her way across the floor. The stairs that led to the balcony took her perilously close to Lord Jake. She just hoped he would let her pass by and not feel the need to make polite conversation.

Out of the corner of her eye she could see him excuse himself from his group and move across the room, towards her.

Should she make a dash for it? It was so tempting, but running in a ballroom and pushing people out of her way would, unfortunately, attract much unwanted attention. Instead, she walked as quickly as etiquette allowed, moving with small, rapid steps towards the staircase, which seemed to get no closer.

'Lady Violet,' he said, stepping in front of her and bowing low. 'It's a pleasure to see you again.'

She bobbed a curtsy. 'And you, too, Lord Jake. Now, if you'll excuse me, I need to perform my duties as Bianca's chaperon.'

He looked out at the dance floor. 'But first, would you do me the honour of a dance?'

'Oh, I don't think… I need to…' She looked up at the balcony. 'I have to…'

While she was still thinking of excuses, he took her hand and led her out on to the floor for the first waltz.

Chapter Fourteen

What was he doing? Jake had been determined to pay Lady Violet no more attention than any other young lady at the ball. In other words, do absolutely nothing more than good manners demanded. She had made her feelings plain when they had parted at Maidstone House. When he had seen her enter the ballroom, he had tried not to look in her direction. He had forced himself to act as if the conversation of Lord Winstone, his mother's elderly friend, fascinated him, although he'd heard not a word the man had said.

Then she had crossed the room, heading his way. He continued to not look at her, but when it was obvious she was heading towards the balcony so she could hide herself away with all the other chaperons he had acted before thinking. That had been the end of his plan. Within minutes of her arrival it had failed dismally.

But what else could he do? He could not let her disappear without even speaking to her. Surely good manners dictated he acknowledge her presence. After all, he had recently been a guest in her home. Then he had asked her to dance. That hadn't been part of any plan, but one dance wouldn't hurt. Would it? So that was how she had ended up in his arms. Now that she was there, he needed to say something, make light conversation. He was more than capable of doing that, wasn't he? So why was he behaving like a tongue-tied schoolboy?

Relax, man. She's just another woman.

Jake had never been uncomfortable in female company, even when he *was* a schoolboy.

'Lovely weather for the time of year.' He could kick himself. Had he really just talked about the weather?

She glanced up at him, her brow creased. She was no doubt thinking exactly the same thing. *What an imbecile Lord Jake Rosemont is.*

'You look lovely tonight, Lady Violet.' Complimenting a lady's appearance was another standard conversation opener, but he meant every word. She did look lovely, beautiful even, but didn't she always? Whether she was wearing a plain brown dress and serving pints behind a bar, or bedecked in her finery, or in sensible clothing and scrambling around in the bottom of a boat, she was always the most attractive woman he had ever seen.

'Thank you,' she murmured and said no more, leaving him back where he'd started, desperately searching for something, anything, to say. Or perhaps he didn't need to. Perhaps he should just enjoy having her in his arms. After all, it might be the first and last time that he danced with her. His hand moved further round her waist. Yes, why bother talking at all?

He lowered his head and gently inhaled her soft, delicate perfume. Violets. He smiled to himself. How appropriate. It was almost whimsical that she should choose such a perfume. Soft and delicate were not words most people would attribute to Lady Violet Maidstone, but underneath that stern exterior Jake had glimpsed a softer side and he suspected her strong outer shell had been deliberately constructed to protect that delicate, vulnerable inner core.

Her head lowered and skimmed against his shoulder. Was she going to relax into him? He hoped so. But no. As if catching herself doing something shameful, her back suddenly went rigid. 'I'm supposed to be chaperoning Bianca. Please lead me closer to where she is so I can watch my sister and Mr Fortescue.'

'They're in a room full of people. I believe she is perfectly safe.'

She tilted her head and he knew he was about to be told she expected him to do exactly as she commanded. He gave a light laugh. 'As you wish, m'lady.' He looked over her head at the couples whirling around them. Herbert and Lady Bianca were nowhere in sight.

'I can't see them. Perhaps they have retired to the drawing room for an early supper.'

'What?' She stopped dancing, almost causing another couple to crash into them. 'Where have they gone?' She looked around the room, turning in small circles, her face furious.

'Don't worry. We'll find them. They can't have gone far.' Taking her arm and placing it through his, he stopped her frantic movements and led her off the dance floor.

'I should never have danced with you. I should have

been watching her carefully. I should have known that Mr Fortescue would lead her astray. This is a disaster.'

'I promise you we'll find them. And I also promise you no harm will come to your sister.'

'How can you possibly know that?'

'I know Mr Fortescue. And I know that the last thing he wants to do is lead Lady Bianca astray.'

She merely scoffed a reply.

'Where's the drawing room? We'll check that first.'

Jake pointed to the doors at the far end of the ballroom, pleased that she had said 'we' and included him in this quest.

She quickly skirted the edges of the ballroom, moving as rapidly as her silk ballroom slippers would allow. Trying not to laugh, he followed in her path. It wasn't really funny. She was genuinely worried. But he knew she had nothing to worry about. Herbert was a man in love. He all but worshipped Lady Bianca and would soon marry her. Lady Violet's sister could not be in safer hands.

Jake was tempted to break his confidence. If Lady Violet knew her sister was engaged to Herbert, she would not be so anxious. She could relax and they could enjoy this dance. But he had promised his friend and presumably Lady Bianca had her reasons for wanting to keep it a secret from her sister. Although Jake could not fathom what those could be. The ways of women never ceased to confound him.

They entered the drawing room, where indeed they found the errant couple, standing by the supper table, where Lady Bianca was feeding wobbling green jelly to a laughing Herbert.

'What are you doing?' Lady Violet said.

Bianca turned towards her, a spoon suspended in mid-air in front of Herbert's open mouth. 'We got rather hungry.' She bit her upper lip as if to stop herself from laughing, while Herbert's mouth shut with an audible click.

'Well, stop it.' Lady Violet ripped the bowl and spoon out of her sister's hand and practically threw it on to the table, where it wobbled just like its contents before settling down at a precarious angle.

'We got a bit hungry, didn't we?' Herbert repeated, winking at Lady Bianca, who giggled behind her gloved hand. Jake winced. If Herbert wanted to make a good impression on Lady Violet, winking in front of his future sister-in-law was not the way to go about it.

'We need to return to the ballroom.' Lady Violet attempted to grab her sister's hand, which Bianca stubbornly placed behind her back.

The two sisters indulged in a somewhat bizarre game of grab the arm, watched on by two bemused men, before a laughing Bianca conceded defeat and stopped dodging her sister.

'Oh, yes, all right,' Lady Bianca said, sending a wink of her own at Herbert. 'The quadrille is about to start and I believe I promised that to you, didn't I, Mr Fortescue?'

'Indeed, you did, my lady,' Herbert said, taking her now extended arm and rushing out of the room, at a faster pace than Jake had ever seen the man move.

'Well, I never.' Lady Violet stared at the door through which they had hurriedly departed.

'Your sister is correct,' Jake said. 'No harm has been done. You worry unnecessarily.'

She turned towards him, her hands on her hips, her face the picture of wrath. 'Someone has to worry about her. Someone needs to keep an eye on them. That's the second dance they've had together. People will talk, they'll make assumptions.'

Jake shrugged. Now would be the perfect time to inform her that if people did make assumptions, then those assumptions would be correct. But a promise was a promise and he would not betray Herbert. Lady Bianca wanted the engagement kept a secret and he would abide by that.

'Then perhaps you would like to join me for the quadrille,' he said instead. 'We can both keep an eye on them from the dance floor.'

Her frown grew deeper. 'Oh, yes, and that was such a success last time, wasn't it? No, from now on I will take my duties more seriously.'

She commenced to stride out of the room, but he caught her before she reached the door and took her arm. 'Then let me escort you to the chaperons' balcony.'

She stopped and frowned at him again, as if this was all somehow his fault. 'I have no intention of dancing again this evening, so perhaps you should find Lady Alice or some other debutante and dance the night away with them.'

'You seem to be blaming me for Lady Bianca and Herbert retiring to eat jelly, so perhaps I had better make amends. I'll join you on the balcony and the two of us can watch them as if we're hawks soaring in the sky.'

'This is no laughing matter.'

'No, but it could be fun. While we're monitoring Herbert and Lady Bianca's every move, we can also have fun discussing all that is happening below us. We'll have the perfect vantage point.'

Her expression became quizzical. 'Why would you want to do that? Shouldn't you be dancing?'

Good question. Why was he offering to spend the ball with the very woman he had promised himself he would avoid?

'I could say the same to you,' he responded, deflecting his thoughts from the more pertinent question.

'I'm not here to dance. I'm here to chaperon.'

'It seems we're both here on sufferance. I'm here because my mother insists I attend this ball. And I have to admit, the idea of hiding away on the chaperons' balcony definitely has its appeal.'

Her expression of disbelief did not leave her face, but at least she took his extended arm.

Couples were lining up for the quadrille as they entered the ballroom. The rapid pace at which Lady Violet continued to stride across the floor signalled as loudly as words that there was no point asking again if she would do him the honour of another dance.

'Lord Jake, there you are,' Lady Alice said, stepping in front of him and blocking his progress. 'I knew you had to be here somewhere. I believe this is our dance.'

This was news to Jake. Lady Alice slid her arm through his as if Lady Violet did not exist. Was Jake now about to become the subject of a tug of war between these two women? But no, Lady Violet released his arm and hurried away without another word.

It seemed he had no choice but to dance with Lady Alice. He could hardly insult the young lady in front of her friends.

Lady Violet raced up the stairs, took her seat with the other chaperons and glared down at the dancers below her. She had been adamant that she would not dance because she had to supervise her sister, yet she was not watching Lady Bianca and Herbert. Her disapproving gaze was firmly fixed on him and Lady Alice.

Violet forced herself to look away. She was such a fool. When Lord Jake had held her on the dance floor, for a moment she had lost all sense of purpose. She had allowed herself to drift off into a fantasy, where she was a young woman again, being swept round the dance floor by a handsome man during her own Season. But she was not a young woman any more. She was now six and twenty, officially an old maid, and a woman with responsibilities. Responsibilities she had so easily forgotten.

Lord Jake and Lady Alice lined up for the quadrille. She fought to ignore the clenching in her stomach and told herself not to glare at them. She was not jealous. Of course she wasn't. If for no other reason than it was obvious that Lord Jake had no interest in Lady Alice. He'd already had ample opportunity to express his interest in the lady and had not.

At the house party, hadn't he said he avoided the Season mainly because he did not wish to be preyed upon by the debutantes in search of a husband? He had told her the Rosemont ball was the only event he attended, for the simple reason that he had no choice.

What better way to keep those young ladies at bay than to spend your time with one of the old maids? That was all she was to him. A way of avoiding debutantes like Lady Alice who, when they looked at him, saw a man with a good fortune and connections to a duke, and was therefore an ideal husband.

Well, she would not be used in such a manner.

She looked over at Bianca and Mr Fortescue. They were now part of a group of four couples, twirling around and circling each other according to the intricate steps of the dance.

Bianca and Mr Fortescue had their gazes firmly fixed on each other. Even when the steps demanded they swap partners, they did not look away. And Violet had to admit, Bianca looked supremely happy. Her sister often smiled, being by nature of a cheerful disposition, but had she ever smiled so brightly? And the look on Mr Fortescue's face was that of a man enraptured, as if he was in the presence of a piece of artwork of such rare and exquisite beauty that it had him spellbound.

Was that the look of love? Randolph had never looked at her like that. He had smiled; he had flattered; he had laughed when she said things she hoped would amuse him, but he had never once looked at her the way Mr Fortescue was looking at Bianca. Was Lord Jake right? Did Mr Fortescue love her sister?

She looked over at Lord Jake and Lady Alice. A sense of relief flooded through her. Lord Jake was not looking at Lady Alice like that. He appeared to be merely making polite conversation, as he did with the other women in their set when they changed partners.

Not that it really mattered how he looked or who

he was looking at. She was not here to observe Lord Jake. Her gaze returned to Bianca and Mr Fortescue. The dance had come to an end and he was escorting her off the dance floor. The way they were staring at each other, their arms tightly entwined, their bodies so close they were actually touching, sent a loud message to all that they did not want to be interrupted.

If Bianca continued to behave like that, it was unlikely that she would attract the attention of any other men. Perhaps that was her intention.

Her gaze once again moved over to Lord Jake, who had returned Lady Alice to a group of young women. He made a quick bow and a hasty retreat.

Violet almost laughed at the look of concentration on his face. Walking as quickly as decorum would allow, he moved across the dance floor, his gaze fixed straight ahead. It was as if he was making a run for it. He walked towards the stairs. He was going to do as he said, hide out on the balcony. With her.

She quickly adjusted her gown, moving the straps on her shoulders, brushing down the skirt and pulling up her elbow-length gloves.

He arrived and took the seat beside her, causing quite a stir among the other chaperons. It was most unusual for an eligible man to join them. Several women smiled and cocked their heads in question. She wanted to tell them this meant nothing. He was merely trying to escape the relentless husband hunting.

'Thank goodness that's over,' he said. 'If only I'd thought of coming up here before. It means I can attend my mother's balls without having to actually attend them.' He leant forward. 'Look at poor old Luther.'

He gave a wicked laugh. 'That debutante has got him cornered. There will be no escape for him now.'

He glanced over at Violet. Despite herself, his infectious laughter caught her and she smiled.

'Oh, and look at Lord Fitzherbert. The man is actually surrounded. He's almost in as much demand as my brother. He'll one day inherit an earldom and several estates. He's definitely a prey worth pursuing. Look at that expression on his face. I suspect it's just how a fox looks when he sees the hounds coming.'

The other chaperons looked at him sideways, their disapproval evident. It was possibly their charges who were vying for the attention of Jake's brother, or Lord Fitzherbert, or the other titled men down on the dance floor. They quite obviously did not like their daughters' attempts to attract the attentions of a suitable future husband depicted as a blood sport.

'And you do have a perfect vantage point from which to watch your sister.'

Her gaze moved to Mr Fortescue and Bianca, who were taking the floor once again, this time for the polka. This would not do. They must not dance together again tonight. It was utterly scandalous.

She rose from her chair. Lord Jake placed his hand on her arm to halt her progress. 'Leave them be, Lady Violet,' he said quietly. 'They are in love. Can't you see it on their faces? I saw the same expression on my brother's face just before he proposed to his wife.'

She looked down at the dance floor, at Bianca's dewy-eyed expression and Mr Fortescue's rapturous gaze. She wanted to dismiss his claim, but hadn't she been thinking the same thing only moments ago? Instead, she took her seat.

'Herbert is in love with your sister, of that there can be no doubt,' he continued. 'And from the look on your sister's face, I believe she, too, is in love. Do you believe it right to actually try to thwart true love?'

Violet wanted to contradict him, but was he right? Had she been letting her own experiences taint her attitude towards Mr Fortescue?

'Is he in love with Bianca? Or is he in love with her dowry?'

'Look at the man. I'm surprised you even have to ask that.'

'Well, if he thought we were in…' She lowered her voice. 'If he knew about our problems with the estate manager, that it might affect Bianca's marriage settlement, do you think he'd still be looking at her like that?'

Lord Jake shook his head slowly, as if unable to believe what he was hearing. 'Herbert would adore your sister even if she was reduced to penury. It's Lady Bianca he's in love with, not her dowry. I could say it's an insult to your sister to think otherwise, but I won't. All I'll say is many a mother here tonight would be pleased to see their daughter being courted by Mr Fortescue. One day he will be a viscount. He has numerous estates, is fully solvent and will be a loyal, loving husband.'

Violet did not want to agree with him, but could think of no reason to dispute his claim.

He turned to face her. 'Is it Mr Fortescue you object to, or is it the concept of love, or is it the thought of your sister finding love so easily and being so happy?'

Her breath caught in her throat. Was that how he saw

her? As a woman who did not want others to be happy? She loved her sister. She only wanted what was best for her. 'I am not… I do not…it's not…' She choked to a halt, as if not sure what it was or wasn't that she believed.

She swallowed and drew in a long, deep breath. 'Bianca is too young to know her own mind. I am merely offering my guidance so she finds the perfect husband.'

'And what makes you such a good judge of what man is right for your sister? How do you know who would make your sister happy? Or is no man ever going to be good enough for her?'

'That's not true.'

'What exactly are your objections to Mr Fortescue?'

She fought to remember why she did not want that match. Surely it had nothing to do with what she thought of men. Surely it was not because she no longer trusted men, all men.

He waited as she fought for an answer. None came. Was he right? Would no man ever be good enough for Bianca? Had her own experiences made her dismissive of all men?

'Why not just accept that your sister is in love with a man who returns her love in abundance?' he said gently. 'Then you can relax and just let Lady Bianca enjoy her Season. And talking of relaxing and having an enjoyable time, I think we should partake in the next dance. Don't you?'

He stood up and offered her his hand. All the other ladies seated on the balcony smiled at them, as if they were watching a courting couple.

He leant down and whispered in her ear, 'You can't

leave me standing here looking like a fool, Lady Violet. That would be too cruel.'

He was right. What choice did she have? She could never be that badly mannered and embarrass him in front of others. She placed her hand lightly on his and he led her down the stairs and out on to the floor. It was another waltz. How many waltzes were there going to be at this ball? Far too many, in Violet's opinion.

As if doing something forbidden yet enticing, she placed her hand tentatively on his shoulder. His hand slid around her waist and she stifled a gasp to avoid revealing how much his touch affected her. He pulled her in closer to his body. Surely they were now too close? And yet she put up no objection. The music started, and they glided across the parquet floor. He was a superb dancer, and it did feel good to be in his arms.

Her hand lightly slid along the breadth of his shoulders and she gently squeezed the site where shoulder joined arm, loving that hard touch of muscle. Warmth flowed through her. She had glimpsed the muscles in his arms when he had been rowing, had felt them when she had fallen on him in the boat. What would it be like to run her hands over their sculpted form? What would he look like without the covering of his shirt and jacket? What would those muscles feel like under the gentle caress of her fingers?

Her hand quickly moved back on to his shoulder. What was wrong with her? Why did she lose herself so easily? Now was neither the time nor the place to think of such things. There would never be a time nor a place where she should have such thoughts.

He smiled down at her. Her thoughts strayed again,

as if she had no control over them. Her hand inched closer to his neck. She so wanted to run her fingers slowly up his neck to his hairline and wind them through those dark locks, just as she had done when he had kissed her.

He had kissed her.

Memories of that kiss flooded her mind and body. She could almost feel her lips on his. She released a shuddering sigh, suddenly aware that she had moved so close to him that her breasts were skimming his chest. But she didn't move back. Couldn't move back. What she wanted was to move even closer.

His hand slid slightly down her back. It was now resting lightly on the very top of her buttocks. The pounding of her heart intensified, almost drowning out the sound of the music. Would his hand slide lower? Her back arched towards him, wriggling slightly in response to the tension building up in her body. This was torture, pure, exquisite torture. She both wanted it to stop and for it to never end.

But it did end. The band ceased playing, couples stopped dancing and, as if in a trance, she allowed him to take her hand and lead her off the dance floor, out through the French doors, away from the lights flooding from the ballroom, down a path, to the dark, secluded end of the garden.

Before she had time to speak, she had her wish. She was back in his arms and his lips were on hers.

This was nothing like that first, gentle, tentative kiss. His lips crashed on to hers, hard, hungry, demanding, as if he had to have her, right now. A surge of desire engulfed her. This handsome, virile man, this man who so many other women wanted, wanted her.

He drew back, his lips still a few enticing inches from her own. He stared into her eyes, the brown black in the subdued lighting. 'I shouldn't have done that. I'm sorry, but I couldn't...'

'Kiss me again,' she said, her words coming out on a soft breath.

'We shouldn't.'

'Yes, we should.' She reached up, her parted lips touching his. He gave a low groan that was almost a growl and kissed her back, parting her lips wider with his tongue and entering her mouth.

She sank into his kisses, her burning body hard up against his, her breasts rubbing against his chest. His hands slid down her back, pulling her in even tighter, so the entire length of her body touched his. When his hands cupped her bottom, she moaned softly, wanting him to explore more of her, to relieve her pulsating, consuming needs.

His lips left hers and he kissed a tantalisingly slow line down her neck, kissing and nuzzling the sensitive skin until she lost all ability to think. But she did not want to think. All she wanted to do was feel. His tongue and lips moved lightly over her collarbone.

Silently, she begged him to kiss and caress more of her body. As if he had heard her plea, his hand cupped her breast and she cried out in both surprise and excitement.

His hand instantly flew from her breast, his lips stopped their nuzzling progress and he stood back.

'No,' she whispered, hardly able to talk.

'I'm sorry,' he said, his voice husky.

'No, I mean, don't stop.'

He started to speak, but before the words were out, she took his hand, placed it back on her breast and kissed him again, stifling any objections he might have.

His hand slid inside the top of her gown and Violet was sure she was about to die from pleasure as he cupped her breast, his thumb rubbing over her hard, tight nipple.

Could any experience be more exquisite, more exciting, more arousing? The throbbing that had taken over her body continued to mount with each rub of his thumb. She moved in closer to him, her hands tracing down his back, moving under his swallow jacket and cupping his firm buttocks.

As if under a power over which she had no control, she rubbed herself against him, her back arching with each stroke, trying to relieve the delicious pressure that continued to rise and rise.

His lips once again nuzzled into her neck, moving down to her collarbone and along the mounds of her breasts.

He stood back and looked down at her, his breath coming harder and faster. She waited, wanting him to do something, anything, to relieve her of this mounting tension.

His hands moved back to her breasts, but instead of caressing them as she hoped, he undid the line of buttons at the front of her gown, then parted the soft silky fabric. With one firm tug, he pulled down her chemise and exposed her breasts to his gaze.

Hardly able to breathe, she gazed up at him. He was

staring at the round orbs, pale in the moonlight, the tight nipples pointing up at him, as if in invitation. The ardent expression on his face made her feel so beautiful, so desirable. He liked what he saw, liked what she was offering him.

Her breathing resumed, her breasts rising and falling rapidly with each shallow breath as she waited for him to do more than just admire, but to caress her again. When he failed to do so, she could wait no longer and took her breasts in her hands and watched him as she rubbed her thumbs over the tight, hard peaks, showing him how desperate she was for his caresses.

A look of raw, primal desire swept over his face. He pulled her hands away from her breasts. She expected, hoped, he'd resume his delicious tormenting caresses. But he didn't. Instead, he lowered his head and took one hard peak in his mouth.

Liquid excitement shot through her body and she cried out in rapture. She wasn't sure what she said. Was it yes? Was it his name? Was it please? Or was it all three? Whatever she asked, begged, she didn't care. As long as this glorious sensation did not stop. She cradled his head, running her fingers deep into his hair. His tongue stroked her increasingly sensitive nipples, while his lips suckled, causing Violet to all but pant as the throbbing deep within her continued to mount, until she was possessed by a shuddering that radiated out from the core of her body. She gave a long, rapturous sigh and leant back against the low garden wall, her eyes closed.

'That was…that was…' Violet didn't know what

that was. All she knew was it was beyond what words could express.

She opened her eyes and looked up at him. He sent her a slow, sensual smile. 'And we've only just begun, my sultry vixen. There's so much more I can show you.'

Violet's pounding heart had been slowing down. Now it once again throbbed in expectation as he placed his hands around her waist and lifted her up on to the stone wall. She didn't know what he was going to do next, but whatever it was, she knew she wanted it. His hand moved under her dress and she smiled. Yes, that was exactly what she wanted him to do. That was exactly where she needed his hands to be.

His fingers lightly ran up the inside of her calf. She closed her eyes and tilted back her head, relishing the way her skin came to tingling life under his touch. With exquisitely, painfully slow progress, his hand moved further upwards, tracing a line along the inside of her leg. She was sure he was enjoying tormenting her. He reached her knee. Acting on instinct and without thought, her legs parted. He moved up higher, his hands gently caressing the delicate naked skin of her inner thigh, above the restriction of her silk stockings.

'Please,' she whispered, not knowing what she was begging for, but knowing that only he could ease the demanding need that was once again possessing her.

A bush rustled behind them. His hand left her leg and he pulled down her skirt.

'No, I, please, I…' Violet begged, her thoughts and words confused.

'Don't worry, my dear.' A strange man's voice

reached her, as if coming out of a dense fog. 'No one will see us way down here.'

Violet's eyes shot open. Before she had fully registered what was happening, Jake had lowered her from the garden wall, restored the top of her gown and brushed down her skirt.

'I hope not,' a giggling female responded. 'I wouldn't want anyone to know what we were getting up to.'

The man laughed, then the woman's giggling was stifled.

Without a word, Jake took her hand and led her along the side of the garden wall to the gravel path. They were soon back in the light and walking arm in arm as if doing nothing more scandalous than taking the night air.

Music, light and laughter spilled out from the ballroom. Other couples were also outside, chatting together or walking in the garden. It was as if nothing had happened between her and Jake, but her still-tingling body knew that something had indeed happened. Something marvellous. Something that she wanted to happen again. As soon as and as often as possible.

Chapter Fifteen

Jake should be feeling guilty, but how could you feel guilty for doing something over which you had no power? The moment he had her in his arms on the dance floor his control had started to slip away. When her breasts had touched his chest, he had become like a man possessed. He had wanted her more than he had ever wanted a woman before. As if a demon had taken control of his mind and body, he had ceased to think straight. All that was left was a demanding, primitive need. So he had taken her hand and led her away, to a quiet, dark place where he could have what he so desperately desired.

But did that really excuse him, or was he merely trying to justify his lascivious behaviour?

They walked closer to the house, her arm through his, her beautiful, luscious body close against him, his hunger for her still unsated.

He should say a silent thank you to the couple who had interrupted them. Thanking them and yet cursing them from the bottom of his soul. Cursing them for denying him his gratification, cursing them for bringing him back to reality, cursing them for ruining something so beautiful, so precious, and yet so wrong.

And it *was* wrong. The small part of his brain that could still think knew he should have controlled himself. What he'd done was unforgivable. And what he had wanted to do was beneath contempt. If that couple hadn't interrupted them, he would not have stopped, not until he had taken her completely, and satisfied his hunger to have her, to make her his own.

Yes, he should thank that couple, not curse them. They had saved him from himself.

He took hold of Lady Violet's hand and lightly kissed it, then brushed a stray hair that had come free from her coiffure back from her forehead. She looked up at him and smiled. Had a woman ever looked more radiant?

It might be wrong, but having her in his arms had indeed been beautiful and precious. Kissing her had been unlike anything he had experienced before. It wasn't just her soft lips. It wasn't just her glorious, curvaceous body. It wasn't just the pleasure of watching her writhing under his touch. It was all those things, but it was also so much more. Something indescribable had possessed him, had made him not just want to make love to her, but to love and cherish her. That was something he had never experienced before, something he could not define, something that was both wonderful and unsettling.

But the question he had to ask himself was, what did he do now? She had every right to expect a proposal from him. After such an encounter, any other woman would be already thinking about what style of gown she would wear and deciding on the floral arrangements. But Lady Violet was not any other woman. She was unique.

'I should say I'm sorry,' was the closest he could come to making an apology. 'But I have no regrets,' he added with all honesty. If she required a proposal, he would do what was expected of him and make one.

She smiled at him, a delicious, enticing smile. 'Nor do I. And don't look so worried. I'm not going to insist that we now have to rush up the aisle.'

He was about to deny that was what he was thinking. After all, what woman wants to know that the man with whom she has just had an intimate encounter is concerned about how to hang on to his freedom?

'And you're right.' She bit her bottom lip as if to rein in her smile. 'Perhaps we shouldn't have done what we did.' Her teeth ran seductively over her lip as she released it and she sent him a delightfully saucy smile. 'But I, too, have no regrets at all. It was astonishing. I had no idea that it was possible to feel like that.' She pointed towards the bottom of the garden. 'If I promise not to hold you to account, I hope we can do it again, soon.'

Jake was sorely tempted to take her up on that offer. Right now. He looked around the garden, which suddenly seemed full of annoying couples, talking together in the moonlight, strolling in the garden and generally being an inconvenience.

'I'd be delighted to be of service any time you desire,' he said, causing her smile to grow even brighter.

This woman never failed to surprise him and, despite himself, despite the seriousness of what they were discussing, he couldn't help but laugh. 'At any time, in any place, anywhere that takes your fancy. Lady Violet, I will always be at your command.'

She joined in his laughter. 'And I think, after what has just happened, you might call me Violet, at least in private.'

'Violet,' he said softly, loving the sound of her name, loving the new intimacy between them. 'And you must call me Jake whenever and wherever you like.'

And in particular if you're calling my name out in ecstasy.

'Jake,' she whispered on a gently exhaled breath. His name had never sounded so seductive.

They continued to stare at each other, as if exchanging names was an intimate experience that they needed time to savour fully.

'But I think, Jake, that we should return to the ballroom. Our absence might have been noticed and I am supposed to be chaperoning my sister.'

'Yes, Violet,' he whispered, but remained transfixed to the spot, staring down at those warm brown eyes.

She took his arm and laughed again. 'Although, right now, I think I am probably the least qualified woman in the room to enforce standards of morality. Hopefully, Bianca and Mr Fortescue have been behaving themselves better than we have.'

Jake laughed again, but this time it had a forced note to it. He could make no comment on whether Lady Bianca and Herbert would or would not behave themselves, but what he did know was that Herbert's intentions towards Lady Bianca were always honourable.

The same could not be said for himself. He had acted on impulse, had followed his own needs without thinking. Despite her enthusiastic response, his behaviour was still unforgivable by any social standards.

And despite recent actions that suggested otherwise, Violet was still an innocent, something he should not have forgotten, not for one second. She might be unlike any other woman, but she was untouched and was expected to remain so until she married. If they had not been interrupted, he would have taken her virtue and done so with no intention of offering his hand in marriage. He was truly a man without honour.

Part of him wished she were angry with him. If she was raging against him for taking advantage of her, it would be no less than he deserved. He did not deserve for her to be laughing with him, smiling at him in that warm and affectionate manner. She should not be letting him off the hook so easily.

They entered the ballroom and were immediately joined by Lady Bianca and Herbert.

'Where have you two been?' Lady Bianca asked, as if she was now the chaperon.

'It was getting so hot and stuffy in here. We decided to take some air,' Violet responded lightly.

Lady Bianca raised her eyebrows, a knowing smile on her lips. 'The night air seems to have done you the world of good, sister. You are simply glowing. Perhaps we, too, should go for a walk in the garden. Then I might glow in the same manner. What do you think, Herbert?'

Herbert smiled and opened his mouth to speak, but was too slow.

'You do not need to,' Violet cut in. 'If you want colour in your cheeks, dance a polka. One's about to start. Off you go.'

Lady Bianca laughed and put her arm through Herbert's. 'It seems my sister has given us our orders, Herbie. We have no choice but to dance together once more.' With that, the two all but skipped away.

Violet shook her head as she watched them dance, twirl and jump around the dance floor. 'I think you're right about those two. They do seem made for each other and I don't know which one is the sillier.' She looked up at him and gave a delighted laugh.

She continued to be full of surprises tonight. Herbert was going to be a very happy man when he discovered that his future sister-in-law's animosity towards him was starting to thaw, even if she did still think him silly.

She frowned slightly and patted her cheeks. 'But is Bianca correct? Is my face really flushed?'

'Yes, and you look beautiful,' he whispered.

'But what might people think?'

That you look like a woman who has recently been in a state of ecstasy, who has been brought to the crescendo of arousal, then sent crashing over its peak and into sated rapture.

'Perhaps you'd like to dance,' he said instead. 'Then they'll think you're flushed from your exertions on the dance floor.'

'Another dance, Lord Jake?' she said with a delightfully cheeky smile. 'Won't such behaviour set the tongues wagging?' She laughed lightly and took his arm. 'Well, let them wag.'

Jake returned her smile as he led her out on to the

dance floor. Dancing repeatedly together would indeed make people wonder, but he was no longer capable of caring. All he wanted was for this beautiful woman to remain in his arms. No, that wasn't correct. What he really wanted was to take her by the hand and lead her back to the garden, to finish what they'd started. For now, he would have to be satisfied with having this dance.

He did not know what the outcome of their new-found intimacy would be, but for the moment, Jake was enjoying himself. Something he had never before done at a society ball.

Violet was enjoying herself. That was most certainly not what she expected when she arrived at the Rose-mont ball. She could almost say she was a changed woman. She certainly felt different. It was as if she had suddenly moved from darkness into the sunlight. Her body had never felt so alive, with every inch of her skin seemingly tingling with the memory of his touch. Her lips burned deliciously from his impassioned kisses and it was best not to think about how her breasts and her most intimate areas were reacting to once again being in his arms. That was something the old Violet would have considered to be thoroughly wanton. But after what she had just experienced, wanton was exactly how she wanted to be.

If she never had to leave Jake's arms, she was sure she would spend the rest of her life smiling.

Violet knew she should be feeling guilt and shame over their behaviour. If she was as respectable as she had believed herself to be, she should not have let it happen. But she had done more than just let it happen, she had wanted it so desperately she had all but begged him to continue. That was the very definition of shameful behaviour for a woman. And yet it was neither guilt nor shame that was making her feel giddy. No, all she felt was deliriously happy. She moved closer to him, wishing she could kiss him, right here, and to hell with what everyone thought.

He placed both arms on her waist and lifted her up. Every other man in the room did the same with their partner in accordance with the steps of the polka, but for Violet it caused her to briefly close her eyes as contentment swept through her. He had lifted her up in the garden as well, placed her on the wall then ran his hand up the inside of her leg. How she wished he would do that again.

He lowered her to the ground and they resumed the dance, but her inner leg continued to tingle, all the way up to her core. Oh, how she loved that feeling. How she loved having him touch her, kiss her, hold her.

They exchanged private smiles, as if both knowing what the other was thinking, and continued to stare deep into each other's eyes. Violet wished he could go on looking at her like that for ever, as if she was the only woman in the room, the only woman for him.

The polka ended and supper was announced.

As if in a daze, Violet followed Jake as he led her out of the ballroom and into the drawing room, where footmen were serving punch. Guests were helping themselves to the plates laden with a wide array of food, while maids rushed about removing empty platters, replacing them with full ones and ensuring every guest wanted for nothing.

Violet was too excited to eat, but she took the glass of punch Jake offered her and couldn't resist the temptation to surreptitiously run her fingers lightly over his as he handed it to her.

Just then, they were joined by his mother, the Duchess of Southbridge, and his brother the Duke.

'Mother, Luther, may I present Lady Violet Maidstone,' Jake said quickly.

Violet gave a low curtsy, desperately wanting to make a good impression on his family.

'It's delightful to meet you, my dear,' the Duchess said with a smile. 'And I'm delighted that for once my son has decided to remain for the entire ball. He usually escapes at the first opportunity.' She sent a pointed look in Jake's direction, causing him to shuffle and looked delightfully embarrassed.

The Duke took her hand and bowed over it. 'But I'm not going to let my brother monopolise your attention, Lady Violet,' he said. 'After supper, would you grant me the honour of the next dance?' He looked at Jake. 'With my brother's permission, of course.'

What was happening? Was the family treating her as if she and Jake were courting? It certainly seemed that way. This had to be a dream. Surely she would wake up soon and discover she had drifted off to sleep and none of this had actually happened.

Once supper finished, they joined the jostling, happy crowd as they made their way back to the ballroom, for yet another waltz.

The Duke placed her arm through his and led her on to the floor. This was such an honour, but Violet couldn't stop herself from looking round to see whether Jake was asking another young woman to dance.

He was.

He bowed to Bianca and, while Mr Fortescue smiled at them, he escorted her on to the dance floor.

Violet released her held breath.

She made polite conversation with the Duke and tried hard to look at her partner while he spoke to her, but her gaze kept moving over to Jake. He really was magnificent. So tall, so handsome, and did any man dance as well as he did? Violet doubted it. The Duke was also an accomplished dancer, she had to admit, but it was nothing like being in the arms of Jake.

When the dance was over, the Duke crossed the room to where Jake was standing. He in turn was handing Bianca over, not to her chaperon, but to Mr Fortescue.

'Here she is, back safe and sound,' the Duke said to Jake, giving him a quick wink before departing.

Violet must be in seventh heaven. Only in a place such as that could she feel this wonderful. She assumed Bianca went back to dancing with Mr Fortescue. She hardly cared as Jake once again led her back on to the dance floor.

And that was how they spent the rest of the evening. In each other's arms, dancing the night away.

Still in a dream, the ball came to an end. Somehow, she found herself in the carriage, travelling back through the early morning London streets.

Neither sister spoke, but both continued to smile all the way home.

The carriage pulled up in front of their town house and they walked up the path, arm in arm, still lost in their thoughts.

'Your father has requested you join him in the drawing room on your return,' the butler said the moment they entered the house.

Bianca and Violet exchanged confused glances. What on earth was their father doing here, in London?

There was only one way to find out. They entered the drawing room to find their father reading a scientific journal, a glass of brandy on the side table, a cigar burning in a nearby ashtray.

'There you are, my dears,' he said, placing the journal on the table. 'I've come down to London to attend a series of lectures at the Royal Astronomical Society, but as I'm here for the next week or so, I thought I should take the opportunity to get to know my future son-in-law a bit better.'

Violet looked at her sister, whose expression could only be described as sheepish. 'Bianca, what's going on? What is Father talking about?'

Her father was so absent-minded, there had to be some mistake.

'At the house party, Herbie asked Father for permission to marry me and he said yes.'

Violet looked to her father. 'Is this true?'

'What?' Her father looked up at her in bewilderment.

'I said, have you really given your permission for Bianca and Mr Fortescue to marry?'

'He seems a nice enough young man. Comes from a good family and all that. He doesn't know much about astronomy, though, which is a shame.' Her father took a long sip of his brandy, picked up the journal once more and buried himself back in its pages, as if that was the last word that needed to be said on the subject of his younger daughter's marriage.

She turned back to Bianca, feeling hurt. 'And when did you plan to tell me?'

Bianca shrugged. 'Well, I thought it best to keep it a secret for now.'

'Why?'

'I was worried that if you knew I was already engaged you wouldn't come down to London with me for the Season, and that would ruin everything.'

Violet waited for her to explain further.

'Oh, Violet, you can be so simple sometimes. It was obvious at the house party that you had feelings for Lord Jake. I knew that, well, after what had happened to you, you'd be reluctant to admit to those feelings. I had to make sure the two of you spent time together so that nature could take its course. And I was right, wasn't I?'

Bianca smiled at her sister in a manner that could only be described as triumphant.

'Did Lord Jake know about this?'

'Well, I swore Herbie to secrecy, but apparently he spilled the beans and told Lord Jake.'

Violet stared at her sister, unsure how to feel about having a trick played on her, and unsure how she felt about everyone being in on something about which she had no knowledge.

'Don't look at me like that, Violet.' Bianca laughed, taking hold of her hands. 'It worked, didn't it? You and Lord Jake danced nearly every dance together tonight. I believe that makes my plan a success.'

Violet slowly smiled. 'You're right. It did work. It was a clever scheme. I can't believe I ever called you a ninny.' She took her sister in her arms and gave her a hug.

Bianca laughed, then abruptly stopped. She disentangled herself from Violet and frowned. 'You called me a ninny?'

'Yes, sorry. I did, but I was wrong. That wasn't the only thing I was wrong about. You're a very clever, extremely perceptive young woman. I was wrong about you and about Mr Fortescue, too.'

'And?'

Violet nodded in glorious defeat. 'All right, I admit it. You were also right that I do have feelings towards Lord Jake.'

Bianca squealed with delight and hugged her sister, as if this news was as exciting as her own engagement.

Chapter Sixteen

Just as the Rosemont Ball was a tradition, so was the discussion over breakfast the next morning. The after-ball breakfast was usually dreaded by the three brothers, almost as much as the ball itself. This Season, the youngest brother, Ethan, was safe from their mother's scrutiny, having become the one and only Rosemont brother to surrender himself to the state of matrimony.

While the two unmarried brothers, Jake and Luther, were pleased their brother had found a woman who made him so happy, they would rather he hadn't proposed to her in such a dramatic fashion. It had set such a terrible precedent. Now all of society saw the Rosemont ball as a place where debutantes were swept off their feet and romantic gestures were made by besotted men to love-struck young ladies.

And their mother was foremost among those who now had such high expectations. Luther and Jake would be furious with their brother if he wasn't so deliriously happy and oblivious to any criticism. While Luther and Jake were expected to attend the breakfast aftermath,

Ethan was excused. He was still secreted away in his bedchamber with his wife.

'So, Lady Violet Maidstone?' Luther said the moment the family took their seats at the breakfast table. Jake knew exactly what he was doing, deflecting their mother's attention from himself. Well, he would not be allowed to succeed.

'And did you find a suitable future Duchess of Southbridge last night? After all, isn't that the whole point of putting us through the ordeal? And there were rather a lot of attractive young women with the suitable pedigree present.'

Jake smiled to himself and commenced eating his bacon and eggs, waiting for their mother to recite the various virtues of each debutante present and inform Luther to whom he would be expected to pay a follow-up visit.

'Yes, Lady Violet is a lovely young woman,' their mother said instead. 'And she deserves to be courted by a decent man with honourable intentions.'

He looked up to find his mother staring intently at him, her face set in a serious countenance. 'Yes, Jake, I *did* notice that you two spent rather a lot of time together and a decidedly long time out of the ballroom as well. I do hope you are serious about her. It would be cruel to lead her on. No woman deserves to be dallied with, and Lady Violet more so than most.'

Jake swallowed, his breakfast suddenly as dry as ash. 'Yes, of course, Mother, I will treat her with the utmost respect.'

'Good, I would expect nothing less from one of my

sons.' She gave him another appraising glare, then turned her attentions to Luther.

'So, Luther, I was pleased to see you danced with Lady Amelia Howard. Lovely girl, excellent family.'

Luther adopted that familiar look of resignation whenever she discussed his future bride while his mother continued to list all of Lady Amelia's Duchess-like qualities.

Jake pushed away his plate, no longer hungry. He was uncertain how he felt about Violet or what their future would hold, but there was one thing about which he *was* certain. Last night, he *had* dallied with her, as his mother so quaintly put it. And his mother was also right that it was not what she deserved. She deserved to be with a man who was seeking a bride, who wished to court her, who wanted to marry her. She should be wooed by an honourable man who would not take liberties and, if he did, would make his intentions to marry her very clear.

He threw his napkin on to the table. This was why he avoided balls. This was why he did not get involved with unmarried society women. The rules were clear and the outcome for men who transgressed those rules just as clear. Marriage.

And if his mother had noticed their long absence from the room, had others? Had he already put her reputation at risk? Had he already joined that group of men who were forced to marry to save a young woman from the horror of being classed as an unvirtuous woman?

She had said she had no interest in matrimony, had even joked that, despite what had happened between them, she was not expecting them to march down the aisle, but no society lady could cope with the ignominy of a tarnished reputation. When that happened, there was only one cure. Marriage.

Damn it all. He should have done what he always did, left the ball as early as he possibly could. Then he would not be in this predicament. And yet, when he had seen Violet, the thought of escaping had not entered his mind. All he had wanted was to be with her. And now look at the quandary he was in.

But wasn't that always the case when he was in her company? He lost the ability to think. All he could do was react, surrender himself to desires that should be kept firmly under control. He became like a man incapable of logical thought, or even the most basic sense of self-preservation. Even now, here in the drawing room, surrounded by his family and servants, the mere thought of her was making him want her so desperately he could almost smell her feminine scent, feel her soft skin, hear her gentle moans.

He moved uncomfortably in his chair. This would not do. His mother was right. She deserved respect, deserved not to be dallied with. And he was a man who desperately wanted to dally with her until she was left panting and exhausted.

There was only one thing for it. He knew what he had to do. He had to avoid seeing her again and certainly never be alone with her again. Too much danger lay in wait if he did otherwise.

Wasn't last night enough of a warning of what little control he had whenever he was with her? Only the fortuitous arrival of that courting couple had prevented him from completely compromising her in the garden. If he had done so, they would now be announcing their engagement and Jake's life as a carefree bachelor would be over.

That was it. His mind was made up. He would not see her again. He never attended society events during the Season and this year would be no different.

If he couldn't resist temptation, then the sensible thing to do was to not put temptation in his way. When it came to Violet, he was a weak man; therefore he would ensure his willpower, or lack thereof, was never put to the test.

With that in mind, he excused himself from the breakfast table. Luther looked up at him and drew his face into the comical expression of a man being led to the gallows, while his mother continued to list off all the social events he would be expected to attend in the next week and which young ladies he should pay particular attention to.

Joining in the charade, Jake raised his hands and eyebrows, to show he could do nothing to save his brother. He could only try to save himself. To that end, he departed the dining room and retired to his study, where he opened the lid of his roll-top desk and removed a piece of crisp white card from the shelf. Despite his resolve, Violet still deserved the courtesy of a card and some flowers to be sent to her address. After all, they'd spent almost the entire time at the ball together, not to mention what had happened in the garden. It was only polite to do so.

He agonised over each word, tore up several attempts, before settling on simply telling her he had enjoyed their time together and she had made the

Rosemont Ball more agreeable than he would ever have thought possible. Every word of which was the truth, although no words were adequate to describe just how agreeable their time together had been.

That done, he could rest a bit more easily. He would never again be doing what his mother had warned him against, dallying with Violet Maidstone. Never seeing her was going to be hard, but he had made the right decision. What was the point of testing yourself when you already knew you would fail?

He handed the card to the footman, with instructions to order a large bouquet and for both to be delivered to Violet's home.

That done, he tried to put all thoughts of Violet Maidstone out of his mind.

It was a task that proved nothing less than impossible. At the most inopportune moments, the memory of how she looked in the moonlight would come unbidden into his mind. He'd have to contain the groan that welled up inside his throat when he remembered her standing before him, half-naked, her hands caressing her breasts. Was any woman more sensual, more bewitching? He had been right to suspect she had untapped passions. And he had been right to decide he should not see her again. Otherwise, he would be incapable of preventing himself from further exploring her passionate nature.

While in the midst of another fantasy about where her passionate nature might take her, a footman coughed and brought him back to the uncomfortable reality of sitting in the drawing room, taking afternoon tea with his family. The footman handed him a white embossed card, laid out on a silver tray. It bore the crest of Violet's father. Despite himself, he ripped it open with almost boyish enthusiasm, wondering what message she had sent him.

It was an invitation to a dinner to celebrate the engagement of Lady Bianca Maidstone to the Honourable Mr Fortescue. He stared at the card. They had made it official already. This presented a problem. His close friend's engagement dinner was one social occasion he could absolutely not avoid. He tapped the card against his fingers.

He was going to see her again. It looked as though his weak will was going to be put to the test once again and Jake did not know if he could ever be strong enough to avoid succumbing to the temptation that was Lady Violet Maidstone.

Violet hardly had a minute to herself, but she was never so busy that she couldn't indulge in her new favourite pastime, thinking about Jake and reliving what had happened at the ball.

She paused, mid-conversation, which earned her a curious look from the housekeeper. Violet shook her head to drive out her latest imaginings, a fantasy involving her, Jake, rows of flickering candles and a four-poster bed draped in soft red velvet curtains. She needed to focus. This was neither the time nor the place for such inappropriately ribald indulgences.

In her usual manner, Bianca had decided on a whim that she wanted to host a dinner to announce her engagement. She had declared she would invite the same twenty guests who had attended the house party and that she wanted it to be something special. She had immediately sent out invitations, then had left the organisation of the dinner party to Violet.

Just a few days ago, Bianca's presumptions would have irritated her, but nothing seemed to irritate her now. Part of her knew it was due to the strange state in which she had found herself, as if she was floating on a cloud, where nothing and nobody could upset her. Organising the party was a joy, not a chore, especially as it would provide the perfect opportunity to see Jake again, to hopefully be alone with him, preferably somewhere with lots of candles and yards of draping red velvet.

'Do you agree, my lady?' the housekeeper asked. 'The entire floral scheme should be in soft pastels and that theme could then continue through to the wedding.'

It seemed Violet had once again lost the thread of their conversation.

'Perfect, Mrs Hampton. And has Cook made any suggestions for the menu?'

Mrs Hampton indicated the card in Violet's hand.

'Oh, yes.' Violet scanned the card. 'Well, that all seems perfectly in order.' She handed it back to Mrs Hampton. 'And have we received replies to Bianca's invitations?'

'Yes, my lady. Everyone has said they will be attending.'

Mrs Hampton excused herself and Violet settled back in her chair. She still had a lot to do, but it wouldn't hurt to spend a few moments indulging in thoughts of Jake. Yes, the engagement party would be a perfect time for them to be alone together again.

She hadn't seen him since the ball, which was a disappointment, but he had sent her a lovely card and a large floral arrangement the following day. And soon she would see him again.

She smiled secretly to herself as she remembered their conversation in the garden. He had promised her he would be available to her whenever and wherever she wanted.

That meant he would be available to her at the engagement party. Her toes curled up inside her shoes as she contemplated where and how they could get away from the other guests and repeat what they had done in the garden.

It was all just too deliciously naughty. Violet knew she should not be thinking such things, but she could not help it. It was as if she was a new woman, one who could only live for the moment and live for seeing Jake again. After what she had experienced in the garden, how could it be otherwise? The desire to feel Jake's hands on her body again drove out all other thoughts. All she wanted was for him to kiss her again, to undress her the way he had on the night of the ball, to run his fingers over every inch of her body, to kiss and nuzzle her until she was once again consumed by desire.

Bianca burst into the room, crashing into Violet's latest fantasy.

'What are you doing?' Violet gasped out, trying to hide her discomposure. 'What's wrong?'

Bianca stopped and sent her a knowing smile. 'There's nothing wrong with *me*. But we're supposed to be visiting the dressmaker today. Or had you forgotten?'

'No, I did not forget,' Violet lied. 'I'll just get my hat and gloves and we can be off.'

'Good, because my wedding gown has to be perfect. I know exactly what I want. Tiny mother-of-pearl buttons down the back, delicate lace sleeves, a sweeping, embroidered train and...'

Violet followed her sister from the room, murmuring in agreement, but no longer hearing the long list of requirements that would make Bianca's wedding dress perfect.

The days had passed both quickly and slowly. Violet had much to do and wished she had more time to organise the dinner party, but also wanted the time to rush by so she would see him again.

Then, as if all of a sudden, it was the night of the party. Nerves and excitement possessed Violet as she completed the final preparations then retired to her bedchamber to dress for the evening.

She held up the gown she had chosen and frowned at it. It was entirely unsuitable. The neckline was too high, the sleeves too long. She placed it back in her wardrobe and looked for something more acceptable. Gown after gown was rejected.

'I'll be back in a moment,' she informed her lady's maid as she pulled on a robe over her chemise and corset and rushed down the corridor to her sister's bedchamber.

'Bianca, I need your help.'

'Oh, no, what's wrong?' Bianca was already dressed

in a stylish pale pink gown with grey embroidery, and her lady's maid was just adding the finishing touches to her hair.

'I've got nothing suitable to wear. May I borrow one of your gowns?'

'Of course you may.' She crossed the room and removed several gowns before she made her selection. 'I believe this one will suit you perfectly. The skirt doesn't have to be pulled in quite as tightly as I like it and the loose bodice should accommodate your rather generous…'

She circled her hands in front of Violet's chest and giggled.

'And the scooped neckline should also show off your rather generous…' she circled her hand once more in front of Violet's chest '…to perfection.'

Violet lightly bit her lip as Bianca handed her the gown. It was an exquisite creation in gold silk with silver lace at the neckline and embroidered motifs of leaves and flowers flowing from the bodice and down on to the train. 'Are you sure, Bianca? It's so beautiful. Don't you want to save it for your next ball? All your friends will see me wearing it and you won't be able to wear it yourself.'

Bianca waved her hand in dismissal. 'I'm about to become officially an engaged woman. It's not as if I need to wear a gown that will catch a man's gaze.' She giggled again. 'And I suspect I could turn up in sackcloth and Herbie would still tell me I looked beautiful.'

Violet placed the gown gently over her arm, thanked her sister and returned to her room, where Agatha helped her dress.

Observing herself in the full-length mirror, Violet was more than satisfied with what she saw. The way the fabric flowed over her hips was certainly flattering. The neckline was lower than Violet would ever usually dare to wear. And Bianca was right, it really did show off her generous proportions and was a gown designed to capture a man's attention. The silver lace at the neckline caught the light each time she moved, while the lace was supposed to give the appearance of modesty. In reality, the way it glittered and sparkled drew the eye to the wearer's decolletage.

The straps were made of the same lace and rather than covering the skin, as they were supposedly meant to do, they gave a tantalising hint of the naked skin underneath.

She could hardly wait for Jake to see her so attired, to watch his reaction. Would she once again see raw desire on his face? Would passion overcome him? Would he take her hand and lead her away to somewhere private, as he had at the Rosemont ball? Would he slide the lacy straps off her shoulders?

She ran her hand lightly across the neckline, closed her eyes and imagined his hand caressing her. Would he then…?

'Do you want to wear the garnets tonight, my lady?' Agatha asked, causing Violet's eyes to spring open and reminding her she was not alone.

'No, just a single string of pearls, I think.' Violet wanted nothing to impede Jake's view.

Her stomach fluttering with anticipation, she descended the stairs to join Bianca, Mr Fortescue and their guests in the drawing room. The footman opened the door and she paused on the threshold.

The room was full of elegantly dressed men and women, but her gaze was instantly drawn to the man standing at the far side of the room, and all the other guests seemed to merge into a colourful haze.

He looked across the room. They smiled at each other. She entered, moving straight towards him as if pulled by a magnetic force.

'You look beautiful, Violet,' he whispered, his voice husky, as his eyes skimmed up and down her body, causing the fluttering in her stomach to intensify. Her breath caught in her throat, her breasts rose higher, as if she was further inviting him to observe what was on offer.

'As do you,' Violet responded. It was a silly thing to say. Ladies did not compliment men on their appearance, but he did look magnificent. She rubbed her fingers lightly together, itching to run them along the breadth of his chest, to explore what was hidden under that formal dinner jacket and stiff white shirt. She should have taken the opportunity to do so when they had been alone in the garden and she hoped to have the chance to do so tonight. The sooner the better. He had kissed her neck, her chest, and she longed to do the same. To press her lips against every inch of him, and she just knew he would taste delicious.

Several other guests joined them and Violet stifled a giggle. What would they think if they knew what salacious thoughts were going through her mind, what she was imagining doing and having done to her?

But she mustn't think of that now. Until they could

find time to be alone together, she would have to act with at least a modicum of decorum.

Polite conversation flowed around her, although Violet heard little of it. She hopefully laughed in the right places, smiled when required, and nodded when a thoughtful response was expected. But if she failed to do so in the right places and at the right times, what did it matter? All she wanted was for this dinner to be over, to lead Jake away. Then conversation would be unnecessary, and what she hoped he would do to her could never be described as polite.

Violet smiled to herself, a wicked, delighted smile, and he smiled back in a similar fashion. Was he thinking the same thing? Was he just waiting to get her alone? She hoped and prayed that was so.

The footman announced that dinner was served, and the guests paraded into the dining room. Once again, she was seated next to Jake, but tonight she had no objections as to where Bianca had placed the cards.

She took her seat and angled it slightly so she would be closer to him. Her thigh was tantalisingly close to his. Her arm was so near to his jacket she could almost feel the fabric stroking her naked skin.

They hardly spoke through the seven-course meal, but it was as if an unspoken conversation was taking place with their bodies: a slight smile exchanged, a gaze held longer than propriety would demand, the light touch of his fingers as he filled her wine glass, a gentle stroke of her leg as he placed his napkin on his lap.

This was all so enticing, so intoxicating, as if they

were playing out a seductive ritual in public, and no one seated at the dinner table had any idea what they were doing.

Finally, the dinner was over. Her father rose from his chair and made a brief speech, officially announcing the engagement and expressing his joy at the coming wedding.

Bianca smiled at her father, then at the happy man sitting beside her. Bianca and Mr Fortescue not only looked as if they were in love, but seemed to be bathed in a gentle glow, one not caused by the candelabra on the table. In fact, the entire room seemed to be bathed in a silky glow. It was as if the entire world had softened and lost all its harsh edges.

Mr Fortescue got unsteadily to his feet. It seemed his glow wasn't just caused by love. He had indulged a bit too much in the claret, but Violet could forgive him for that. He had just become engaged. He was in love. He had every right to celebrate.

'I just want to let you all know how happy I am. When I first met my darling Bianca, I knew she was far too good for me. At that time, I doubted I would ever have a chance of winning her hand.'

Violet smiled at her future brother-in-law, who was saying all the right things, and at her sister, who was basking in his admiration.

'I still can't believe she actually agreed to marry me and can hardly believe it is possible to feel this happy. So I want to toast my beautiful future bride, Bianca.'

Everyone raised their glasses to toast a smiling Bianca.

'And I want to thank my future father-in-law for being so generous in allowing me to marry his precious daughter.' Herbert drank another glass in toast, then refilled his glass.

'And I also want to toast my friend, Lord Jake Rosemont, without whose help I might not be here tonight—'

'No need to thank me,' Jake cut in, signalling with his hands that Mr Fortescue should take his seat.

'No, I must thank you properly. If you hadn't taken on the task of keeping Lady Violet distracted from her role as chaperon, I might never have had a chance to woo my beautiful future wife. I know you didn't want to do it and you really did take some convincing.' Herbert looked around at the assembled guests and gave a small chuckle.

Violet froze. The temperature in the room plummeted. She couldn't breathe.

'So for making such a sacrifice I am doubly grateful.' He lifted his glass and took another long swallow. Everyone else followed suit, raising their glasses towards Jake and Violet.

Assaulted by their cheers, Violet fought to keep her dignity. This had all been a sham. Everyone else had known. And everyone was laughing at her. With supreme effort, she unclenched her jaw so she could smile back at them, hoping they would think that she, too, was in on the joke and never realise she was dying inside.

Herbert dropped back down into his seat, signalling that the toasts were now over, and chatter once again erupted.

It was her opportunity to escape.

Jake placed his hand on her arm. 'Violet, I—'

She threw off his arm and jumped to her feet before that abhorrent man could make some paltry excuse. 'Ladies, it is time for us to retire to the drawing room,' she all but shouted over the sound of twenty people talking at once.

Without waiting for the other ladies to respond, she took a step backwards, her rapid movement almost causing her chair to topple over. Only the quick movements of a footman saved her from the further indignity of it crashing to the floor. She rushed to the door, no longer capable of caring about decorum. The moment the door shut behind her, she ran. Down the corridor, away from her utter humiliation, which was somehow worse than what had happened to her eight years ago.

Ignoring protocol, Jake followed Violet out of the room. He caught sight of the edge of her gold skirt disappearing around the corner. She was not retiring to the drawing room, but fleeing, possibly to her bedchamber. He sprinted down the corridor, ignoring the questioning look of the footman walking towards the dining room with a carafe of brandy.

At the bottom of the stairs, he caught up with her, grabbed her arm and stalled her progress.

She pulled against him, refusing to even look in his direction.

'Violet, please, let me explain.'

'I don't want your explanations.' Her constricted voice contained muffled tears. He winced as if she had slapped his face. He had to make this right.

'Herbert has had far too much to drink.'

She made no reply. Nor did she look at him.

'Yes, it's true that he wanted me to distract you so he could court Lady Bianca,' he rushed on, his words tumbling over each other. 'But that was just at the beginning. I was never trying to distract you at the ball.'

Despite the tense situation, he couldn't help but smile at the memory of what had happened between them in the garden. 'Well, perhaps I was trying to distract you at the ball, but by then I was doing it all for my own benefit, not Herbert's.'

His attempt to make light of the situation failed dismally.

She pulled against his grip, refusing to even look in his direction. 'Let me go, immediately,' she seethed.

'Not until I have explained myself.'

Slowly, she turned to face him, her eyes now cold, her chin lifted in haughty dignity. 'I don't want your explanations. I want nothing from you.'

'I'm sorry, Violet. Herbert should never have said that and certainly not in such a public place. I know he embarrassed you, but—'

'Yes, I'm embarrassed,' she cut in, her voice harsh but level. 'I'm embarrassed that I ever let a man like you into my life. I'm embarrassed that I let myself think you were anyone other than who you are. I'm embarrassed that I've been so gullible. But as for how you treated me, I'm not embarrassed about that. Why should I be? You're the one who acted like a cad. You're the one who has no regard for other people, their feelings or how your actions could affect them. You're the one who thinks he's so irresistible that women will just fall into his arms.'

He released her arm and stepped back, shocked by the intensity of her words.

'No, I didn't...' Jake was unsure what he wanted to say. He should say that she was wrong. But how could he? He *had* been a cad. He should never have agreed to Herbert's scheme. He hadn't thought of how it would hurt her.

She stared at him with narrowed eyes. 'When I first met you, I made the assumption that you were a vain, privileged man who only ever thought about his own pleasure. And nothing you have done has changed that opinion. You are indeed a worthless wastrel whose only skill is the ability to take money you don't need off other men at the gaming tables. In other words, a useless good-for-nothing who has never amounted to anything and never will.'

Jake dragged in a sharp breath, stunned. Weren't those exactly the same words his father had used against him, over and over again? Was that how she saw him, too? Did she really hold him in such low regard? He knew the answers to those questions. Yes, she held him in low regard and, yes, she had every right to do so. For a brief, deluded period of time, he had thought she was the one person who did not see him as a good-for-nothing. But he was wrong.

'You seem to be under some sort of misconception that what happened between us meant something to me,' she continued coldly. 'Well, yes, I admit for a passing moment I did forget what you were really like and thought you were someone good, someone honourable and decent. I should be grateful to Mr Fortescue for reminding me of your true nature and bringing me back to my senses. I would never see you as a man I could actually take seriously. A man as frivolous as you could never be anything other than an enjoyable pastime for a woman like me. Yes, it was fun, I'll admit that. You're certainly experienced with women. But you're far too shallow. You know that as well as I do.'

He stared at her, incapable of even thinking, let alone defending himself.

'I have to admit I was affected by what happened between us in the garden.'

Hope surged. Perhaps she did not entirely despise him.

'But it meant nothing. All we were doing was using each other for our own ends. Now, you can go back to all your other women, back to your superficial life, and I can get on with living one that has some substance.' She turned towards the stairs. 'Now, if you'll excuse me, I wish to retire. You'd better return to your friends so you can all continue trying to think of ways to fritter away your endless amount of time in yet more pointless pursuits.'

With that, she walked up the stairs, her head held high, leaving Jake reeling in her icily contemptuous wake.

Chapter Seventeen

Violet ignored the quiet knock on the door. How dare that man think they had anything more to say to each other. And how dare he think he could follow her to her bedchamber. His arrogance knew no bounds. She would not be seeing him again, ever.

'Go away,' she called out, her voice cracked, her throat thick. She coughed. 'Go away,' she called out again with more authority.

She needed to be alone, alone with her mortification. Once again, she had been publicly shamed. When Randolph had abandoned her, she had been left standing at the door of a country church in her wedding finery. All the guests inside had witnessed her rejection, as had all the village people standing outside the church, waiting to see the happy couple emerge. And now it had happened again. It was not quite so public this time, but it was just as humiliating. No, it was worse. Much worse.

On her wedding day, when the news had reached her that Randolph had been obliged to marry another young lady he'd thoroughly compromised and the gossip swiftly filtered through the assembled guests, she had been forced to weather the pity on everyone's faces. Tonight, the guests did not pity the deluded old maid who had been hoodwinked by the handsome charlatan. They had simply laughed at her. It had all been a big joke at her expense.

She was such a fool. A stupid old fool of a spinster.

That knock came again. 'Go away,' she cried out, then buried her head in her pillow to block out the sound.

The door opened slowly. She tossed the pillow away, sat up and looked towards the door, her face defiant. She could not let him see her in a vulnerable state, would not let him think he could hurt her.

Bianca quietly slipped into her room. 'Violet, are you all right?' Her voice was low, as if she were entering a sickroom.

'I'm perfectly fine, but I think you should get back to your guests and your fiancé.'

Bianca waved her hand towards the door. 'They can entertain themselves, and as for Herbie, I think it had better wait until the morning before I speak to him again, because he's certainly going to get a piece of my mind.'

'He said nothing that wasn't the truth.'

'Hmm, but he could have not said it at all. One of Herbie's good qualities is that he doesn't think before he speaks. It's also one of his most annoying qualities. But don't worry, I will be putting him straight and letting him know what he has done wrong.'

Violet climbed down from her bed, straightened her

crumpled gown and moved over to her dressing table. 'It's not his fault,' she said as she pulled the pins out of her hair and threw them on the dressing table. 'Well, not entirely his fault. The man who is truly to blame is Lord Jake Rosemont.'

She picked up her brush, but hardly had the energy to brush out her hair, nor did she have the energy for this conversation. She sank down on to the bench in front of the dressing table. 'I mean it, Bianca, you should return to your guests. I'm sorry for storming off and making a scene at your engagement dinner.'

Bianca seated herself on the edge of the bed and stared at her sister's reflection in the mirror. 'I don't believe anyone noticed as rather a lot of claret has been consumed tonight. Perhaps a bit too much, especially by my husband-to-be.'

Violet turned to face her sister. 'Did you know about this, too, Bianca?' She placed her hands on her stomach to quench the pain. 'Did you know Lord Jake was instructed to keep me busy while Mr Fortescue wooed you?'

'No, of course not.' Bianca rushed to Violet and placed her arms around her. 'I would never do such a thing to you.'

Violet closed her eyes and held back her tears.

'It was all Herbie's idea, apparently, and a silly one at that. Even if his plan did have a good outcome.'

'Bianca,' Violet cried out, standing up and disengaging herself from her sister's arms. 'How can you possibly say that? Nothing about this is good. It's…it's…'

Bianca held up her hands. 'I'm not saying I approve

of what happened, but, well, no real harm was done, was it?'

'No real harm,' Violet spluttered, hardly able to believe what her sister was saying. 'I have been humiliated.'

'Why? How?'

Violet stared at her sister. Could she really be that deluded, or was love and the thought of marriage making her totally blind?

'Lord Jake misled me.'

'Only at the house party.'

'Yes, exactly. Oh, how he must have been laughing at me.'

'But not at the Rosemont ball.'

'What?'

'At the ball he knew that Herbie and I already had Father's permission to wed. He did not need to distract you and yet he was still so attentive, hardly ever leaving your side.'

Violet sat back down at her dressing table, picked up her brush and stroked it vigorously down her long hair, trying to block out Bianca's words.

'So, anything that happened between you and Lord Jake after the house party had nothing whatsoever to do with anything Herbie had asked him to do.'

Violet continued to brush her hair, the brush scraping along her scalp, while Bianca smiled, as if everything had now been explained away sufficiently. 'I'm right, aren't I?'

'No, Bianca, you are not right,' Violet said slowly. 'Lord Jake is a cad. He used me, tricked me and humiliated me. His behaviour is unforgivable.'

'Oh, Violet, you shouldn't be so headstrong, especially when it is your own happiness that is at stake.'

She kissed the top of Violet's head. 'I'll leave you
to think about what I said while I return to my guests.'

Violet remained staring at the door, her brush suspended over her head. Bianca was wrong. Lord Jake
was a scoundrel. She could, perhaps, acknowledge that
Bianca had a point that he was only expected to distract
her during the weekend party, but that did not make his
behaviour any less unforgivable. He had still been hiding things from her and had made a fool of her.

And Bianca did not know as much as she thought
she did.

Lord Jake had said he abhorred society events, but
he'd had no choice but to attend his mother's ball. Continuing to spend time with her meant she'd provided
him with a necessary distraction. Being with her that
night had simply kept all those young debutantes at
bay, that was all. Once again, he had used her for his
own ends.

And as for what happened in the garden, wasn't that
further proof of just how low he'd sunk? How he must
have laughed at the way he had given the old maid a
bit of excitement.

Her flaming cheeks grew even hotter and she
clenched the brush to her chest, her nails scraping
against the ceramic back. How it must have amused
him, the way she so readily surrendered herself. All he
had to do was pay her a few compliments, show her a
little attention, and she was almost begging him to do
with her whatever he wanted.

One kiss, one touch, and she was his. She would

have done anything, let him do anything, and probably have thanked him for it afterwards.

She threw the brush on to the dressing table. She could imagine him turning it all into a big joke for the entertainment of the other ne'er-do-wells at his club.

Bianca said the fact that he continued to show her attention after she was engaged meant there had been a good outcome. She was wrong. He had gone on to use her for his own entertainment. That was even more unforgivable. And what was worse, she had told him she did not expect them to get married, the way most young ladies would. That, too, would no doubt be turned into a funny anecdote with which to entertain his friends.

Without calling for her lady's maid, she pulled off her gown, mortified that she had actually dressed with the misguided intention of impressing him, had even hoped to captivate him. Him, the man she now utterly despised.

She really was a joke.

Throwing the pile of gold silk into the corner, she pulled on her nightdress and climbed into bed. She had expected this Season to be a trial, but she could never have imagined it would be so devastating. But at least now, for her, it was over.

Bianca was, however, right about one thing. Now that she was engaged, there was no reason for Violet to remain in London. Bianca's lady's maid would make an adequate chaperon to the engaged couple. Violet could return to their Norfolk estate. Never attend another Season and never see that reprobate Lord Jake Rosemont ever again.

* * *

A worthless wastrel. A good-for-nothing. A man who would never amount to anything. How could she say such things? To him? The fact that every word was true did not make it any easier to bear. He had heard those same words, many times before, from his father. He'd hardened himself to his father's contempt so the insults usually bounced off him, but when they came from Lady Violet's lips they had cut deeper than any physical wound.

For one brief moment, when he had been with her, he had thought he was a better man than that, but she was right. And there were more insults she could have levelled at him. He was a philanderer who had done more than dally with a young lady's virtue. And a self-centred coward whose only thought had been for maintaining his own freedom. Yes, she was right to despise him. He deserved nothing less.

Now that she had made her opinion of him clear, there was nothing left to be said or done. Jake did not return to the dining room. While the other guests continued with their merrymaking, he quietly slipped out of the Maidstones' house.

Dismissing his carriage driver, he chose to walk home, to clear his head of thoughts of this turbulent night and that even more turbulent woman.

And turbulent was exactly what she was. From the moment he had seen her behind the bar at the Golden Fleece, his emotions had been in a state of constant flux. If she really had been Betsy, the beauteous barmaid, life would have been so much simpler. He would have indulged in a bit of harmless flirting that would have gone nowhere. Instead, she'd turned out to be Violet, the voluptuous, volatile Violet.

Then his voluptuous Violet became the cantankerous chaperon, then a seductive, sensual siren. He stopped walking. Damn it all, why did he have to think of that? It was going to take a long time to get the seductive siren out of his mind, but that was exactly what he must do. All he had to remember was that the seductive siren despised him.

What a joke he was.

He had worried that she would expect more from him than he was willing to give, had even laughingly thought she might expect a marriage proposal from him. And worthless wastrel that he was, he had been trying to find a way to avoid that fate. A worthless weasel is what she should have called him. What other words would describe a man who nearly compromises a woman's reputation then tries to weasel out of it and take no responsibility?

Yes, she was right about him and she was better off without him in her life.

So what now? Jake stopped walking aimlessly and looked up and down the road. How would a worthless weasel, a useless good-for-nothing, cope with such a situation? How did such a man deal with all the images possessing his mind, the unfamiliar emotions coursing through his body? The answer was obvious. He did what he always did, wasted his time on pointless pursuits.

He commenced walking faster. For the sake of his sanity, he had to forget all about Violet Maidstone. Forget those rare and beautiful smiles and not think about how his heart soared when she laughed. And most of all, forget how she had looked in the subdued light of the night-time garden at the Rosemont ball. Never again would he think about her head tilted back, her lips parted, her breath coming in a series of shaking gasps as she came to a shuddering climax...

He turned the corner, the Maidstones' residence no longer in view.

She had made her feelings for him perfectly plain. There was nothing for it but to return to his life and put that vexatious woman behind him, and that was what he intended to do. He would get her out of his mind in the time-honoured manner of jilted men. By indulging himself—no, overindulging himself in every vice on offer.

She already thought he was worthless. Well, he was about to show her just how worthless he could be. She'd said all he thought of was his own mindless pleasure. Well, that's what he would do, take his pleasure whenever and wherever he could find it and with whomever he wanted. And the more mindless that fun, the better.

Starting tonight. Starting right now.

Parties that catered to worthless weasels could be found throughout London. They were the perfect place for a man like him. And while he was indulging himself, he wouldn't give Lady Violet Maidstone one more thought.

He turned and headed in a different direction, trying to think of which den of iniquity had the worst reputation. He wanted to find a place fit only for the lowest of the low. A place to confirm every contemptuous opinion Lady Violet had of him.

He arrived at the door of his friend, the Earl of Chesterton. Every room in the Kensington house was lit up. Laughter, music and female squeals of delight rang out from the house into the otherwise quiet street.

'Hello, darling,' the young lady leaning against the portico column said. 'If you're looking for a good time, you've come to the right place.'

'Indeed, I have, madam,' he said, tipping his hat and causing the young woman to giggle.

Yes, this was where he needed to be. None of the women who attended the Earl's parties cared whether he was worthless or not. If all he thought about was his own pleasure and filling his pointless days with pointless activities, they would not give a fig. In fact, such women encouraged such behaviour and no doubt could suggest new and interesting pleasurable activities with which to indulge his baser nature.

Yes, he needed to be among people who did not despise him so completely. He walked up to the door, raised the knocker then gently lowered it again without making a sound.

He tipped his hat to the young lady once more and retreated down to the street.

He still intended to spend his days at parties, gambling houses and the like, but perhaps not tonight. His argument with Lady Violet had left him strangely depleted of energy. But tomorrow he would put her firmly in the past where she belonged. Tomorrow he would return to his old life as if she had never existed. Tomorrow, everything would be back to normal.

Chapter Eighteen

Arranging the packing of her trunks, giving instructions to the household servants on what would be expected of them for the remainder of the Season and providing detailed instructions to Bianca's lady's maid on her new role as a chaperon, had kept Violet physically busy as she'd prepared for her trip back to Norfolk, but hadn't stopped her busy mind from dwelling on unwanted thoughts and memories.

Even worse was the train journey home. After she and Agatha had taken their seats and she had exchanged a few pleasantries with the other passengers in the first-class compartment, Violet had nothing to do except sit and watch London pass by outside the window. She hoped that once the bustling, smoky city disappeared from sight, to be replaced by the pleasant greenery of the passing countryside, her tense body would start to relax.

She was on her way home. Away from him. Surely the gripping in her shoulders and neck should now release, the agitation in her stomach start to settle down.

Perhaps she needed to be at home, back to her normal routine. Then she would be free of those thoughts that constantly tormented her. Then she could stop going over and over their last conversation, thinking of things she should have said, creating his responses, which were always contrite as he admitted that everything she said was right. Or, alternatively, she imagined him putting up feeble arguments, which she would immediately shoot down with some caustic comments, while watching with satisfaction as he crumbled before her.

And, when she was finally free of thinking about him, hopefully she would also be free of the harrowing memory of him holding her, kissing her, caressing her. When that unwanted image invaded her mind, her body reacted with such powerful longing it was physically painful. As if she were an empty pit and every part of her was craving his touch to fill her up and make her whole again.

She coughed, smiled tightly at the other passengers, pleased that they could not read her mind, and picked up her abandoned book. As she stared at the page, the words swam in front of her eyes. The journey passed at an excruciatingly slow pace, but finally she was back in Norfolk. Home. Now she would be able to heal. Now she would be able to get back to who she really was before she'd so foolishly lost herself to Jake Rosemont.

She walked in through the familiar entrance of Maidstone House and waited for the weight to be lifted off her shoulders. Her home had never sounded so quiet. There was no Bianca, greeting her with her cheerful chatter. No Father emerging from his study to acknowledge her arrival, list off all that needed doing, before retreating once more to his solitude. There was just Violet. She was going to have to get used to this silence. Bianca would soon be gone, leaving her all alone.

But she would not sink into self-pity. She had plenty to keep her busy. Unlike some other people she wasn't even going to think about, she was not a worthless wastrel who had to find pointless ways to fill her time. She had a house to run, tenants to care for, an estate that still needed a manager. Yes, she had plenty to occupy her time.

And at the end of the Season, once Bianca had finished enjoying every ball and soirée and had her fill of the theatre and the opera, Violet would also have a wedding to arrange. That, too, would keep her busy.

She sank down on to the bench by the entrance-way. A wedding where she would inevitably see Lord Jake again. He would probably even be Mr Fortescue's best man.

No doubt he would look splendid in a morning suit. Dove grey would probably suit him best and would contrast well with his dark hair.

This will not do. Pull yourself together.

She stood up and walked briskly down to the kitchen. The housekeeper had remained in London, at Violet's insistence, so she could attend to any entertaining needs Bianca might have. That was all for the best. Violet would enjoy managing the house herself.

She entered the kitchen. The scullery maid was seated at the table, languidly peeling some potatoes, while the kitchen maid sat by the stove, reading the newspaper. They both jumped to their feet on her arrival and bobbed quick curtsies.

'Mrs Hampton has remained in London, so I alone will be organising the household.'

'Very good, my lady,' the maid said with another quick bob. 'And will you be hosting any dinner parties any time soon that we need to prepare for? Will we need the services of Beryl and Myrtle again?'

'No.'

'Very good, my lady. And will there be any guests arriving that we need to buy provisions and prepare rooms for?'

'No.'

The kitchen maid and the scullery maid exchanged quick glances. Violet knew what they were thinking. If she was the only person in residence and she was not planning on entertaining, what did she actually have to organise?

'Well, everything seems to be in order,' Violet said, looking around as if giving the kitchen her final approval. 'I'll leave you to it.'

She left the kitchen and looked up and down the corridor, trying to decide what needed her attention next.

The village. The tenants probably needed her help in all sorts of ways, particularly poor, broken-hearted Mr Armstrong. She would visit the Golden Fleece and help him find a permanent new barmaid.

With a fresh determination to sort out this problem, she strode down the pathway and through the village, greeting each tenant as she passed.

* * *

Unlike the last time she had visited the tavern, today the doors were wide open, and the sound of laughter and men's loud voices spilled out into the road. She entered to find the place full of farmworkers, all enjoying their tankards of beer after their day working in the fields.

A few men looked up from their tables when they saw her and rose to their feet, but most were too busy enjoying their beer and the companionship of others to notice her.

Mr Armstrong was behind the bar. Gone was the sullen man who could barely lift his head. He was smiling and chatting with the patrons as he refilled their tankards. And Rosie, the temporary barmaid Violet had organised, was still working by his side.

Rosie looked completely at home, flirting, laughing and exchanging banter with the patrons. She pushed past Mr Armstrong and reached for another tankard hanging from hooks above the bar. To Violet's horror, as she did so, Mr Armstrong grabbed hold of her buttocks and gave them a squeeze.

Violet expected her to slap his face as he deserved and storm out, leaving Violet to sort out the mess he had made. Instead, she squealed with laughter, turned and gave him a quick peck on the lips. The tavern keeper's smile grew wider, and he almost appeared to be purring like a cat just given a bowl of cream.

Unbelievable. It had not been long since that man had been inconsolable, vowing he would never get over Betsy. Now it seemed he was completely healed and had already moved on to pursuing another woman.

Men. It didn't take them long, did it? Lord Jake would be no different. He would have forgotten all about her, if he had even thought about her in the first place. That was another good reason why she should not be wasting any time thinking about him.

Violet strode up to the bar. 'Mr Armstrong, I believe you are still in need of a permanent barmaid.'

The smile died on his lips. 'No, my lady. All's been taken care of. My Rosie here is happy to continue.' He looked over at the barmaid. His smile returned, as did that dopey look on his face.

'And what of Betsy? Have you heard anything from your wife?'

Mr Armstrong stared at her in confusion. 'Oh, her... no, nothing.' He went back to gazing at Rosie. Violet huffed her disapproval and strode out of the tavern.

She looked up and down the village street. People were going about their daily tasks. Women were chatting over fences to their neighbours, couples were strolling in the late afternoon sunshine, while children pushed hoops and played with spinning tops. No one within sight appeared to need her help.

She strode back to the house.

An estate manager. Good. She still needed to find an estate manager. That should occupy her time. With new determination, she rushed down to the butler's pantry, now occupied by the head footman in the butler's absence. Like the kitchen maid, he was absorbed in reading the newspaper, but quickly jumped to his feet the moment she entered.

'Samuel. I need to organise a new estate manager. How does one go about doing that?'

Samuel looked uncharacteristically uncomfortable. 'That has all been taken care of, my lady.'

'No, it hasn't.'

'Yes, my lady. Your father appointed a new man before he left for London. He starts at the end of the month.'

'My father?' When had her father ever taken any interest in the running of the estate or organising the staff?

'Yes, one of your guests, a Lord Jake Rosemont, contacted your father with a suitable appointment and your father hired him.'

'Lord Jake? My father?' What was going on? Was Lord Jake trying to ruin her life? Was he conspiring against her so she would have nothing to do? Nothing except to spend her endless days thinking about him.

'Will there be anything else, my lady?'

'No, no, that is all. Thank you, Samuel.' She remained standing, wondering what to do now, then turned abruptly, left the butler's pantry, stopped in the corridor and looked both ways. She had to keep busy, but what to do now?

She walked back out the entranceway. She would go for a long, brisk walk. That would exhaust her. By the time she returned, she would be so tired she would not be able to think, and when night came, she would fall into a deep, dreamless sleep.

She walked up the gravel path, kicking up the small stones as she went, then strode across the grassy field, determined not to think of Lord Jake and not to relive her recent humiliation, but it was impossible to do so.

It was hard to believe that, after eight years of protecting her heart so vigilantly, she had let her guard down so easily and so quickly. And she could no longer deny why her pain was so intense. Fool that she was, she had actually fallen in love with Jake Rosemont.

If such a realisation didn't hurt so much it would actually be laughable.

She had been humiliated before and knew well what that felt like. But this time, the emotion was more extreme. It wasn't just that she had not learnt her lesson and had once again fallen for a charming man who had secrets of which she alone was unaware, but because she had fallen in love with Jake.

With Randolph, it had never really been love. She had loved the thought of having a wedding, being his wife, of being a married woman with a home of her own, but she had not loved him, not the actual man. She had enjoyed his company, had found him dashing and exciting, and had been proud to be by his side, but she did not feel the same intensity of emotion that she felt for Jake.

When Randolph had picked her out from all the available debutantes, she had been flattered to be selected by the most handsome man available that Season. She had quickly got caught up in the romance of being married and had been so proud of herself for finding a husband in her first Season. She had even felt sorry for those young ladies who were on their second, third, even their fourth or fifth Season and were still not being courted. But hadn't they all had the last laugh and hadn't they been able to pity her in the end?

That had been the main thing she had felt, a wound to her pride and an abhorrence of being pitied. But this time it was different. This time, she was in real pain. This time, she had felt something deep for the man. This time, it was Jake himself, and not the idea of a big white wedding or being a married woman, that she missed.

She had never really missed Randolph, but every inch of her seemed to ache for Jake.

Or was she just missing a fantasy?

He had never really been the man she thought he was. The man she had fallen in love with did not play tricks, did not manipulate other people's emotions the way he had manipulated hers.

She had fallen in love with a man who didn't really exist.

The man she thought she loved would not treat anyone the way he had treated her. Yes, she needed to forget all about him. She needed to once again be a woman who did not need a man in her life and certainly did not need Lord Jake Rosemont.

She approached a stile, placed a hand on the top to climb over, then sat down, her energy sapped. Taking her head in her hands, the tears she had been keeping at bay ever since Bianca's engagement party finally rolled down her cheeks.

Chapter Nineteen

For the first time in his life, Jake had lost. He stared at the empty space in front of him, the spot where only moments ago there had been a large pile of money. Now there was nothing, just the green baize of the table.

His fellow players were as equally bamboozled by this turn of events as he was, although the gambling parlour owner was for once treating him like an honoured guest, encouraging him to stay longer, plying him and the rest of the table with complimentary drinks.

But his interest had waned some time ago and he had no desire to stay.

Jake rose from the table. Ignoring the come-hither looks of the young women who plied their trade at the gaming houses, he made his way out into the evening air. He knew the devastating sense of loss that was gripping him had nothing to do with the money he had just given to the gambling house and his fellow card players. The emptiness inside him had a completely different cause.

He looked both ways, up and down the alleyway,

trying to get that damn woman out of his head, but he couldn't stop thinking about their last conversation, repeating what she had said to him and each time reacting as if the insults had been flung at him anew. Worthless, a wastrel, of no benefit to anyone.

She had angrily accused him of doing nothing other than enjoying himself, and now he didn't even seem capable of doing that.

He wandered through the London streets, her words running repeatedly through his mind. How could she say those words to him? How could she see him like that? He had thought they had grown close, but then, just as he was trying to explain himself, she had lashed out at him and revealed her true feelings. If it hadn't been for Herbert's speech, he would still be under the delusion that there was something between them, something tangible, something special.

He stopped walking, standing still in the middle of the pavement, causing the pedestrians to part around the obstacle he was causing.

Her expression as she'd listed his innumerable faults came into his mind, as clear as if she was standing in front of him. He was wrong. That wasn't anger. That wasn't an irate woman dismissing him for his deficiencies. Nor was it the look of a woman labelling him as worthless.

That was pain, and he had been too stupid to see it. He had been too caught up in his own sense of injustice to realise what she was expressing. He really was a scoundrel. All he had thought of was the pain she was inflicting on him, not on how she was feeling, how he had offended her.

How could he do such a thing? How could he so badly hurt the woman he loved?

He looked around at the passing pedestrians, as if one of them had put that surprising thought into his head.

The woman he loved?

He was in love with Lady Violet Maidstone. His hand covered his mouth as if he had said those shocking words out loud.

He lowered his hand slowly, taking in the magnitude of this realisation. Then he smiled. He was in love with Lady Violet Maidstone.

Why had it taken him so long to realise that? His smile died. And why did he finally realise it now, after he had caused her so much pain that she likely hated him?

He commenced walking, his gaze fixed on the pavement as he tried to digest the ramifications of this sudden awareness and consider what he was going to do about it.

There was no denying that he had hurt her. He had tried to justify his actions to her, but there was no justification for causing her pain.

What he had done was unforgivable. He could not change what happened. He had hurt the woman he loved and there was only one thing for it. He had to try to make it right. She might never forgive him, but he owed her a heartfelt apology. Who cared if she thought he was a worthless wastrel? After all, he *was*, and she had said nothing that wasn't the truth.

He had to stop caring about his own wounded feelings. He needed to let her know that she never deserved to be treated as badly as he had treated her. He needed to apologise.

To that aim, the moment he arrived home he summoned his manservant and asked him to pack his bags so they could take the first available train tomorrow to Norfolk.

Then he settled down for a restless sleep, wishing tomorrow would come, wishing he could see Violet immediately and tell her just how deeply, how sincerely sorry he was.

Throughout the train journey, he went over and over what he would say. Each time he came up with an apology that adequately expressed what he felt, he would sit back on the leather bench and relax. Then, almost immediately, he would see something wrong with his words, and would start again, formulating a new, better way of saying it, until his mind became completely confused.

When he arrived at the country station, he was no more certain of what he needed to say than he had been when boarding the train in London. He headed straight to the tavern and booked a room for the night. A much friendlier young woman was behind the bar, causing a pang in his heart at the memory of the first time he had seen Violet. Was she still angry about the way he had treated her when they first met? He had flirted with her when it was obvious she did not want his attentions.

Should he apologise for that as well? And how many other offences had he committed? He was unsure. All he knew for certain was his behaviour had been that of an unforgivable cad.

'I sleep above the tavern as well,' the barmaid said as she handed him the key, sending him a saucy smile that made her intention very clear.

'Well, you can rest easy. I promise I won't be disturbing your sleep.'

She shrugged and went back to talking to one of the locals.

While his valet unpacked Jake's bags, he washed and changed out of his travelling clothes, then walked over to the Maidstone estate. It was somewhat inappropriate to arrive unannounced and uninvited, but what did it really matter? She would be angry with him for this impropriety, but she was already angry with him. She would think him a rude, inconsiderate man, but she already thought that as well.

He stopped at the edge of the formal garden. There she was, talking to the gardener. She was just as beautiful as he remembered her, maybe even more so. Dressed in a simple brown skirt and white blouse, an old straw hat on her head and wearing thick gardening gloves, she appeared to be instructing the gardener on his topiary techniques.

The man was staring at her with a resigned look on his face, causing Jake to smile. That was his adorable, bossy Violet.

She caught sight of him. The pruning shears dropped from her hand and her mouth fell open. Her gaze darted to the entrance of her home as if she was about to flee back to her sanctuary. Then she pulled back her shoulders, excused herself from the gardener and approached him.

'What are you doing here?' Her words held not the slightest suggestion that he might be forgiven.

'I've come to talk to you.'

'Well, I don't want to talk to you, so leave.' She pointed imperiously towards the end of the tree-lined drive.

'No, I won't leave, and if you don't want to talk to me, that's fine, but please just listen, because I definitely want to talk to you and I won't leave until I've said my piece.'

She glared at him, her hands firmly on her hips.

'The sooner you let me speak, the sooner I will be out of your life and you can get back to whatever it was you were doing.'

She continued to glare at him, then gave a curt nod. 'If you must.' She led him over to a stone bench in front of the formal garden, sat down and continued staring straight ahead, as if she was prepared to listen to what he had to say, but had no intention of taking part in the conversation.

Jake sat down and tried to gather his thoughts. Now that he had her attention, he was uncertain how to begin. 'I'm *not* sorry for what I did,' he finally said.

She turned towards him, her face the picture of bubbling rage. 'You are even more despicable than I thought. I'd assumed the reason you had come here was to offer me an apology.'

'Well, you're wrong.'

She stood up. 'In that case, you might as well leave. Now.'

He did not want to stand and he most certainly did

not want to leave, but he had never remained seated while a woman stood and could not do so now.

'I said I'm not sorry because I would never be sorry about meeting you, even if the way in which we met was somewhat unconventional.'

'Somewhat unconventional,' she spluttered. 'That, I believe, is what is called an understatement. You lied to me, tricked me, manipulated me, all so you could do a favour for your friend.'

'At the time, I did not think it would cause any harm. I was just giving Herbert the opportunity to court the woman he loved and for your sister to decide for herself whether Herbert would make a good husband. Something which had a happy outcome.'

'And you did that by lying to me.'

This was not going well. He had come to apologise, not to make her even more angry with him.

'Yes, and I shouldn't have done that, but can you think of any other way those two lovebirds would have got together if I hadn't been involved and if I hadn't, as Herbert said, kept you occupied?'

Her angry eyes grew wider, her chin tilted higher. 'But what about me? What about my feelings?'

Jake closed his eyes briefly and winced. 'Yes, for that I am truly sorry,' he said quietly. 'I never meant to hurt you.'

'And yet you did. You hurt me more than you could possibly know.' She sank back down on to the stone seat. He sat down beside her. He had finally apologised but his sorry sounded so inadequate and could never express the depth of the remorse he felt.

'You humiliated me.'

'I'm sorry,' he said quietly, knowing that his apologies, even if they were sincere, were as worthless as he was.

'You know I was once engaged to be married to Lord Randolph Simeon,' she said, quietly, as if talking to herself.

'Yes, I believe Herbert may have mentioned that you had once been engaged.'

'And did your friend tell you what happened to me? When you and Mr Fortescue were concocting a plan that would further humiliate me, did you think about what I had been through before?'

Jake frowned, his sense of inadequacy increasing with every word she spoke. He knew Randolph Simeon, a rascal of the worst kind. A married man who cheated repeatedly on his wife and was known to keep at least one mistress. 'I didn't know who you were engaged to. But Lord Randolph was never worthy of you. You deserve so much better than a scoundrel like him.'

She gave a quick shrug of one shoulder. 'Perhaps, maybe. But that does not make my humiliation any the less. On the day of my wedding, I discovered Randolph had been forced into a hasty marriage to the debutante who was carrying his child. I was humiliated in front of all my guests.'

'It was a lucky escape, if you ask me.'

'I'm not asking you and that is not the point. You humiliated me, just as Randolph did. And once again, I found out in public that the man I thought cared for me was actually lying to me. I had thought I knew what humiliation felt like, but that was nothing compared to how I felt when Mr Fortescue made that speech at

Bianca's engagement dinner and I discovered you, too, were a fraud, that everything that had happened between us was a lie.'

He went to speak, but she held up her hands to stop him, then drew in a shuddering breath. He wanted to put a consoling hand on her arm, but knew he must not. He was the last person whose sympathy she wanted.

'Once again, the man I thought…the man I thought I could trust had made a fool out of me.'

She drew in a deep breath, then released it slowly. 'You would think I would have learnt my lesson the first time, wouldn't you?' She gave a harsh laugh that contained no humour.

'Oh, Violet, I am so, so sorry.' He moved towards her to take her in his arms, to offer what comfort he could.

She held up her hands to repel him. 'Don't.'

'I'm sorry,' he repeated and lowered his arms.

'You're not sorry. You said you weren't. Just like Bianca, you think no harm has been done.'

'Bianca?'

'Yes, my sister has this insane idea that you did nothing wrong.' She waved her hands to indicate she had no intention of repeating what her sister had said.

'I've always said your sister was an astute, intelligent woman.'

She shook her head slowly, but made no comment.

'But you're right, I am both sorry and not sorry for what happened. I'm sorry that I hurt you, caused you to feel humiliated, made you angry. But I'm not, and never will be, sorry that I met you.' He needed courage for what he was about to say, so he breathed in slowly and steadily. 'And I'm not sorry I fell in love with you,' he said quickly before he could prevent himself from doing so.

Her body went rigid. The world seemed to fall silent.

He waited for her to reply. Waited for her to say something, anything. She said nothing, just continued staring straight ahead, his words hanging in the air.

He drew in another breath. He had to say this. It didn't matter how she reacted, but he might never get another opportunity to tell her how he felt, so he would not let this moment pass him by. 'I suspect I started to fall in love with you the moment I saw you standing behind the bar at the Golden Fleece. The fire in your eyes was unlike anything I had ever seen in a woman. You have such an indomitable spirit that it is intoxicating.'

He smiled to himself at the memory. 'I could hardly believe it when I discovered that the chestnut-haired beauty with the flashing eyes was the woman I was supposed to keep entertained for the weekend. Suddenly the favour I was doing my friend turned from a burden to an enjoyable task and there was no other way I would have wanted to spend that weekend.'

Still, she made no response.

'And then we kissed.'

She shuffled slightly on the seat.

'It was a kiss like no other I have experienced. It set off something inside me I couldn't understand at the time. Now I know what it was. It was love, hammering at me, trying to get my attention, but I was too stupid to notice.'

He laughed lightly at his own inability to see at the time what was now so glaringly obvious.

'Once the house party was over, I knew I still wanted

to spend time with you,' he continued doggedly, appealing to her to understand, but getting no reaction. 'I had to attend my family's ball and was so pleased I had an official reason to see you again. Very pleased.'

Once again, she shuffled on the seat, but still said nothing.

He turned to face her. 'What happened between us in the garden that night, that was an expression of my love for you,' he said quietly. 'I didn't know it at the time, but I was obsessed with you. I had to have you. That, too, was unforgivable, as were all my actions since the moment I first met you. I know I have no right to ask you for your forgiveness, but I just wanted to tell you I *am* sorry. Sorry for hurting you. Sorry for all my behaviour. Sorry for letting my love for you get the better of me when we were alone together. And sorry that I am indeed a worthless wastrel who would never be worthy of you.'

'No.' She finally turned to him and took hold of his arms. 'I didn't mean what I said. I was angry. I was hurting, and I wanted to hurt you, too, to make you feel some of the pain I was feeling. But I don't think you're a worthless wastrel. I think you are...' She paused and bit her lip.

He waited. She said no more.

'So am I forgiven?' he asked, his voice still quiet.

'Yes, you are forgiven.'

Jake sat back on the stone bench. That was the most he could hope for, and much more than he deserved.

Violet didn't know how to feel. She was familiar with being angry, but this was new and unsettling.

When she had seen him standing at the entrance of Maidstone House, that anger had bubbled up inside her like a volcano set to explode and she had been longing to give full vent to her rage.

And now he had not only said he was sorry, but had said he loved her.

She swallowed. He had made a declaration. Now it was her turn to do the same. She did love him, had done so for some time. Even when she thought she hated him, she still loved him.

But could she say it? Could she be that brave? Could she let down her guard and take such a risk? She gripped the edges of the cold stone seat. She had two choices. Open her heart and leave it exposed to even greater pain or run and hide so she could protect herself and her vulnerable emotions.

But before she could take that risk, there was something else she had to say.

'And I should also ask for your forgiveness,' she said, her voice calm.

'You? For what? No, you've done nothing wrong.' He reached up to push a lock of hair back from her forehead, then, as if catching himself doing something he had no right to do, he lowered his hand.

'I should not have said those cruel things to you. You are certainly not worthless. It was you who discovered the estate manager was cheating us. You helped me with the books and you even found a new estate manager.'

'So, I'm not completely hopeless then.' He smiled at her, that lovely, lazy smile that made her bones seemingly melt.

'No, you're not hopeless.' She, too, was tempted to reach up and brush a tousled curl back from his forehead. 'And you are extraordinarily good at managing the servants,' she continued, keeping her voice matter of fact. 'Our substitute cooks adored you. Just yesterday Myrtle visited and informed me that as Cook is still in London, she would be more than happy to fill in. Although I don't think she realised you would not be here.'

'I'm just pleased that I did some good while I was here for the weekend party. Along with all the harm I caused.'

She shrugged. 'I think, maybe, Bianca *was* right. No *real* harm was caused.'

'Thank you, Violet, that means so much to me.'

She looked down at the ground, placed her hands on her stomach to still the fluttering and willed herself to be strong. 'Did you mean what you said?' she asked.

'I've meant everything I've said to you today.'

'That you love me.'

'I meant that more than anything else. I do love you.'

'I love you, too,' she whispered as quietly as she could.

He reached over and took her hand. Slowly, she raised her head and looked at him. They stared at each other, their faces a mirror of shocked expressions. Then slowly, as one, they smiled.

'I love you,' they both said, their smiles growing wider.

'Oh, Violet, do you really mean that?' He clasped her hand close to his chest. She could feel the pounding of his heart under his muscles. Was he as nervous as she was? It seemed he was.

She nodded, unable to speak, unable to express all the emotions welling up inside her.

'I love you, Violet,' he repeated. 'Your love has taken me over. It's like a physical presence in my heart. You're always with me, in my every waking thought and my night-time dreams. It is as if you are now my entire life.'

She continued to nod. 'Yes, yes, that's exactly how it feels.'

His smile died. His face became sombre, but he did not release her hand. 'I came here to apologise and to let you know of my love. I had hoped for your forgiveness, but expected nothing from you. I can hardly believe that you love me as well.' He looked around, his brow creased. 'I had thought about how I would apologise, but not what I would say if you shared my love. I have prepared nothing to say. I so wish I had.'

'You don't need to say anything more.'

'Yes, I do.' He dropped to his knee in front of her, still holding her hand and causing her breath to catch in her throat at this unexpected turn of events.

'Violet, I am hopelessly in love with you. You captured my heart the moment I saw you and my heart is still yours and always will be. I know that we have only known each other for a short time, but I feel as if I have been waiting my entire life for you. Now that I have found you, I never want to let you go. I want to spend my life proving to you that I love you. Every day, I want to show you how deep my feelings are for you. I know I have a lot to make up for, but if you agree to be my wife, that is what I will do. I will prove to you

I am worthy of your love every day for the rest of our lives. You said I had no purpose in life.'

'No, I'm sorry, I...'

He held up his hand and she stopped. 'But if you agree to become my wife, you would give me a purpose. My purpose would be to make you happy, to love you as you deserve to be loved.'

'You are worthy of my love already,' she said. 'And, yes, I would love to be your wife.'

'Oh, Violet, my love.' He stood up, pulled her to her feet, and his lips found hers. Violet melted into his arms as happiness engulfed her. She kissed him back, showing him with her passion what words were inadequate to express. She loved Jake Rosemont. Wanted to spend the rest of her life in his arms. He was the man she loved, the man she trusted, the man she knew would never hurt her again.

'Let's do it now,' he said, his lips a few tantalising inches from her own. 'Let's marry right now.' He sent her a wicked smile. 'I for one can't wait a moment longer for our wedding night.'

Violet was tempted to say, *why wait until we are married*, but instead, she laughed. 'We can't.'

'Why not?'

'Well. We need to inform our families, there's the banns to read, the wedding breakfast to organise.'

'But I don't want to give you time to change your mind.'

His face was so earnest she couldn't help but laugh again at his unfounded fears. 'I won't change my mind. I promise. I want to marry you. That will never change.'

'Do you really promise?'

'Yes, I promise.'

Pulling her back into his arms, he kissed her again. With that, all her past dissolved. He loved her. She loved him. Nothing else mattered. Any past pain and humiliation drifted away. Yes, she had suffered, but all that suffering had led up to this glorious, euphoric moment. If she hadn't been left at the altar, she would never have met Jake. If she hadn't felt so angry and betrayed by the world, she would not have felt the need to be so strict with Bianca and she would never have met Jake. It was as if everything in her past had happened for a reason and that reason was the wonderful man who was holding her tight and expressing the intensity of his love with the power of his kiss.

Epilogue

He had been right. They couldn't wait. Within a week they were married.

Jake had offered to delay the marriage for as long as she wanted. He had said, even though he wanted her as his bride, the sooner the better, he would exercise supreme self-control and provide her with the romantic courtship she deserved. He'd also offered to delay their marriage until they had arranged a large wedding, sent out hundreds of invitations and had the perfect wedding gown made.

But it was Violet who could not wait. She wanted him too much, more than she would ever want a courtship, more than she could ever want a large white wedding.

Propriety demanded that they have the banns read at the local church over three consecutive Sundays, but Violet could not even endure that torture.

Instead, Jake purchased a special licence so they could marry immediately. This possibly caused a great deal of speculation as to the reason for such haste, but neither Jake nor Violet cared what the gossips might say.

Some might have thought she feared history would repeat itself and she would once again be left waiting at the altar, or that their behaviour had been completely scandalous and a hasty marriage was required to restore Violet's reputation before the proof of their transgression was born.

Neither was true.

The simple truth was Violet wanted her promised wedding night with an urgency that grew each day. Even one week was too long to wait. Violet was sure she would have gone completely mad if she had been made to wait any longer.

If his kisses could cause her body to thrum with excitement, if his caresses could send her soaring up to a pinnacle of excitement, crashing over, and left gasping in a state of exhausted ecstasy, she was desperate to discover what it would be like when they were finally together in their marriage bed.

And that night did not disappoint. After a simple ceremony, attended by just their families, and an interminably long wedding breakfast, where she was itching to get her hands on her new husband, they finally retired to their bed. At least, they'd intended to retire to their bed. They didn't quite make it that far. In fact, they didn't even make it to their bedchamber. Their clothes had been discarded in the corridor, ripped off in their frantic desire for each other, and their marriage was first consummated on the stairway leading to their room, then again against the wall outside their bedroom. Finally, they made it to the bed, where they spent the next week unable to leave, their need for each other growing more intense each time they made love.

Eventually, they emerged, but Violet's dreamlike state never quite left her.

She was happy, exquisitely, completely happy.

And it seemed that everyone she met was infected by that happiness. The village people all smiled at her. Men tipped their hats when she passed by and none wore that look of trepidation that had once been so common.

Together, she and Jake assumed the running of the estate, and they couldn't make a better pair. Jake not only worked closely with the new estate manager, managing the estate finances and running the farm, but had voluntarily taken on the books of several of the local shopkeepers and tradesmen. It was a task they readily handed over to him and he got such satisfaction from the work.

Violet couldn't understand how anyone could actually enjoy messing about with numbers, but it always amused her to see her handsome, debonair husband pouring over columns of figures, his face so serious.

Eventually, the Season came to an end and Violet had Bianca's wedding to organise.

As she sat at her desk and compiled the seemingly endless list of things to do, Jake looked over her shoulder. 'I'm sorry, Violet, you, too, should have had your special day.'

Violet smiled up at her husband. 'My day was special enough.'

'But...' he indicated the list '...it could have been even more special.'

She laughed and took his hand. 'Darling, I don't believe you would have had the energy to make it more special than it was.'

Jake laughed, lifted her hand to his lips and kissed it. 'I suspect you are right, my lovely, insatiable wife.' He lowered her hand and his face became serious. 'But I would hate it if you thought you were missing out. Didn't you want all of this, the flowers, dresses and so on?'

She stood up and wrapped her arms around him. 'I've missed out on nothing. Bianca's day is going to be perfect for her and my day was perfect for me. You're perfect for me.'

And she was right on all counts. The day of Bianca's wedding was indeed perfect. As the matron of honour, she stood beside her sister as she took her vows. As the best man, Jake stood beside his friend Herbert. Throughout the ceremony, they exchanged knowing, secret smiles, because they did know a special secret.

Violet would do nothing to take the attention off her sister on her wedding day, but they had exciting news they were dying to share with their families. Soon, Jake and Violet would be parents. She was to be the mother of Jake's child, a child she knew they would love and cherish, just as they loved and cherished each other.

* * * * *

If you enjoyed this story,
be sure to read the first book in Eva Shepherd's
Those Roguish Rosemonts miniseries

A Dance to Save the Debutante

And whilst you wait for the next book, why not check
out her Young Victorian Ladies miniseries

Wagering on the Wallflower
Stranded with the Reclusive Earl
The Duke's Rebellious Lady